SOME TAME GAZELLE

Barbara Pym

Introduced by Mavis Cheek

WINDSOR
PARAGON

First published 1950 by Jonathan Cape Ltd
This Large Print edition published 2010
by BBC Audiobooks Ltd
by arrangement with
Little, Brown Book Group

Hardcover ISBN: 978 1 408 46096 2
Softcover   ISBN: 978 1 408 46097 9

British Library Cataloguing in Publication Data available

Printed and bound in Great Britain by
CPI Antony Rowe, Chippenham and Eastbourne

INTRODUCTION

From the opening line of *Some Tame Gazelle* you are safely and deliciously in Pym Country. 'The new curate seemed quite a nice young man, but what a pity it was that his combinations showed, tucked carelessly into his socks.' The curate in question is visiting Belinda and Harriet Bede, unmarried, middle-aged sisters living in the heart of a village parish. Plump Harriet likes to tuck young, pale, thin curates under her substantial wing, while the more circumspect Belinda potters through her life, comfortably loving the Archdeacon from afar.

Harriet is much more flamboyant than her sister, and given to wearing fashionable frocks in which she is well buoyed up by corsets. (Barbara Pym is awfully good at writing about clothes.) These corsets, under constant strain, frequently need mending, and are often to be found thrust beneath a cushion when an unexpected visitor comes to call. Harriet is loved, unrequitedly, by an adoring Italian count who asks for her hand in marriage on a regular basis and which, on a regular basis, is declined. Both seem quite content with this.

Belinda, who little cares for fashion, asks for nothing more than to continue to adore the handsome, self-satisfied Archdeacon from afar, and to loyally support him as he bemoans the heavy workload of his parish duties which, in fact, are mostly absorbed by said pale, young curates. It is Belinda's task and delight, she feels, to support and explain the Archdeacon's sermons, which are often of great length, and totally obscure. Here, one of the Pym trademarks is used to great effect—the sharp and skilful quoting of poetry and various texts. Barbara was extraordinarily well-read and could find the perfect quotation for any occasion. Robert 'Jock' Liddell wrote that she had 'a genius for quotation which has probably never been equalled'. When the Archdeacon finishes a particularly long and unintelligible sermon, she has him quote Edward Young (a poet also known for his somewhat lengthy and disconnected texts):

> *Say dreamers of gay dreams,*
> *How will you weather an eternal night,*
> *Where such expedients fail?*

The bored congregation, she says, 'had been dreaming gay dreams most of the morning . . . and had only allowed their thoughts to wander when it had passed beyond their comprehension.'

Belinda often compares herself, unfavourably, to Archdeacon Hoccleve's capable and more literary wife. Agatha is cool, elegant, and unsympathetic. She is the kind of woman who is a glad martyr to her rheumatism, and takes the waters at Karlsbad for her holidays. And she is based on someone Barbara knew and disliked at Oxford. This is another of Barbara Pym's authorial characteristics: she loved to include real people in her books. Even the sisters, Harriet and Belinda, are loosely based on herself and Hilary, her elder sister. When she began writing *Some Tame Gazelle* in 1934, at the astonishingly young age of twenty-one, she imagined them both, she said in her diary, 'as spinsters of fiftyish'.

Barbara was a great one for falling in and out of love as often, and usually as hopelessly, as possible—and a great one for using her experiences in her books. Archdeacon Hoccleve is also based on a real person, an old flame who rejected Barbara at Oxford. One can only wonder on whom the famous librarian, Nathaniel Mold, and the visiting bishop from Africa, Theodore Grote, are based when they make their unsettling and unwelcome visits to each of the sisters in turn. The sense of glee she shows in the writing of these characters is practically palpable. Beware! Thus fall all miscreants in a sharp-eyed novelist's life— eventually.

High comedy the book may be but perhaps one of her greatest gifts as a novelist is that she puts her own hand up to the frailties and foibles, the affectations and absurdities that her characters contain and endure. As with all the best writers of comedy, she is non-judgemental and, though beady-eyed, she is also sympathetic, particularly in matters of the heart and how foolishly they can make us behave. From the very first she proved herself to be an accomplished novelist of sharply observed comedies of manners where, though life appears to be carrying on calmly and evenly, beneath its façade lie dark undercurrents, hidden desires and unsuitable attachments.

Barbara wrote in her diary that she '*must* work at my novel, that is the only thing there is and the only way to find any happiness at present . . . I want *Liebe* but I would be satisfied if my novel could be published.' That novel was *Some Tame Gazelle*, and it set the pattern for all the rest.

Some tame gazelle, or some gentle dove:
Something to love, oh, something to love!

After many drafts *Some Tame Gazelle* was finally published by Jonathan Cape in 1950. Her friend from Oxford, Jock Liddell, who read it in its first incarnation and in its last before she offered it to publishers said, 'The wonderful thing is that you haven't spoiled it—it is still the book we knew and loved—and yet it is tidy and shapely, and every blot removed.'

It was received with ecstatic reviews. The *Observer* said, 'She creates a small well-bred Eden, but contrives to insert a little old Adam as well.' The *Daily Telegraph* wrote, 'Miss Pym's sharp fresh fun is all her own', while the *Manchester Guardian* called it 'An enchanting book about village life, but no more to be described than a delicious taste or smell.' And the *Church Times*, which might be expected to be a little sour, given the harsh light her books shone upon the life and ways of the clergy, had nothing but praise for it: 'We needn't bring Jane Austen into it, but Miss Pym is writing in a great tradition and she knows it.' Yes, she most certainly does. She knows exactly how to take a small community of folk and make its story timeless, universal and very, very funny.

Barbara went on to publish a further five critically well-received novels before, in 1963, with quite extraordinary lack of foresight, Cape's Tom Maschler refused to publish her next, *An Unsuitable Attachment*. Many years later she wrote to Philip Larkin that she and her sister Hilary had invented a pudding which they called 'a Maschler—a sort of milky jelly'—which is just the kind of thing that might happen in a Barbara Pym novel.

When Philip Larkin, perhaps Barbara's greatest fan and champion, discovered that Cape had rejected her, he was outraged at the Maschler decision, writing to her that:

> I can't understand why the publishers are taking this line ... it seems a sad state of affairs if such tender, perceptive and intelligent work can't see the light, just because some tasteless chump thinks it won't 'go' in paperback.

Suffice it to say that when *An Unsuitable Attachment* did get published, posthumously in 1982, it was received with rave reviews.

But to begin at the beginning . . . For those readers who have yet to discover Miss Barbara Pym, this debut novel will be full of delights and surprises; for those of us who have read and loved her books for years, this new edition of the first of her novels is a fitting tribute to her brilliant, humorous story-telling and the enduring charm of her writer's eye. *Some Tame Gazelle* is still my personal favourite for its sparkling high comedy and its treasury of characters, but rereading the entire canon, ten novels in all, has been pure bliss. She makes me smile, laugh out loud, consider my own foibles and fantasies, and, above all, suffer real regret when I reach the final page. Of how many authors can you honestly say that?

Mavis Cheek
November 2008

Some tame gazelle, or some gentle dove:
Something to love, oh, something to love!

THOMAS HAYNES BAYLY

CHAPTER ONE

The new curate seemed quite a nice young man, but what a pity it was that his combinations showed, tucked carelessly into his socks, when he sat down. Belinda had noticed it when they had met him for the first time at the vicarage last week and had felt quite embarrassed. Perhaps Harriet could say something to him about it. Her blunt jolly manner could carry off these little awkwardnesses much better than Belinda's timidity. Of course he might think it none of their business, as indeed it was not, but Belinda rather doubted whether he thought at all, if one were to judge by the quality of his first sermon.

'If only we could get back some of the fervour and eloquence of the seventeenth century in the pulpit today,' she had said to her sister Harriet, a plump elegant spinster in the middle fifties.

'Oh, we don't want that kind of thing *here*,' Harriet had said in her downright way, for she had long ago given up all intellectual pursuits, while Belinda, who had never been considered the clever one, still retained some smattering of the culture acquired in her college days. Even now a light would shine in her mild greenish eyes, so decorously hidden behind horn-rimmed spectacles, at the mention of Young's *Night Thoughts* or the dear Earl of Rochester's *Poems on Several Occasions*.

Neither she nor Harriet had ever married, but Harriet was making her usual fuss over the new curate and was obviously prepared to be quite as

3

silly over him as she had been over his predecessors. She was especially given to cherishing *young* clergymen, and her frequent excursions to the curates' lodgings had often given rise to talk, for people did like a bit of gossip, especially about a respectable spinster and church worker like Miss Harriet Bede. There was naturally nothing scandalous about these visits, as she always took with her a newly baked cake, some fresh eggs or fruit—for the poor young men always looked half starved—or even a hand-knitted pullover or pair of socks, begun by her in a burst of enthusiasm and usually finished, more soberly, by Belinda. And then of course she would ask them to supper.

Was it tonight he was coming? Belinda wondered vaguely. It must be tonight, she decided, catching sight of a bowl of exceptionally fine pears on the little table by the window, and expensive bought chrysanthemums in the vases when there were perfectly good Michaelmas daisies in the garden. Dear Harriet, she wasn't really extravagant, only rather too lavish in her hospitality. The Reverend Edgar Donne was surely a simple young man and would not expect much. Naturally one did not think of the clergy as expecting anything in the way of material luxuries . . . Belinda paused, for she was remembering the vicar, Archdeacon Hoccleve, and how one couldn't really say that about him. But then dear Henry was different, in some ways not like a clergyman at all. For although Belinda had loved him faithfully for over thirty years, she sometimes had to admit that he had very few of the obvious virtues that one somehow expected of one's parish priest. His letter in this month's parish magazine, announcing the arrival of the new curate, had a peevish and condescending tone that a stranger might have thought not quite the thing for an archdeacon. But the village was used to it.

'The Reverend Edgar Donne—the name is of course pronounced *Dunne*—will be with us by the time you read these words', he wrote. 'Nobody will be more glad to welcome him than I myself, for whom these last few weeks have been more trying than any of you can possibly imagine. Without a curate it has been impossible for me to take the holiday I so badly need and I have been forced to cancel some of the services because I have not felt equal to taking them, as the ready help I looked for from fellow priests in neighbouring parishes has not been forthcoming . . .'

Of course that was a dig at the Reverend Edward Plowman, who disliked the Archdeacon so much, and as he had quarrelled with Canon Glover what could he expect? thought Belinda, almost wishing that she were Deaconess Bede and could enter the pulpit herself. But even a deaconess was not permitted to celebrate Holy Communion—it was of course the *early* services which had been cancelled—whereas in the Nonconformist churches, she believed, women ministers had equal status with men . . .

'B'linda!' Harriet's impatient voice interrupted her thoughts, 'it's nearly seven and Mr Donne will soon be here.' Harriet appeared in the doorway, wearing only a celanese vest and knickers, as if her actual presence in the room would make Belinda realize more fully how late it was.

'Why, Harriet, the curtains aren't drawn,' exclaimed Belinda in an agitated tone. 'Anybody might see into the room! And you know I never take as long to get ready as you do.'

'All the same Mr Donne will probably be punctual,' said Harriet, 'and it would be terrible if neither of us was ready. I've borrowed your lace scarf, as I must have something to cover up the neck of my green frock. Perhaps it would have been better if I hadn't tried to alter it to a Vee.'

'Yes, dear.' Belinda spoke rather absently, for by now she was occupied with the problem of what *she* should wear. She hoped that Harriet had not also borrowed her black velvet bridge coat, as she wanted it herself on these late September evenings. But then Harriet was probably too stout for it, although she liked her clothes to fit tightly and always wore an elastic roll-on corset.

In her room Belinda took out her blue marocain, a rather dim dress of the kind known as 'semi-evening'. Quite good enough for the curate, she decided, though if the Archdeacon had been coming as well she would probably have worn her velvet. She did hope that Harriet wouldn't put on a lot of lipstick, it was so unsuitable . . .

At that moment there was a ring at the bell and an agitated call from Harriet.

'Belinda, you go! I haven't finished doing my hair.'

'But surely Emily will go?' said Belinda. She was wondering whether to wear her little seed-pearl brooch or not.

'No, Emily can't go. She's putting the sauce on the chicken.'

Belinda hurried downstairs without the little brooch. She felt flustered and incomplete.

The figure on the doorstep might have been any

6

of the other curates, except that Mr Donne favoured a rather unfashionably high clerical collar. He doesn't remember me, thought Belinda, as she replied to his rather puzzled greeting.

'This *is* Miss Bede's house?' he asked, hesitating on the threshold.

'Yes, I am Miss Bede,' said Belinda with simple dignity, 'but I expect you know my sister better.'

'Ah, you must be Miss *Belinda* Bede,' he announced, triumphant at having placed her. 'I've heard a lot about you from the Archdeacon.'

'Oh, really? What did he say?' Belinda tried not to sound too coy and eager.

'He—er—said you did a lot of good work in the parish,' replied the curate primly.

'Oh . . .' Belinda could not help feeling disappointed. It made her sound almost unpleasant. If that was what he had really said, of course. It didn't sound at all like the Archdeacon, who never said the sort of things clergymen ought to say. It was so odd to think of him as being a clergyman at all . . . Belinda's thoughts slipped back to her college days when they had been students together. *Most* odd . . . and yet there was no sadness or bitterness in her mind as she thought of him. It was obvious that poor Agatha had a very difficult time with him, although by her scheming she had made him an archdeacon. Their cook had told the Bedes' Emily who had told Harriet that the Archdeacon was very difficult to get up in the mornings, and of course one knew that he always made his curates do the early services which was really rather slack, because it wasn't as if he were very old or weak in health. And yet he had such charm, even now . . .

The curate coughed nervously and ventured a remark about the weather.

'Yes, I love September,' agreed Belinda, guilty at having let her thoughts wander from her guest. 'Michaelmas daisies and blackberries and comforting things like fires in the evening again and knitting.'

'Ah, knitting,' he smiled, and Belinda could see him glancing round the room as if he already expected to see the beginnings of a pullover for himself. But all that Belinda's cretonne work bag contained was a pink lacy-looking garment, a winter vest for herself. It was so annoying of Miss Jenner not to have any more 'Perliknit' left. She had had to buy a slightly thicker wool of a rather brighter pink to finish it off.

Fortunately at this moment, for the conversational going was heavy, a firm step was heard on the stairs and Harriet came into the room, radiant in flowered voile. Tropical flowers rioted over her plump body. The background was the green of the jungle, the blossoms were crimson and mauve, of an unknown species. Harriet was still attractive in a fat Teutonic way. She did not wear her pince-nez when curates came to supper.

The curate sprang up eagerly and seemed suddenly to lose some of his shyness.

'Good evening, Mr Donne,' said Harriet, 'I'm afraid I haven't my sister's punctual ways, but I'm sure she has been entertaining you better than I could have done. I had a classical education and it isn't a very good training for scintillating conversation.' She sat down rather heavily on the sofa beside him. 'Now we must not forget that the name is pronounced *Dunne*,' she declared

8

roguishly.

'Well, actually, as a matter of fact . . .' the curate looked embarrassed, 'I don't pronounce it that way. I can't imagine why the Archdeacon thought I did.'

'He was of course thinking of the seventeenth-century poet of that name,' said Belinda stoutly. The truth was, of course, that dear Henry could never resist a literary allusion and was delighted, in the way that children and scholars sometimes are, if it was one that the majority of his parishioners did not understand.

'He will have to put a correction in the magazine next month,' chortled Harriet. 'I should like to see the Archdeacon having to climb down.'

'It makes one feel quite odd to have one's name mispronounced or misspelt,' said Belinda evenly. 'Almost like a different person.'

'Oh, yes,' agreed Harriet, 'like Gorringe's catalogue.'

The curate looked politely interested but puzzled.

'You see,' Harriet explained, 'they once sent me a catalogue addressed to Miss *Bode*, and somehow I'm so lazy that I never bothered to correct it. So now I have a dual personality. I always feel Miss Bode is my dowdy self, rather a frumpish old thing.'

'She must certainly be most unlike Miss *Bede*,' blurted out Mr Donne with surprising gallantry.

Harriet protested amid delighted giggles. Belinda felt rather left out and found her eyes fixed on the curate's combinations, which still showed. Surely it was much too warm for such garments, unless perhaps he wore them all the year round?

During the short silence which followed, the tinkling of a cowbell was heard. The sisters had brought it back from a holiday in Switzerland and it was now used as a gong.

'Ah, dinner,' said Harriet. 'Come, Mr Donne, you shall take me in,' she added with mock solemnity.

Mr Donne was quite equal to the occasion, for he had all the qualifications of a typical curate. Indeed, his maternal grandfather had been a bishop.

In the dining-room Harriet sat at one end of the table and Belinda at the other, with the curate in the middle. Harriet carved the boiled chicken smothered in white sauce very capably. She gave the curate all the best white meat.

Were all new curates everywhere always given boiled chicken when they came to supper for the first time? Belinda wondered. It was certainly an established ritual at their house and it seemed somehow right for a new curate. The coldness, the whiteness, the muffling with sauce, perhaps even the sharpness added by the slices of lemon, there was something appropriate here, even if Belinda could not see exactly what it was.

'I called at the vicarage on the way here,' said the curate. 'Mrs Hoccleve very kindly promised me some apples.'

Harriet looked rather annoyed. 'Their apples haven't done at all well this year,' she said, 'and I always think those red ones are rather tasteless. You must take some of our Cox's Oranges with you when you go.'

The curate murmured grateful thanks.

'How is Mrs Hoccleve's rheumatism?' asked

Belinda.

'Not very much better,' he replied. 'I hear she is going to Karlsbad in October. Apparently the waters there are very good.'

'Nettles are an excellent thing, I believe,' said Harriet.

'Indeed?' Mr Donne looked so interested that he must have found it quite a strain. 'How should they be used?'

'Oh, I don't really know,' Harriet beamed. 'Just nettles. Boiled, perhaps. People will try all sorts of odd remedies,' she added, with the complacency of one who is perfectly healthy.

'Poor Agatha,' murmured Belinda, although she could not really feel very sympathetic.

There was a slight lapse in the conversation.

'I hear you are a rowing man,' said Belinda, with what she felt was rather forced enthusiasm.

'Oh, how splendid!' Harriet was of course delighted, as she would have been with any piece of information. 'I can just imagine you stroking an eight.'

'Well, actually, I haven't done any for some time, but I used to be very keen.' The curate looked down at his chicken bone as if he would like to take it up in his fingers and gnaw it. He was not very well fed at his lodgings and the evening meal was particularly scrappy.

Harriet picked up her bone and began to eat it in her fingers. She beamed on Mr Donne and said brightly, 'Like Queen Victoria, you know, so much more sensible and convenient.'

He followed her example eagerly. Belinda looked on with some distaste. If only Harriet could see how foolish she looked. The white sauce was beginning to smear itself on her face.

'I expect you are quite bewildered meeting so many new people,' she said, leading the conversation back into suitable channels.

'Yes, in a way I am, but I find it fairly easy to remember them so far. I came across Miss Liversidge this afternoon in the village and have persuaded her to address a meeting of the Mothers' Union. She seems to have had a great many interesting experiences.'

Belinda smiled. The idea of Edith Liversidge addressing the Mothers' Union amused her. One never knew what she might say to them and she would hardly set them a good example of tidiness. Dear Edith, she was always such a mess.

'She's a kind of decayed gentlewoman,' said Harriet comfortably, helping the curate to trifle.

'Oh *no*, Harriet,' Belinda protested. Nobody could call Edith decayed and sometimes one almost forgot that she was a gentlewoman, with her cropped grey hair, her shabby clothes which weren't even the legendary 'good tweeds' of her kind and her blunt, almost rough, way of speaking. 'Miss Liversidge is really splendid,' she declared and then wondered why one always said that Edith was 'splendid'. It was probably because she hadn't very much money, was tough and wiry, dug vigorously in her garden and kept goats. Also, she had travelled abroad a good deal and had done some relief work after the 1914 war among refugees in the Balkans. Work of rather an unpleasant nature too, something to do with sanitation. Belinda hoped that Harriet wouldn't mention it in front of Mr Donne. 'Of course she has made a home for poor Miss Aspinall, who's a

12

kind of relation,' she said hastily. 'I always thinks it's very unselfish to have a comparative stranger to live with you when you've been used to living alone.'

'Ah, well, we ought to share what we have with others,' said Mr Donne with rather disagreeable unctuousness.

'Oh, Mr Donne, I can't imagine you sharing your home with Connie Aspinall,' Harriet burst out, 'she's so dreary.'

Mr Donne smiled. 'Well, perhaps I didn't mean to be taken quite literally,' he said.

'Now she's a decayed gentlewoman if you like,' said Harriet. 'She can talk of nothing but the days when she used to be companion to a lady in Belgrave Square who was a kind of relation of one of Queen Alexandra's Ladies-in-Waiting.'

'She plays the harp very beautifully,' murmured Belinda weakly, for poor Connie was really rather uninteresting and it was hard to think of anything nice to say about her.

'Let's have coffee in the drawing-room,' said Harriet rather grandly. At one time she had wanted to call it the lounge, but Belinda would not hear of it. She had finally won her point by reminding Harriet of how much their dear mother would have disliked it.

In the drawing-room they arranged themselves as before, Harriet on the sofa with the curate and Belinda in one of the armchairs. Belinda took out her knitting and went on doing it rather self-consciously. It was beginning to look so very much like an undergarment for herself. The curate's combinations must be 'Meridian', she thought. It was nice and warm for pyjamas, too, in fact Harriet

13

herself wore it in the winter. The close fabric fitted her plump body like a woolly skin.

While they were drinking their coffee, Harriet went to the little table by the window and took up the bowl of pears which Belinda had noticed earlier in the evening.

'Now you must have a pear,' she insisted. 'Do you know, when we were children our mother used to say that we could never keep fruit on the sideboard.'

Belinda would have liked to add that they couldn't now, and that it was only because they had been having the curate to supper that there had been anything more than a withered apple or orange in the bowl this evening. Harriet's appetite was just as rapacious in her fifties as it had been in her teens.

The curate helped himself to a pear and began to peel it. He seemed to be getting rather sticky and there was some giggling and interchange of large handkerchiefs between him and Harriet.

Belinda went on quietly with her knitting. The evening promised to be just like so many other evenings when other curates had come to supper. There was something almost frightening and at the same time comforting about the sameness of it all. It was odd that Harriet should always have been so fond of curates. They were so immature and always made the same kind of conversation. Now the Archdeacon was altogether different. One never knew what he might say, except that it was certain to be something unexpected and provocative. Besides, it was really more suitable to lavish one's affection on somebody of a riper age, as it was obviously natural that one should lavish it on somebody. Indeed, one of Belinda's favourite quotations, taken from the works of a minor English poet, was

> *Some tame gazelle, or some gentle dove:*
> *Something to love, oh, something to love!*

Belinda, having loved the Archdeacon when she was twenty and not having found anyone to replace him since, had naturally got into the habit of loving him, though with the years her passion had mellowed into a comfortable feeling, more like the cosiness of a winter evening by the fire than the uncertain rapture of a spring morning.

Harriet's tittering laugh disturbed Belinda's quiet thoughts. 'Oh, Mr Donne, I'm not quite as stupid as you think! I used to know some Latin. *Ah quotiens illum doluit properare Calypso,*' she retorted, flinging at him triumphantly the last remnants of her classical education.

Can she be hinting at me to go? he wondered, but then decided that she had probably long ago forgotten the meaning of the line. All the same it was getting late. He mustn't outstay his welcome and the elder Miss Bede had yawned once or twice, although she stifled it very politely.

Despite protests from Harriet, they were soon in the hall and the curate was putting on his overcoat. Harriet was fussing round him like a motherly hen.

'Why, of course, it's the garden party tomorrow,' said Belinda, suddenly feeling very tired. 'There will be such a lot to do.'

The curate sighed with an affectation of weariness. 'I shall be almost glad when it is over,' he said. 'These functions are always very tiring

15

for us.'

Harriet smiled understandingly, as if including herself in the select brotherhood of the clergy. 'Never mind,' she said, 'there will be the coconut shies. I always love them. And you'll get a good tea. *I* am in charge of the tea garden.'

'Oh, *well*, Miss Bede . . .' the curate moved towards the front door and Belinda was able to slip quietly into the background. She went into the drawing-room and began to tidy it, plumping up the cushions and removing the remains of the pears they had eaten. She put her knitting into its cretonne bag and took the parish magazine to read in bed. There was a nice new serial in it, all about a drunken organist and a young bank clerk, who was also a lay reader and had been wrongfully accused of embezzlement. And of course the Archdeacon's letter was always worth a second reading.

CHAPTER TWO

Although the Misses Bede had a maid they were both quite domesticated and helped her in various small ways, clearing away the breakfast things, dusting their own bedrooms and doing a little cooking when they felt like it. On this particular morning, however, which was the day of the vicarage garden party, Belinda decided that she could miss doing her room with a clear conscience, as there were so many more important things to be done. It was unlikely that Miss Liversidge would be visiting them and putting them to shame by writing 'E. Liversidge' with her finger, as she had

16

once done when Emily had neglected to dust the piano. Typical of Edith, of course, going straight to the point with no beating about the bush. Not that she could talk either, with dog's hairs all over the carpet and the washing-up left overnight.

This morning, as she went about humming *God moves in a mysterious way*, Belinda wondered what to do first. She had to arrange for some deck-chairs they had promised to be taken over to the vicarage. The cake she had made to be raffled—the Archdeacon was broad-minded and didn't disapprove of such things—must be finished off with its mauve paper frill. The seams of Harriet's crêpe de Chine dress had to be let out, as Harriet seemed to have grown stouter since she had last worn it. Perhaps that was the most important thing of all, for Harriet intended to wear it that afternoon.

While she was sewing, Belinda began to wonder what everyone would be wearing at the garden party. Agatha Hoccleve would of course wear a nice suitable dress, but nothing extreme or daring. As the wife of an archdeacon she always had very *good* clothes, which seemed somehow to emphasize the fact that her father had been a bishop. Then there was Edith Liversidge, who would look odd in the familiar old-fashioned grey costume, whose unfashionably narrow shoulders combined with Edith's broad hips made her look rather like a lighthouse. Her relation, Miss Aspinall, would wear a fluttering blue or grey dress with a great many scarves and draperies, and she would, as always, carry that mysterious little beaded bag without which she was never seen anywhere. Undoubtedly the most magnificent

17

person there would be Lady Clara Boulding, who was to perform the opening ceremony. It was of course fitting that this should be so, as she was the daughter of an earl and the widow of their former Member of Parliment, an excellent man in his way, although he had never been known to speak in the House except on one occasion, when he had asked if a window might be opened or shut.

By now Belinda had tacked the seams of the dress and was fitting it on her sister, who twitched about impatiently, while Belinda ran round her with her mouth full of pins.

Harriet was having one of her tirades against the Archdeacon.

'All that nonsense in the parish magazine about him needing a holiday,' she stormed. 'If that's so, why doesn't he go to Karlsbad with Agatha? Unless she wants a holiday away from him—you could hardly blame her if she preferred to go alone. *I* certainly would.'

'But surely Agatha isn't going to Karlsbad *alone*?' asked Belinda eagerly.

'Well, their Florrie told Emily that she and cook aren't looking forward to managing the Archdeacon by themselves, so it looks as if he isn't going with her. I think it would be nicer if he went too, then we might have a good sermon for a change. I never heard anything so depressing in my life as that horrid thing he read last Sunday—all about worms, and such stilted language. Edith Liversidge walked out in the middle, and'— Harriet chortled at the memory of it—'one of the churchwardens ran after her with a glass of water, thinking she felt faint or something.'

'But Harriet,' said Belinda gently, 'Henry was

reading a passage from *Urn Burial*, I thought he read it magnificently,' she sighed. Of course the real truth of the matter was that poor Henry was too lazy to write sermons of his own and somehow one didn't think of him as being clever in a theological kind of way. That is, no scholarly study of any of St Paul's Epistles had as yet appeared under Archdeacon Hoccleve's name, although he had once remarked to Belinda that he thought the Apocalyptic literature remarkably fine.

Harriet continued her tirade. 'If it weren't so far to walk,' she said, 'I should certainly go to Edward Plowman's church; he does at least preach good homely sermons that everyone can understand. He works systematically through the Ten Commandments and the Beatitudes, I believe; much the most sensible thing to do. Besides, he's such a nice man.'

'But Harriet,' said Belinda anxiously, 'he *is* rather high. He wears a biretta and has incense in the church. It's all so—well—*Romish*.' Broad-minded as she was, Belinda was unable to keep a note of horror out of her voice.

Harriet became defiant. 'Edward Plowman is such a fine-looking man, too,' she declared. 'Like Cardinal Newman.'

'Oh, no, Harriet,' protested Belinda. 'Cardinal Newman had a much bigger nose. And besides, he really did go *over*, you know, and I'm sure Edward Plowman would never do that.'

'Oh, then I must have been thinking of somebody else,' said Harriet vaguely. 'Anyway,' she went on, 'Mr Donne could certainly preach better sermons than the Archdeacon, I'm sure.' She pulled the dress off over her head. 'You needn't bother to oversew the seams—they won't show.'

When Belinda had finished the sewing she decided that she had better go over to the vicarage to see if she could help Agatha in any way. It did not take her long to reach the vicarage gate, as it was very near her own house. When they had finally decided to spend their old age together, Harriet had insisted that they should be well in touch with the affairs of the parish. Belinda had not felt so strongly about it, although when Archdeacon Hoccleve had been made vicar she was naturally glad that their house was so near his. She imagined friendly poppings in and out but somehow, dear Henry not being quite like other clergymen, it hadn't worked out like that. And then of course there was Agatha. It was difficult to be completely informal with her, either because of her father having been a bishop or for some more subtle reason, Belinda had never been quite sure which.

She walked up the vicarage drive. The Archdeacon had a hankering after the picturesque and would have liked a ha-ha, a ruined temple, grottoes, waterfalls and gloomily overhanging trees. He fancied himself to be rather like one of those eighteenth-century clergymen suffering from the spleen, but Agatha was a practical woman, who liked neat borders and smooth lawns, flowers in the front garden and vegetables at the back. So the vicarage garden, as Belinda saw it on this September morning, was admirably suited to a garden party but there were no grottoes.

Belinda walked up to the front door, but before she had time to ring the bell Agatha appeared, carrying many bundles of brightly coloured paper.

She was wearing a plain but well-cut dress of striped Macclesfield silk and looked rather harassed.

'How are you, Agatha?' asked Belinda. 'I've come to see if there's anything I can do to help and I must see the Archdeacon about the Sunday School children's recitations.'

'Henry is having a bath,' said Agatha shortly.

Surely rather late? thought Belinda. It was past eleven and oughtn't an archdeacon to rise earlier than that?

'So of course you can't see him now,' continued Agatha in the same tone of voice, which implied that she had the privilege not allowed to Belinda of seeing an archdeacon in his bath. 'You will have to wait,' she concluded, with a note of something like triumph in her voice.

'Why, of course,' said Belinda meekly. Agatha always seemed to be most formidable in the mornings. In the evenings she was often quite affable and would talk about begonias and the best way to pickle walnuts.

'You seem very busy,' said Belinda, moving towards Agatha as if to help her. 'Can't I do something while I'm waiting for the Archdeacon?'

Agatha nodded reluctantly. 'I was going to arrange the garden-produce stall,' she said, thinking that Belinda Bede was rather a nuisance although she no doubt meant well. 'You might help me to pin the coloured paper round it. I thought green and orange and perhaps red would show off the vegetables rather nicely.'

'What lovely marrows!' exclaimed Belinda, catching sight of them among a heap of miscellaneous garden produce. They were

21

gleaming yellow and dark green, with pale stripes. Surely the poor soil of the vicarage garden could not have produced such beauties?

'Yes, they are fine,' agreed Agatha. 'They are from Count Bianco's garden. He brought them round himself early this morning.'

'Poor old Count Bianco,' said Belinda gently. Ricardo Bianco was an Italian count, who for some unexplained reason had settled in the village many years ago. He was a gentle melancholy man, beloved by everyone for his generosity and courtly manners and he had admired Harriet Bede for more years than could now be remembered. He had the habit of asking her to marry him every now and then, and Harriet, although she always refused him, was really very fond of him and often asked his advice about her gardening problems. Gardening and his childhood in Naples were his chief topics of conversation, though he would occasionally enjoy a melancholy talk about his old friend John Akenside, who had been killed in a riot in Prague, when he had just been sitting at an open-air café taking a glass of wine, as was his custom in the evening, doing no harm to anybody. 'Ricardo is so *devoted* to Harriet,' said Belinda, giving the words a full meaning which was not lost on Agatha Hoccleve.

Agatha went rather pink and said angrily, 'Count Bianco comes of a very old Italian family. I always think he and Lady Clara Boulding would be very suited to each other, but of course her father's earldom was only a nineteenth-century creation,' she mused.

Belinda was rather annoyed at this. 'I don't think Lady Clara and Ricardo would be at all suited to each other,' she said, repeating his Christian name with triumph. 'Harriet and Ricardo have a great many tastes in common, especially gardening. Why, whenever he comes to our house he nearly always brings with him some roots or seeds . . .' here Belinda broke off, aware that this sounded rather ridiculous, but Agatha did not seem to have noticed. She was just opening her mouth to say something else, when their attention was diverted by somebody calling out in a loud voice.

Belinda recognized the voice as that of the Archdeacon. He was leaning out of one of the upper windows, calling to Agatha, and he sounded very peevish. Belinda thought he looked so handsome in his dark green dressing-gown with his hair all ruffled. The years had dealt kindly with him and he had grown neither bald nor fat. It was Agatha who seemed to have suffered most. Her pointed face had lost the elfin charm which had delighted many and now looked drawn and harassed. She had rheumatism too, but Belinda realized that she would have to have something out of self-defence and perhaps with the passing of the years it had become a reality. One never knew.

The voice went on calling. It seemed that the moths had got into the Archdeacon's grey suit and why had Agatha been so grossly neglectful as to let this happen? The tirade was audible to anyone in the garden or in the road beyond.

Belinda turned away from the window and began to hang festoons of green paper along the top of the stall. The gardener, who was weeding one of the flower beds nearby, also turned away. He could not bear the Venerable Hoccleve, as the servants called him. He was a bit mad in his opinion, wanting yew trees on the lawn and something he called a ha-ha, which no gardener had ever heard of.

Eventually Agatha returned to the business of decorating, looking extremely annoyed, but not mentioning the incident. She began to take down all Belinda's decorations and arrange them another way. Belinda thought it better to say nothing, so they went on with their work in silence. At last Belinda, who felt rather uncomfortable, drew Agatha's attention to the arrangement of the marrows.

'I think they would look rather effective in a kind of pyramid, if it could be managed,' she suggested, thinking to herself that it would obviously be better if Agatha were to humour dear Henry a little more. But of course Belinda could hardly give an archdeacon's wife a few hints on how to manage her husband.

At that moment one of the marrows fell over and the pyramid had to be rebuilt. While they were doing this, the Archdeacon came out on to the lawn.

'Good morning,' he said, ignoring his wife. 'I see that I have kept you waiting, but so many annoying things have happened that it was quite impossible to be ready any sooner.' He darted a quick, angry glance at Agatha.

Belinda spoke hastily in order to change the subject.

'I've brought a list of the recitations the children have learnt, so you can choose which ones you think best from it,' she said, knowing perfectly well that he would find fault with the pieces and ask why they had not been taught more Middle

English lyrics or passages from Gower and Chaucer.

He smiled with an affectation of weariness and then sighed. 'Ah, yes. There is so much to be done before this afternoon. I haven't been able to sleep for thinking about it. Nobody can possibly know how much I have to do,' he went on, with another meaning glance at Agatha.

'Perhaps if you had got up earlier, Henry,' she said sharply. 'Florrie called you at eight. I was up at *seven*.'

The Archdeacon laughed and began to pace about the lawn with his hands in his pockets. Belinda was embarrassed and began to walk slowly towards the house. Eventually the Archdeacon followed. They walked together into his study. He was smiling to himself in a sardonic way that Belinda found very disconcerting. It was unsuitable for a clergyman to look sardonic. Perhaps Harriet was right to prefer the more conventional Mr Plowman and Mr Donne.

There was an awkward silence and to break it Belinda descended weakly to flattery.

'I did enjoy hearing you read *Urn Burial* last Sunday,' she said. 'It is so *very* fine and you read it so well.'

'Ah, yes. Do you remember when I used to read Milton to you?' he said, his thoughts going back to the days when Belinda's frank adoration had been so flattering. By this time he had forgotten how bored he had been by her constancy. Agatha never asked him to read aloud to her when they were alone together in the evenings. 'Do you remember the magnificent opening lines of *Samson Agonistes*?' he asked, warming to his subject and

25

looking dangerously on the brink of reminding her of them. Indeed, the first words were already out of his mouth when Belinda interrupted him, and directed his attention to the matter in hand. There was of course nothing she would have liked better than to hear dear Henry reciting Milton, but somehow with Agatha outside and so much to be done it didn't seem quite the thing. Also, it was the morning and it seemed a little odd to be thinking about poetry before luncheon.

'Now,' she said, 'what about these recitations? I have a list of the ones they know, so I think perhaps you'd better let me choose the most suitable ones. I know you must be very busy with other things,' she added soothingly, 'and even though Mr Donne can help you, I know that you like to see to everything personally.'

'I doubt whether our friend Donne will be much help,' said the Archdeacon. 'His sermons are very poor. He and Edward Plowman are about a match for each other.'

'Oh, but one must be tolerant,' said Belinda, 'and many people prefer a simple sermon. I've heard people say that Edward Plowman is considered quite a saint in his parish.'

The Archdeacon laughed rather bitterly. 'Do you wonder when his parish consists almost entirely of doting spinsters?' he said. It was one of the Archdeacon's grievances that people never made a fuss of him as they did of Father Plowman or of the younger curates, although he pretended to despise such adulation. And then too, Lady Clara Boulding, whose country seat lay midway between the two villages, had chosen to attend Plowman's church rather than his. The Archdeacon could not help feeling bitter about this, for although Belinda might put a pound note into the collection bag on Easter Sunday, it was hardly the same as Lady Clara's five or ten. In these days of poverty the spirit in which it was given counted for very little.

'You need not make fun of doting spinsters,' said Belinda, roused by his mockery. 'After all, it isn't always our fault . . .' she stopped in confusion, fearing that he might make some sarcastic retort.

'No, women like to have something to dote on,' he said mildly enough, 'I have noticed that. And we in the Church are usually the victims.'

'We are *all* in the Church,' said Belinda gently. 'I think I should go out into the garden again and help Agatha. There must still be a great deal to do.'

Out in the garden, Agatha, surrounded now by several willing helpers, for she was popular among the church workers because of her distinguished ecclesiastical connections, had finished decorating and arranging the garden-produce stall.

The vicarage garden was beginning to look like a fairground. Stalls, coconut shies, bran-tubs and even a fortune-teller's booth had taken root on the lawn. The Archdeacon always hated this annual garden party and tried to have as little to do with it as possible, although he had to put in an appearance to fawn on the more distinguished visitors. There was always a possibility that Lady Clara Boulding might decide to come to his church, which was really nearer if one walked across the fields, although it was difficult to imagine anyone as impressive as Lady Clara doing that.

'It looks as if everything is finished,' said Belinda. 'I don't feel as if I have done my share.'

27

'You have put up with my ill-humour for ten minutes,' said the Archdeacon, 'which is more than anyone else could have done.'

Belinda flushed with embarrassment and secret pleasure. She felt herself to be somehow exalted above the groups of busy women, who had been arranging pyramids of apples, filling bran-tubs and decorating stalls with coloured paper. Once, she knew, she *had* been different, and perhaps after all the years had left her with a little of that difference. Perhaps she was still an original shining like a comet, mingling no water with her wine. But only very occasionally, mostly she was just like everyone else, rather less efficient, if anything. Even her paper decorations had been taken down and rearranged. There was nothing of her handiwork left on the garden-produce stall.

'Why, look,' she exclaimed, unable to deal with the Archdeacon's curious compliment, 'there's Edith Liversidge. Whatever is she doing?' For Miss Liversidge, looking even more dishevelled than usual, was pushing her way through a thick clump of rhododendrons on the opposite side of the lawn.

'Oh, Archdeacon,' she called in her rough, mannish voice, 'there you are! I've been looking everywhere for you.'

'Well, Miss Liversidge, I hardly see why you should have expected to find me in the rhododendrons,' he said.

'Oh, that's the treasure hunt,' she explained. 'I've just been arranging some of the clues. We shall have everybody tied up in knots this afternoon.'

'That will certainly be diverting,' said the Archdeacon politely, 'but I had imagined it was

28

only for the younger people.'

'Oh, nonsense, everyone will be encouraged to join in. Now, what I really wanted to see you about was the cloakroom arrangements. Lavatories, you know. What has been done?' Edith rapped out the question with brusque efficiency.

Belinda turned away in embarrassment. Surely Edith could have asked Agatha and need not have troubled the Archdeacon with such an unsuitable thing? But he appeared to be enjoying the conversation and entered into the discussion with grave courtesy.

'I cannot really say. I had imagined that people would use their own discretion,' he ventured.

'Children are not noted for their discretion,' said Edith bluntly, 'and even grown-ups aren't angels.'

The Archdeacon smiled. 'No, not even the higher orders of the clergy would claim to be quite that. Perhaps you can help us, Miss Liversidge, we all know your experience in these matters.'

'Yes, but of course it wasn't at all the same thing in the Balkans after the war,' said Edith, perhaps unnecessarily. 'Still, I have been thinking things over. We must have clear notices put up. I've got Mr Matthews from the Art School at work on them now.'

'Poor Matthews, a prostitution of his talents, I feel,' said the Archdeacon. 'I think Gothic lettering would be most suitable. What is your opinion, Miss Bede?'

Poor Belinda, confused at being drawn into the conversation, could only murmur that in her opinion the largest and clearest kind of lettering would obviously be the best.

Miss Liversidge looked from one to the other

29

impatiently. 'I thought the ladies should use the ground-floor cloakroom and the gentlemen the place behind the toolshed.'

'The Place Behind the Toolshed, what a sinister sound that has,' mused the Archdeacon. 'I'm sure your arrangements will be admirable, Miss Liversidge, though perhaps hardly necessary.'

'We shall see about that,' she said in a dark tone, and then stumped off in search of her relative, Miss Aspinall, calling her as if she were a dog, 'Connie! Connie! Come along! Time to go home to lunch.'

Miss Aspinall, who had been enjoying a snobbish little talk with Agatha, hurried after her. She could never keep pace with Edith and was always a few steps behind her.

'I think Edith Liversidge is really disgusting,' said Harriet indignantly. 'Mr Donne and I could overhear what she was saying from the tea garden. He seemed most embarrassed.'

'Ah, what it is to be young,' sighed the Archdeacon. 'Or perhaps he is what the higher orders of the clergy would not claim to be. One never knows.'

'He is an excellent preacher,' said Harriet stoutly, if irrelevantly, 'and he seems to have the coconuts *very* well organized. Now Mr Donne,' she called, bringing him into the group, 'don't forget that you promised to let me win a coconut.'

'Ah, Miss Bede, I'm sure your skill will win the biggest one of all,' said Mr Donne gallantly.

At this point Belinda thought it would be as well if they went home to luncheon. They would need to reserve all their strength for the afternoon, she explained.

CHAPTER THREE

'Don't you think you would be more comfortable in low-heeled shoes, dear?' suggested Belinda tentatively. 'One's feet always get so tired standing about.' She glanced down at her own—long, English gentlewoman's feet she always thought them, sensibly clad in shoes that were rather too heavy for the printed crêpe de Chine dress and coatee she was wearing.

Harriet glanced down too. 'I always think low heels are so dowdy,' she said. 'Besides, high heels are definitely the fashion now.'

'Yes, I suppose they are,' agreed Belinda, for Harriet always knew things like that. And yet, she thought, at our age, surely all that was necessary was to dress suitably and if possible in good taste, without really thinking of fashion? With the years one ought to have grown beyond such thoughts but somehow one never did, and Belinda set out for the afternoon conscious that she was wearing dowdy shoes.

As they walked to the vicarage, Belinda regulating her normally brisk step in consideration for Harriet's high heels, they were overtaken by Count Bianco, who was escorting Miss Liversidge and Miss Aspinall, both of whom were dressed exactly as Belinda had anticipated. Count Bianco wore a light grey suit and a panama hat. He carried a stick and grey gloves and there was a fine rose in his buttonhole. As they came together he gave them a courtly bow, which from anybody else might have seemed exaggerated.

'How charming you are looking, Miss Harriet,' he said, 'and you also, Miss Belinda,' he added, as a courteous afterthought. 'Poor old John Akenside,' he went on meditatively, 'how he loved the hot weather.'

'Nonsense, Ricardo,' said Edith Liversidge, 'he always went as red as a lobster in the sun.' She had known the Count's friend in what she called her Balkans Days and it was rumoured that he had been very fond of her, but had been too shy to declare himself. It seemed odd to think that anyone could have loved Edith, who seemed a person to inspire fear and respect rather than any more tender emotion, but, as Belinda had once suggested, perhaps the unpleasant nature of her work in the Balkans had hardened her and she had once been more lovable.

They walked on to the lawn where a group of people had assembled. Belinda could see the Archdeacon standing at the top of the front-door steps, against a background of Victorian stained glass, the vicarage being built in the Gothic style. She thought he looked splendid, and somehow the glass set off his good looks.

Lady Clara Boulding was to open the garden party officially at half-past two and as she had now arrived, there seemed no reason why she should not get on with it at once. But the crowd was obviously waiting for something. Agatha Hoccleve, who was standing by her husband, nudged him and said in an agitated and audible whisper, 'Henry, a *prayer*.'

The Archdeacon started. He had been wondering whether Lady Clara would give some definite contribution to the church-roof fund as well as buying things at the stalls. He cleared his throat.

'Let us ask for God's blessing on our endeavours,' he said, in a loud voice which quite startled some people.

Belinda looked down at the grass and then at Agatha's neat suède shoes, so much more suited to the occasion than her own.

The Archdeacon began to recite a prayer. *O Lord God, who seest that we put not our trust in anything that we do, mercifully grant that by Thy Power we may be defended against all adversity . . .*

Harriet looked at Belinda and frowned. The Archdeacon always chose such unsuitable prayers. *Prevent us O Lord in all our doings,* was the obviously correct one for such an occasion. These little departures from convention always annoyed her.

Belinda, on the other hand, was thinking loyally, what an excellent choice! It strikes just the right note of humility. When Henry prays for defence from adversity, he must mean too much confidence in our own powers. One knew that pride often came before a fall. Or perhaps he was not referring to the garden party specifically, but taking in the larger sphere of life outside it . . . here Belinda's thoughts became confused and a doubt crept into her mind, which was quickly and loyally pushed back. For it could not be that dear Henry had just said the first prayer that came into his head . . .

There was a short pause. Count Bianco replaced his panama hat and everyone began to move, relieved to be normal once more.

But they were not to be released yet. Lady Clara

enjoyed opening garden parties and bazaars. Indeed, apart from attending memorial services in fashionable London churches, it was her chief recreation. She stood on a grassy bank, slightly raised above the rest of the crowd. She was still a handsome woman, and if her speech contained rather too much of her late husband's meaningless parliamentary phraseology, her voice was nevertheless pleasant and soothing. Miss Aspinall, who had detached herself from Miss Liversidge in order to be among the foremost of the little group who would go round the stalls with Lady Clara, was listening with a pathetically eager expression on her thin face. Nobody knew how much Edith got on her nerves and how different it all was from the days when she had been companion to Lady Grudge in Belgrave Square. Treated like one of the family, *such* kindness . . . Connie's eyes filled with tears and she had to turn away.

At last Lady Clara stepped down from her grassy platform and made her way towards the stalls, accompanied by Agatha and the Archdeacon, who had a particularly ingratiating smile on his face. At a respectful distance behind them came Miss Aspinall with a group of lady helpers, who were hurrying to get to their places at the stalls. Lady Clara's progress was slow and stately but profitable. She bought some jam, two marrows, half a dozen lavender sachets, a tea cosy, a pair of bed socks, some paper spills in a fancy case and an embroidered *Radio Times* cover.

Belinda, now busy at the garden-produce stall, was wondering whether she ought to wrap Lady Clara's marrows up, and if so what was the best way of doing it. They had only newspapers for wrapping, so she chose *The Times* as being the most suitable and made them up into a rather clumsy parcel. Lady Clara's chauffeur was to collect them later.

Not long after this Agatha came back to the stall and began to fluster the helpers by rearranging them and collecting all the money together into one tin, so that they were all tumbling over each other to get change instead of each one having her own little pile.

'What's this?' asked Agatha sharply, pointing to the *Times*-shrouded parcel which Belinda had put into a corner.

'Oh, that's Lady Clara's marrows,' Belinda explained.

'Wrapped in newspaper?' Agatha's tone was expressive. 'I'm afraid that won't do at all.' She produced some blue tissue paper from a secret hiding-place and began to undo Belinda's parcel.

'Oh, dear, I'm so sorry, I didn't know there was any other paper,' said Belinda in confusion. 'I saw them lying there and I thought perhaps they ought to be wrapped up and put aside in case anybody sold them by mistake.'

'I don't think anybody would be so stupid as to do that,' said Agatha evenly. 'They were the two finest marrows on the stall, I chose them myself.'

'Oh, well . . .' Belinda gave a weak little laugh. All this fuss about two marrows. But it might go deeper than that, although it did not do to think so.

'Perhaps you would like to go and have tea,' said Agatha, who was having difficulty with the bulk of the marrows and the fragility of the tissue paper and did not want Belinda to see. 'We may as well

35

go in turns.'

'Well, yes, if it isn't too early,' said Belinda.

'Oh, no, Lady Clara is already having hers. She has gone with Count Bianco.' Agatha stood up and reached for a ball of string.

Belinda felt herself hurrying away, routed was perhaps the word, Agatha triumphant. It was a pity they sometimes had these little skirmishes, especially when Agatha was so often triumphant. All over two marrows, even if they were the finest on the stall.

Belinda looked around to see if she could find Harriet. She felt that she wanted to tell somebody about the marrows and perhaps laugh over them. Harriet's healthy indignation would do her as much good as a cup of tea, she thought. But Harriet was nowhere to be seen. And where was the Archdeacon? It would be just like him to retire to the house and have a bath. But he had already had one today, as Belinda knew, so she guessed that he was probably attending on some of the more distinguished visitors.

As she entered the tea garden she saw Harriet sitting at a table with the curate. Harriet was handing him a plate of cakes and urging him in her penetrating voice to try one of the pink ones which she had made specially for him. Perhaps it will be better if I don't disturb them, thought Belinda, turning round to look for a vacant place at one of the other tables. And then she came face to face with the Archdeacon. He also wanted his tea, and as they had so often had tea together in the past what could be more natural than that they should have it together this afternoon?

They sat down at a table for two. Belinda began

to be assailed by various doubts. What would people think to see her having tea with the Archdeacon while his wife was still working tirelessly at the garden-produce stall? It was a pity really to worry about what people thought, but, Belinda flattered herself, she wasn't entirely old and unattractive, even in her sensible shoes, and she still had the marrows on her conscience, although she did not feel that she could tell the Archdeacon about them.

He on the other hand had no such scruples. Belinda began to wish that he wouldn't talk so loudly, for although she knew that it was only one of his little oddnesses to complain about his wife, other people might not realize this. So she put two lumps of sugar into his tea, and tried as tactfully as she could to change the subject of the conversation.

'But Agatha has been so busy arranging things for the garden party and the concert tonight,' said Belinda in a low voice. 'She can't see to everything at once.' Raising her voice, she went on, 'Speaking of the concert reminds me that Harriet is still undecided as to what she is going to play. Of course she has a large repertoire, but one must choose something suitable and not too long . . .' Belinda babbled on. '. . . she's very anxious to play a Brahms intermezzo, but it may be a little heavy for a village concert. I thought perhaps some Mendelssohn, some of the *Songs without Words* are so charming . . .' She looked at the Archdeacon anxiously, to see if he had yet forgotten Agatha's negligence in letting the moths get into his grey suit.

His face betrayed that he had not. In fact all the

bright conversation about the concert seemed to have been wasted on him. 'I don't think you'd have done that,' he said thoughtfully, gazing at a piece of bread and butter on his plate.

Belinda saw that it was no good trying to change the subject yet. He must be humoured out of it. She seemed to be having a difficult afternoon altogether, what with the episode of the marrows and now having to humour the Archdeacon. Archdeacons ought not to need humouring, she told herself angrily. Supposing Henry were a bishop, could one still expect no improvement?

'What are you smiling at?' asked the Archdeacon crossly. 'People look very foolish smiling at nothing.'

'I wasn't smiling at nothing,' retorted Belinda. 'I was wondering if you'd still make such a fuss about unimportant trifles if you were a bishop.'

'Unimportant trifles! The only good suit I have ruined, and you call it an unimportant trifle.'

'We are supposed not to take heed of what we shall wear,' said Belinda unconvincingly.

'My dear Belinda, we are not in the Garden of Eden. That is no solution to the problem. We may as well face the facts. Agatha ought not to have let the moth get into that suit. It was her duty to see that they didn't. I am sure that you would have seen that it was put away with moth balls . . .' the Archdeacon's voice had now grown so loud that people at the other tables were beginning to look at them with interest and amusement. Belinda felt most embarrassed.

'It would have smelt of camphor then and you would probably have disliked that,' she said, almost in a whisper.

The Archdeacon gave a shout of laughter at this. Suddenly he was in a good temper again, fell on a plate of cakes and began to eat ravenously. 'I was too busy to have any luncheon,' he explained. 'So many tiresome things to do.'

'It will be nice for you to go away for a holiday,' ventured Belinda.

The Archdeacon sighed heavily. 'Ah, if only I could.'

'But now that Mr Donne is here, surely it can be managed?'

'One cannot leave the flock without a shepherd,' said the Archdeacon in a mocking tone.

'But he said—I mean we heard—that Agatha was going to Karlsbad in October,' said Belinda, urged on by curiosity. 'Surely you will be going too?'

'Alas, no.' The Archdeacon finished the last cake. 'And even if I were, it would hardly be a holiday for me.'

Belinda could think of no reply to make to this and none seemed to be expected. She could neither agree nor protest, she felt, but did what seemed to her the best she could by getting up. from the table and saying that she really must get back to the stall. 'I must go and relieve Agatha,' she said. 'I see she hasn't been for her tea yet.'

'It will please her not to have any,' said the Archdeacon. 'I wonder that you have had any. I thought women enjoyed missing their meals and making martyrs of themselves.'

'We may do it, but I think we can leave the enjoyment of it to the men,' said Belinda, pleased at having thought of an answer. But Henry was really too bad, there was no knowing what he

39

might say next. And he was not going to Karlsbad
. . . She hoped nobody had overheard their
conversation. It had really been most unsuitable,
but somehow she felt better for it and had almost
forgotten the episode of the marrows.

Back at the garden-produce stall, Belinda saw
Agatha, looking rather tired and flustered,
bundling what remained of the flowers, fruit and
vegetables on to the front of the stall.

'Oh, there you are,' she exclaimed, making
Belinda feel that she had been away too long.

'Yes, you must be longing for your tea, but surely
you could have gone before now? Wouldn't Miss
Liversidge or Miss Aspinall have taken charge of
the stall?' said Belinda, doing the best she could.

'Oh, well, I may as well go now,' said Agatha
grudgingly, 'we seem to have taken quite a lot of
money.'

'Yes, and the tea garden has been crowded. The
Archdeacon was still there when I left,' Belinda
added, thinking that this might encourage Agatha.

'I have had no luncheon,' she said. 'I shall really
be glad of a cup of tea.'

'Oh, dear, I wish I'd known that, then you could
have gone first,' said Belinda. Had there been no
luncheon at all at the vicarage today? Surely a bad
arrangement, or had the Archdeacon and his wife
wished to outdo each other in self-denial?

'Well, Belinda, I expect *you* enjoyed your tea,'
said Harriet, advancing towards the stall.

Belinda was thankful that Agatha was out of
hearing. 'Yes, I thought the cakes were lovely,' she
said.

'You and the Archdeacon looked so cosy. Having
a nice conversation about moth balls, too, most

domestic. What a *pity* it is about Agatha. They have really nothing in common.'

'Oh, Harriet, you're quite wrong,' said Belinda stoutly. 'Agatha is a most intelligent woman. She knows a great deal about medieval English literature. And then there's *palaeography*,' she continued, as if her emphatic tone would explain its importance in the married life of Agatha and the Archdeacon.

'Oh, yes, that's about apes, isn't it?' said Harriet, losing interest in the subject. 'Do you think a fur cape would be too hot for the concert this evening? The gold lamé jacket doesn't really go so well with my blue as the white fur. Besides, it's rather severe and needs something to soften it.'

Eventually Harriet decided to wear the white fur cape, and everyone agreed that she looked very handsome, although one of the more spiteful Sunday School teachers whispered to her friend that she suspected it was not real ermine, but only shaved coney.

At the beginning of the concert, the Archdeacon, looking very striking in clerical evening dress, made a charming little speech. He seemed to have recovered completely from his bad temper of the afternoon, because they had made a splendid lot of money at the garden party and there was a good attendance at the concert. He beamed on the crowd of zealous church workers, as he praised their untiring efforts, and they in their turn were so greatly carried away by his charm that they forgot all his annoying oddities and began to think themselves fortunate to have such a distinguished-looking vicar.

Belinda was sitting by Count Bianco. She had

41

seldom seen him so animated. He did not refer even once to the sad death of his friend John Akenside. After Harriet had played her Brahms intermezzo, he declared in an enthusiastic mixture of English and Italian that for him everything would be an anticlimax after this.

Belinda found herself thinking, as she often did, that it would be an excellent thing if Harriet would marry the Count. He was wealthy and he had a beautiful house and garden: and, moreover, as Agatha had remarked that morning, he came of a very old Italian family. Belinda was sure that he would have no objection to Harriet making cakes and other dainties for the curates. He was such a kind-hearted man.

In the meantime a child was reciting, rather too fast, but Belinda caught one or two lines.

> *In dingles deep and mountains hoar*
> *They combatted the tusky boar.*

She tried to remember why the Archdeacon had been anxious to include this, for it was not a particularly suitable poem. Then she realized that it was in order that he might explain to an audience not really interested in such linguistic niceties, the history of the rare word *dingle*. How it is first known in the twelfth or thirteenth century in a work called *Sawles Warde*; then it is revived by the Elizabethans, who gave it to Milton—you remember it in *Comus*, of course . . .

The Reverend Edward Plowman, sitting in the front row by Agatha, listened to the explanations jealously. How like Hoccleve to show off his knowledge on such an unsuitable occasion! Father

42

Plowman, as he was called by his devoted parishioners, was not a clever man. He had failed to take Honours in Theology, but he worked hard in his parish and the elaborate ritual of his services was ample compensation for the intellectual poverty of his sermons. He was greatly beloved by his flock and one Christmas he had received so many pairs of hand-worked slippers that he gave the Archdeacon a pair. The gift was accepted rather grudgingly, especially as they were a size too small. This evening Father Plowman was not wearing his usual costume of cassock and biretta and his evening dress was less well cut than the Archdeacon's. He shifted uneasily, reflecting that even the best seats were hard. But soon there would be an interval. Would there be refreshments? he wondered. He tried to remember whether they had had refreshments at the last concert. He could hardly ask Mrs Hoccleve. These recitations were really rather heavy going, though this was better. *Time wasted is existence, used is life* . . . one might almost use a line like that for a text. He began to meditate on the theme, although he did not really approve of these literary sermons. Still, he had no doubt that he could do them as well as Hoccleve.

In the interval, during which he enjoyed some excellent coffee and cakes, Father Plowman talked to the elder Miss Bede about the death-watch beetle and gave her a short dissertation on its habits. This put Belinda into an elegiac mood and somehow prepared her for the next item on the programme, which was a harp solo by Miss Aspinall. There was certainly something elegiac about poor Connie. Her thin, useless hands, her

43

fluttering grey dress—surely a cast-off from Belgrave Square?—even the instrument itself with its Victorian association, made Belinda think of past glories, of more elegant gatherings than this one, at which Connie might have played. The little beaded bag came with her on to the platform and she took out of it a little lace-edged handkerchief, on which she wiped her hands before she started to play. What she played Belinda hardly knew, but it had a melancholy air and the applause which greeted it was restrained though sincere. The village people thought poor Miss Aspinall was not quite right in the head and considered it very clever of her to be able to play at all.

Certainly their most noisy enthusiasm was reserved for the curate, who appeared last on the programme and had a sensational success. Belinda read in her programme that he was to sing *Believe me if all those endearing young charms* and *The Lost Chord*, both very suitable songs and particular favourites of hers. Like all sentimental people she cherished the idea of loving a dear ruin, and found her eyes filling with tears as he sang the affecting words. Count Bianco too was very much moved, except that he thought of himself as the ruin, perhaps being loved by Harriet.

Belinda could not see the Archdeacon very well, but she could not help feeling that he was a little displeased at the tumultuous applause which greeted Mr Donne's songs. Some of the rougher members of the audience, accommodated on benches at the back of the hall, were even stamping their feet and whistling. There was no doubt of his success and popularity.

'The Archdeacon was looking quite annoyed,'

said Harriet with satisfaction, as they drank their Ovaltine before going to bed that evening. 'Imagine *him* singing, though. I think Agatha was pleased at Mr Donne's success, she would do anything to disagree with the Archdeacon.'

Belinda was too tired to argue. 'I thought poor Connie played very nicely,' she said.

'Oh, yes,' agreed Harriet, 'and you should have heard Edith talking. She seems to think the whole success of the garden party was due to her arrangements. I didn't see anybody disappearing behind the toolshed though, did you, Belinda? At least, nobody we know, that is.'

'No, Harriet, I did not,' said Belinda in a weary but firm tone. 'After all, most of us were there only two or three hours.'

'Yes, I suppose that's really nothing,' said Harriet yawning.

CHAPTER FOUR

'I thought we might have a cauliflower cheese for lunch today,' Harriet announced at breakfast one morning. 'We shall only need a light meal as we are having the duck this evening.'

'Oh, of course, Mr Donne is coming again, isn't he,' said Belinda. 'I think perhaps it's a mistake to ask him *too* often, you know. It seems no time since he was last here.'

'Why, Belinda, it's nearly three weeks,' said Harriet indignantly.

'Yes, I suppose it must be. How quickly the time goes.' Belinda began piling up the plates, scraping fish bones from one to another. Suddenly she stopped, and an expression almost of horror came over her face. 'But Harriet,' she said, 'Miss Prior is coming today. Had you forgotten that?'

'Yes, I had, but I don't see what difference it makes,' said Harriet. 'It's rather a good thing, really. She'll be able to patch that chair cover that's getting so worn, and perhaps start on my new velvet dress.'

'But, Harriet, we *can't* give her only cauliflower cheese,' went on Belinda with unusual persistence. 'You know how she enjoys her meals and we always give her meat of some kind.'

'You surely aren't suggesting that we should have the duck for lunch, are you?' asked Harriet with a note of challenge in her voice.

'Well, I don't know, really . . .' Belinda hesitated. She was a little afraid of her sister sometimes. 'Would it matter if we gave Mr Donne cauliflower cheese? I'm sure he wouldn't mind. We could have some soup and a fairly substantial sweet, and with coffee afterwards it would be quite a nice little meal. I'm sure I would think it very nice. After all, when we had supper with Edith Liversidge on Friday we only had baked beans and *no* sweet, as far as I remember, just some coffee and biscuits . . .' poor Belinda floundered on, disconcerted by Harriet's stony silence.

'Miss Prior will just have to put up with cauliflower cheese,' said Harriet firmly. 'If you expect Mr Donne to, why shouldn't she?'

'Oh, dear, I can't explain exactly. We always seem to have this argument every time she comes,' said Belinda. 'But one feels that perhaps Miss Prior's whole life is just a putting up with second

46

best all the time. And then she's so easily offended. I suppose it's cowardly of me, but I do hate any kind of *atmosphere*.'

The trouble was that Miss Prior wasn't entirely the meek person one expected a little sewing woman to be. Belinda had two feelings about her—Pity and Fear, like Aristotle's *Poetics*, she thought confusedly. She was so very nearly a gentlewoman in some ways that one felt that she might even turn out to be related to a clergyman or something like that. She could never have her meals with Emily in the kitchen, nor would she presume to take them with Belinda and Harriet. They must be taken in to her on a tray. She was so touchy, so conscious of her position, so quick to detect the slightest suspicion of patronage. One had to be *very* careful with Miss Prior.

She arrived at ten o'clock punctually, a little dried-up woman of uncertain age, with a brisk, birdlike manner and brown, darting eyes. Her dress was drab and dateless, but immaculate, and she wore what appeared to be rather a good cameo brooch at the neck.

She did her work in the little morning-room on the ground floor, where Belinda usually did the flowers. This was generally tidied beforehand, but today, on showing her in, Belinda noticed to her dismay that it had not been done. Everything looked dusty, there were bits of cotton on the carpet, and worst of all, two vases of dead chrysanthemums. Their stems showed black and slimy in the yellow water.

'Good morning, Miss Prior,' Belinda's tone was bright and welcoming, but she looked a little harassed, wondering why Emily had not dusted the

47

room and how the dead flowers could have been forgotten. She had taken them out of the drawing-room hastily the day before, when Lady Clara Boulding had been seen coming to the door.

'I think I would like the window open,' declared Miss Prior. 'I'm afraid the smell of chrysanthemums always upsets me.'

'I'm so sorry . . .' Belinda moved in the direction of the window.

'Oh, don't trouble, Miss Bede, I can manage perfectly well.' To Belinda's anxious eyes Miss Prior looked unusually fragile as she lifted the heavy frame.

'There . . .' Miss Prior took a deep breath of the sharp October air, then glanced round the room, alert and birdlike. 'And perhaps I could have a duster?'

'Oh, *dear* . . .' Belinda was almost speechless with confusion. 'I'm afraid Emily doesn't seem to have done it this morning'—that was obvious—'and I know how particular you are.'

Miss Prior smiled. 'Well, I wouldn't like to say that, Miss Bede. I can hardly afford to be in my position, but I think we all work better in bright, clean surroundings, don't you?'

'Yes, of course, I'm *so* sorry . . .'

'That's quite all right, Miss Bede. You will make me think I am being a nuisance.' Miss Prior went to the sewing machine and drew off the cover with a brisk movement. 'Now, what is it to be this morning?'

'I think the chair covers are the most important, and then there are the new bathroom curtains and some sheets to be put sides to middle . . .' Belinda went on rapidly, as if speaking quickly would make

48

the work seem less, 'and my sister was wondering whether you could start on a dress for her out of some brown velvet she's got. Perhaps you could begin to cut it out?'

'Very good, Miss Bede, I will commence with the chair covers,' said Miss Prior.

Belinda was saved any further explanations by the appearance of Harriet, who strode into the room with a bundle of silky velvet in her arms.

'Good morning, Miss Prior,' she said. 'Now I want you to start on this dress first of all, if you will.'

Belinda waited rather fearfully, but she need not have been afraid, for Miss Prior seemed much meeker with Harriet and began to admire the stuff and ask her what kind of style she had in mind.

'Oh, I've bought a *Vogue* pattern,' said Harriet, 'size 38, so you can just follow that.'

Miss Prior darted a doubtful upward glance at the bulk of Harriet towering over her. 'I wonder if it's going to be big enough on the *hips*?' she ventured. 'That's where you usually need it, isn't it?' She took out her familiar tape-measure which was in a little case shaped like a frog. 'Lady Boulding on the bust, Miss Harriet on the hips, that's what I always say to myself,' she chanted brightly.

Belinda laughed. 'Don't you say anything for me, Miss Prior?'

'Oh, well, Miss Bede, you never wear very *fitting* dresses, do you, if you see what I mean? A few inches here or there doesn't make much difference.'

'No, I suppose it doesn't,' said Belinda, depressed by this picture of herself in shapeless,

49

unfashionable garments.

'Now, Mrs Hoccleve,' went on Miss Prior, turning the knife in the wound, 'she *has* got some lovely things. Not that I make much for her, you know, except a few summer dresses, like I do for Lady Clara. But her clothes are from the *best* houses. She's just got a lovely navy two-piece with a lemon blouse . . .' Miss Prior's voice trailed off into a kind of rapture.

It isn't right, thought Belinda indignantly, for a clergyman's wife to get her clothes from the best houses. She ought to be a comfortable, shabby sort of person, in an old tweed coat and skirt or a sagging stockinette jumper suit. Her hats should be shapeless and of no particular style and colour. Like my old gardening hat.

'Would you like a cup of tea, Miss Prior?' she said aloud. 'I am just going to make some.'

'Thank you, Miss Bede, I was just thinking I should like a cup. I find I can start my work better after a cup of tea. There's quite a nip in the air these mornings and I had to breakfast earlier than usual today.'

Miss Prior's tone was uncomplaining, even bright, but Belinda felt she could bear no more and hurried out of the room to put the kettle on.

'I don't think today is going very well,' she remarked to Harriet, when they were alone drinking their own tea. 'First of all the room wasn't dusted and I'd forgotten to throw away those dead chrysanthemums, and then Miss Prior made me feel as if I really ought to have offered tea sooner. I wonder whether she would have preferred cocoa?' Belinda looked worried. 'It's more sustaining if one has had an early breakfast. Still, she is having a piece of cake with her tea.'

'Oh, and there was no paper in the downstairs lavatory,' chortled Harriet. 'She came to me just now, *so* confidential. I couldn't think what she was going to say.'

'Oh, dear,' sighed Belinda, 'I meant to get some more toilet rolls yesterday.'

'I just gave her an old *Church Times*,' said Harriet airily.

'Oh, Harriet, I wish you hadn't done that. I feel Miss Prior is the kind of person who wouldn't like to use the *Church Times*. And I'm still not quite happy about giving her cauliflower cheese.'

Belinda continued to be anxious about Miss Prior's lunch, even though she herself supervised the laying of the tray which Emily was to take in to her.

'It certainly *looked* very nice,' she said, helping herself to a rather smaller portion of the cauliflower cheese than she had given to Miss Prior, 'and I asked Emily to be sure to wash the cauliflower *very* well and to put plenty of cheese in it.'

Harriet helped herself liberally and ate with enjoyment.

'I think the damson flan will make quite a good contrast,' went on Belinda. 'I know she will like that.'

'Oh, I do wish you'd stop worrying about Miss Prior,' said Harriet in exasperation.

'I think I will just look in and see if she is all right,' said Belinda when she had finished her meal. 'I expect she would like some coffee.'

Belinda hesitated for a moment outside the door of the morning-room. She could hear the whirr of the sewing machine inside, but Miss Prior never spent very long over her meals. She did not like to be seen in the act of eating or drinking, it seemed to make her more conscious of her position.

Belinda opened the door and went in. Her heart sank when she saw the tray on the little table, for although everything else had been eaten, the cauliflower cheese had been pushed to one side of the plate and was almost untouched.

'Oh, dear, I'm afraid you haven't enjoyed your lunch, Miss Prior,' said Belinda, who now felt near to tears. 'Don't you like cauliflower cheese?'

'Oh, yes, Miss Bede, I do sometimes,' said Miss Prior in an offhand tone, not looking up from her work.

Belinda went on standing in the doorway watching Miss Prior negotiating an awkward bit of chair cover. Then she looked again at the tray, wondering what she could say next. And then, in a flash, she realized what it was. It was almost a relief to know, to see it there, the long, greyish caterpillar. Dead now, of course, but unmistakable. It needed a modern poet to put this into words. Eliot, perhaps.

Belinda burst into a torrent of apologies. How careless of Emily not to wash the cauliflower more thoroughly! How unfortunate that it should have been Miss Prior who had got the caterpillar!

'I'm afraid I didn't feel like going on with it after that,' said Miss Prior almost smugly.

'No, of course not, I quite understand,' said Belinda. But she did not really understand. If this had happened to her in somebody else's house she would have pretended she hadn't seen it and gone on eating. It might have required courage, but she would have done it. 'You must be hungry still,' she went on, 'perhaps you would like a poached egg, or two poached eggs? Emily could easily do them.'

Miss Prior gave a little laugh. 'Well, no, Miss Bede, thank you all the same. It would seem funny to have a meal the wrong way round like that, wouldn't it? You wouldn't fancy that yourself now, would you?'

'If I were really hungry I don't think I should mind,' said Belinda bravely. 'But you must have an egg with your tea. Perhaps that will make up for it.'

'Thank you, Miss Bede, that would be very nice. I am going to the vicarage tomorrow,' Miss Prior went on conversationally, putting down her work for a moment. 'Mrs Hoccleve wants one or two things done before she goes away.'

'I'm sure you wouldn't get a caterpillar in your cauliflower cheese there,' said Belinda lightly.

Miss Prior made a noise like a snort. 'It might be about all I *would* get,' she said. '*Very* poor meals there.' She lowered her voice, 'Between ourselves, Miss Bede, Mrs Hoccleve doesn't keep a good table. At least, *I* never see any proof of it. An old dried-up scrap of cheese or a bit of cottage pie, *no* sweet, sometimes. I've heard the maids say so, too, you know how these things get about. Scarcely any meat except at the weekend, the Sunday roast, you know. You always have such nice meals, Miss Bede, and you give me just the same as you have yourselves, I know that. After all, it might just as easily have been you or Miss Harriet that got the unwelcome visitor today,' she concluded with a little giggle.

Belinda's eyes filled with tears and she experienced one of those sudden moments of joy

53

that sometimes come to us in the middle of an ordinary day. Her heart like a singing bird, and all because Agatha didn't keep as good a table as she did and Miss Prior had forgiven her for the caterpillar, and the afternoon sun streaming in through the window over it all. 'You're doing that chair cover *beautifully*, Miss Prior,' she said warmly, 'and how well you've got on with Miss Harriet's dress.'

'It really does pay to show her a little consideration,' she said to Harriet afterwards. 'I'm sure she works better when one does. Besides, I'm afraid she's sometimes made to feel inferior, poor soul. Next time she comes we'll have something really nice for lunch, perhaps even a chicken,' she mused.

But Harriet's thoughts were already with Mr Donne and the duck they were to have that evening. Could they perhaps have something original served with it, like the orange salad they had had at Count Bianco's? One wanted to give people really interesting food.

'It was a good idea to give Miss Prior an egg for her tea,' went on Belinda, 'I think it made up for the caterpillar.'

'Of course, Mr Donne *may* prefer apple sauce, though it would be more ordinary,' said Harriet thoughtfully.

So the sisters continued antiphonally, each busy with her own line of thought. But at last they found themselves in agreement on the subject of Harriet's brown velvet dress. It was going to be very successful and the new bracelet-length sleeves were most becoming. 'Not even Agatha has a dress with the new sleeves,' said Harriet proudly.

54

Belinda felt a little depressed at being reminded of Agatha and her clothes from the 'best houses', but soon brightened up when she remembered Miss Prior's remarks about her poor table.

'Do you know, Harriet,' she said, 'Miss Prior told me that the only time they have meat at the vicarage is at the weekend? I can't believe that, really, and yet I've always had a suspicion that Agatha was just the tiniest bit mean.'

'Well, it's a good thing Mr Donne doesn't have to live there,' said Harriet stoutly.

CHAPTER FIVE

One afternoon Harriet set out for the curate's lodgings, carrying a large basket. Besides a cake and some apple jelly, she was taking some very special late plums which she had been guarding jealously for the last few weeks. She hurried along, hoping that she would not meet anybody on the way, as she and Belinda were going to tea with Count Bianco and she had not much time. She therefore felt very annoyed when she saw the Archdeacon coming towards her, and would have hurried on, had they not come face to face on the pavement.

The Archdeacon had been visiting a rich parishioner, who was thought to be dying. The poor were much too frightened of their vicar to regard him as being of any possible comfort to the sick, but the Archdeacon liked to think of himself as fulfilling some of the duties of a parish priest and there was something about a deathbed that appealed to his sense of the dramatic. He had also taken the opportunity of visiting the workhouse that afternoon and was altogether in a pleasant state of melancholy.

'When I visit these simple people,' he said affectedly with his head on one side, 'I am reminded of Gray's *Elegy*.' He began to quote:

> *Far from the madding crowd's ignoble strife*
> *Their sober wishes never learn'd to stray;*
> *Along the cool sequester'd vale of life*
> *They kept the noiseless tenor of their way.*

'Oh, *quite*,' agreed Harriet, annoyed at being delayed. 'One of the finest poems in our language,' she pronounced, hoping that there the matter would end.

But the Archdeacon had had a tiring afternoon and was in no hurry to return to his good works.

'Indeed it is,' he agreed. 'Johnson's criticism of it is so apt, as you will remember—"Sentiments to which every bosom returns an echo."'

But Harriet could stay no longer. 'Oh, yes, like the Apes of Brazil,' she remarked, and moved off, leaving the Archdeacon puzzling over what she meant. He thought it unlikely that it would be a literary quotation and yet it seemed somehow Elizabethan. Perhaps Belinda would know it. She often wasted her time reading things that nobody else would dream of reading.

Harriet walked away in the opposite direction. It would be very annoying if the curate was out, although she supposed she could always leave the things in his sitting-room with a note. His lodgings were situated in what Harriet considered one of

56

the more sordid streets of the village, a row of late Victorian red brick villas called Jubilee Terrace. Every window had its lace curtains and she imagined that she detected stealthy movements behind them as she walked along to the house where the curate lodged. Well, let them watch her and gossip about it too if they liked, she thought stoutly, it would do some of them good to realize that charity began at home. That Miss Beard, a Sunday School teacher too, pretending to be watering the ferns in the front room—Harriet called out 'Good afternoon!' to her, and was pleased to see her scuttle furtively back into the shelter of the lace curtains.

The curate's house was called 'Marazion'. Harriet walked up the little path bordered with shells and rang the front-door bell. Mr Donne himself answered it. He expressed himself delighted to see her and was quite overwhelmed with gratitude when she presented her gifts.

He gazed at the jelly in wonder as if he had never seen anything like it before, but then recovered sufficiently to show Harriet into his sitting-room. This was quite a nice room, not as meanly furnished as Harriet could have wished, though Belinda was relieved that they did not have to provide the curate with furniture as well as food. Harriet looked eagerly round, searching for those personal touches that make a room interesting. Other curates had lodged here, but this was the first time Harriet had visited Mr Donne and there were bound to be differences of detail. The first thing she noticed was a large oar, fastened on the wall over the mantelpiece, with photographs of rowing groups hanging underneath it.

'Ah, now which one is you?' she asked, going up to one of the groups and peering at it. They all looked so alike but at last she discovered Mr Donne and he pointed out to her his best friend who was a curate in London and another who had been called to the Mission Field.

'Oh, dear,' she said, her face clouding, 'I hope you will not go overseas. I mean, you aren't *commanded* to go by your bishop, are you?'

'Oh no, it is a personal matter. The call comes from within, as it were,' explained Mr Donne, rather red in the face.

Harriet seemed satisfied with this explanation and turned her attention to his books, which were not a particularly original selection. Shakespeare, some standard theological works, a few paper-backed detective novels and the *Oxford Book of English Verse*.

'I do hope your electric light is good,' she said anxiously. 'You know how harmful it is to read in a bad light, like Milton or whoever it was, although of course he went blind, so perhaps his eyes were weak to begin with. Oh, good, you have a reading-lamp—I was thinking that I could let you have one that we don't use very much.'

Mr Donne thanked her for the kind thought. 'As a matter of fact,' he assured her, 'I don't work very much in the evenings, except when I'm preparing a sermon. The Boys' Club and the Scouts take up most of my time.'

Scouts seemed to remind Harriet that she had thought of knitting him a pair of socks or stockings.

'That's very kind of you,' he said, 'I wear them out terribly quickly and can never have enough.

I've just had two pairs sent me today, so I shall be quite well off.'

Harriet bristled with indignation. 'Oh? Who made those for you? Your mother or an aunt perhaps?' These occurred to her as the only people who could legitimately be allowed to knit socks for a curate whom she regarded as her property.

'No, as a matter of fact, it was a relation of Mrs Hoccleve's, she was up at the University when I was, at least she was doing research. She's a kind of female Don.'

'Oh, I see.' Harriet was a little pacified, but the whole thing was unsatisfactory and needed to be looked into. It was not somehow natural for a female Don to knit for a curate, especially as she sounded to be quite a young woman.

'Her name's Olivia Berridge and she's awfully nice,' said the curate in a kind of burst.

'Well, I shall have to be going now,' said Harriet, putting on her gloves. 'My sister and I are going to tea with Count Bianco.'

The curate thanked her once more for her gifts and came to the front gate with her. Nevertheless Harriet could not help feeling that the visit had been disappointing. This Olivia Berridge knitting socks for him, that was the trouble. Harriet wondered if there could be anything more between them than that. Of course there had been no photographs other than the rowing groups in his sitting-room, though she had not been able to see his bedroom. There might well be a photograph of Miss Berridge there. And yet it seemed that she must be several years older than he was, so perhaps there was nothing in it after all. Mr Donne was so very young, not more than twenty-three or four, and there was really nobody here in whom he could confide. Agatha was so unsympathetic and the Archdeacon was definitely peculiar, perhaps even the tiniest bit *mental*. He had that odd sloping forehead which was supposed to be a sign of mental deficiency. Harriet had read about it in *Harmsworth's Encyclopaedia*. She let her thoughts wander at random on this interesting point, but by the time she reached home the worry of Olivia Berridge was again uppermost and as soon as she saw Belinda she asked her what she knew about 'a relation of Agatha Hoccleve's doing research at the University'.

Belinda frowned. 'I believe she has a niece who does research in Middle English,' she said. 'Something to do with *The Owl and the Nightingale*, I think, but I'm not sure what aspect. Of course there is still much that is obscure in that poem and several disputed readings . . .'

Harriet interrupted her impatiently. 'Oh, I dare say,' she said, 'but how old is this girl?'

'Oh, I don't think she's very young,' said Belinda, 'at least, she's about thirty, I think, which is young really, isn't it?'

Harriet seemed satisfied and hurried away to change for tea at Count Bianco's. She came downstairs again looking very elegant in a green suit with a cape trimmed with monkey fur. She had decided to break in her new python-skin shoes.

After some delay, because Harriet couldn't walk very fast in her new shoes, they arrived at Count Bianco's house.

They had tea almost at once. The Count had ordered his cook to make all Harriet's favourite

60

cakes and there were four different kinds of jam.

Belinda enjoyed her tea quietly while Harriet and the Count talked. Every time they visited Ricardo's house, Belinda was struck by the excellence of everything in it. The house itself was an interesting continental-looking building with a tower at one end and balconies and window-boxes, filled at all times of the year with suitable flowers. And the garden was delightful, with its perfectly tended herbaceous borders and rockeries, a grove of lime trees and some fine Lombardy poplars. The joys of the vegetable garden, too, were considerable. Belinda wondered how anybody could remain unmoved at the sight of the lovely marrows, and the magnificent pears, carefully tied up in little cotton bags, so that they should not fall before they were ripe or be eaten by the birds. At the bottom of the vegetable garden was a meadow, which Ricardo had planted with such of his native Italian flowers as could be induced to grow in the less sunny English climate. This part of the garden was his especial delight, and on fine evenings he would sit for hours in a deck-chair reading Tacitus or Dante, or brooding over the letters of his friend John Akenside.

This afternoon he was anxious that they should see a fine show of Michaelmas daisies, eight different varieties, each one a different colour and one a particularly rare one, which he had brought back from the south of France, when he was there in the spring. And he was thinking of having a pond made, for water-lilies and goldfish, and where did Harriet think would be the best place to have it?

'Oh, Ricardo, how lovely!' said Harriet, in

raptures at the thought of the pond. 'Will you swim in it? If it had a nice concrete bottom it would be quite clean, and so romantic to swim in the moonlight with the fishes.'

Belinda shivered. The fishes would be so cold and slimy and besides, Ricardo didn't do romantic things like that. 'Leigh Hunt writes rather charmingly about a fish', she said aloud, *'Legless, unloving, infamously chaste'*; she paused. Perhaps it was hardly suitable, really, and she was a little ashamed of having quoted it, but these little remembered scraps of culture had a way of coming out unexpectedly.

'Swans would be nice,' Harriet went on, 'or would they eat the fishes?'

Ricardo was uncertain, but said that he had thought of getting some peacocks, they would look so effective on the terrace.

Harriet agreed that they would, and they moved off together, leaving Belinda bending over the Michaelmas daisies. She did not want to listen to another proposal of marriage and probably a refusal as well. It was some months since Ricardo had last proposed to Harriet and Belinda could feel that another offer was due.

When they came back to the house she could tell that he had once more been disappointed. It seemed a suitable time to talk about Ricardo's old friend John Akenside, and how he must miss him, even after all these years.

Yes, indeed, Ricardo wondered at times whether his own end was near. Would Belinda come into his study and see the photograph which he meant to have as the frontispiece to his long-awaited edition of the letters of John Akenside?

They went into the house, leaving Harriet to collect some plants from the gardener.

Ricardo's study gave the impression that he was a very studious and learned man. The walls were lined with very dull-looking books and the large desk covered with papers and letters written in faded ink. His task of collecting and editing the letters of his friend took up most of his time now, and it was doubtful whether he read anything but a few lines of Dante or a sentence of Tacitus.

A large photograph of John Akenside stood in a prominent position on the desk, showing him in some central European court dress. He looked uncomfortable in the white uniform and faintly ridiculous, like something out of a musical comedy. Perhaps his collar was crooked or the row of medals too ostentatious to be quite convincing, for there was something indefinably wrong about it, which marred the grandeur of the whole effect. Belinda never minded laughing at this photograph, because she felt that somehow John would understand. Indeed, as she looked at the face, she thought she detected a twinkle in the eyes, which seemed to look slyly round the corners of the rimless glasses, and the mouth was curled into a half smile, self-conscious, but at the same time a little defiant.

Together Belinda and Ricardo studied the portrait and for some minutes neither spoke. Then Ricardo said rather sadly, 'I think he would have wished the world to see this one.'

Belinda agreed. 'Yes, perhaps you're right. And yet he never sought worldly glory, did he . . .' she mused sentimentally. 'He was always so humble— hardly downtrodden,' she added hastily, remembering his rather shambling gait and his fingers stained with red ink, 'but I think he never realized his unique gifts, from which we, who were privileged to be his friends, received so much benefit . . .' Belinda stopped, rather tied up in this sentence of appreciation. She felt as if she were writing his obituary notice in *The Times*. Being with Ricardo often made her talk like this. Of course, she thought, I believe John Akenside had a finger in nearly every European political pie at the time of his death, and yet one had never been sure what it was that he actually *did*.

Ricardo continued the funeral oration. 'At the beginning of my edition of the letters,' he said, 'which will also contain a short biographical memoir, I am going to quote that beautiful opening sentence from the *Agricola* of Tactitus— *Clarorum virorum facta moresque posteris tradere, antiquitus usitatum, ne nostris quidem temporibus quamquam incuriosa suorum aetas omisit . . .*' he recited solemnly in his quaint Italian pronunciation.

Belinda waited patiently while Ricardo finished the complicated Latin sentence. She had never been much of a classical scholar.

After he had finished there was a long silence. At last Belinda noticed that it was nearly seven o'clock and at that moment Harriet came into the room, bustling and cheerful, and carrying a basket full of rare rock plants. Her appearance seemed to cheer Ricardo and they began to talk about the care of woolly-leaved alpine plants, a conversation in which Belinda was glad to join.

CHAPTER SIX

On the way home Belinda decided to call at the vicarage to see Agatha. Harriet, calculating that the curate would probably not be there, went home to make some sardine eggs for supper, as it was Emily's evening out.

Belinda found Agatha sitting in the drawing-room, mending the Archdeacon's socks. It was a gloomy, unhomely kind of room, though Belinda could never quite decide why she did not like it. The electric light was too dim or the chair covers too drab or perhaps it was just that Agatha was there and that behind her was a bookcase, where, behind glass, was a complete set of the publications of the Early English Text Society. Belinda noticed rather sadly that the crimson socks Henry had bought in Vienna were not among the pile on Agatha's sewing table. But how stupid of me, she thought, socks don't last thirty years, and how could a man in Henry's position wear crimson socks! The ones Belinda noticed tonight were of the most sober archidiaconal colours. She wanted to say, 'Oh, Agatha, let me help you,' but thought better of it. Agatha might consider it a reflection on her darning, and certainly would not care to be reminded that Belinda had darned socks for Henry before she had ever set eyes on him. 'Never interfere between husband and wife', as Belinda remembered her dear mother telling her, and one could not be too careful, even about an apparently trivial thing like a sock.

Agatha seemed pleased to see her and they

began to talk of parish matters. There would be a great deal to do when Agatha went away, indeed, she was beginning to wonder whether it would be possible to go after all.

Belinda reflected on the truth of the saying that husbands and wives grow to be like each other, for it might almost have been Henry talking. So badly in need of a holiday, and yet who could be left in charge of the Mothers' Union and there was that rather delicate affair of the altar brasses and the unpleasantness between Miss Jenner and Miss Beard . . . listening to her Belinda began to feel very gloomy indeed. It seemed almost as if Agatha had decided not to go.

'I'm sure I should be very willing to do what I could,' she said doubtfully, aware that she was not a mother and was far too much of a moral coward to deal satisfactorily with even the slightest unpleasantness. 'I often go into Miss Jenner's shop to buy knitting wool,' she added, 'perhaps I could say a word . . .'

To Belinda's surprise, Agatha seemed grateful for her offer of help and they found themselves talking about Mr Donne and what a great asset he was to the parish, after which it was the most natural thing in the world for Belinda to ask after the Archdeacon.

Agatha smiled indulgently. He was well, considering everything, she said.

Considering what? Belinda wondered, and ventured to remark that men were really much more difficult to please than women, who bore their burdens without complaining.

Agatha nodded and sighed. There was a short pause during which Agatha seemed to be intent on

66

finding a piece of wool to match the sock she was mending. Belinda took up the *Church Times* and began glancing idly through the advertisements. A priest's cloak for sale, 44-inch chest—clerical evening dress, tall, slim build, never worn—she paused, wondering what story, sad or dramatic, lay behind those words. She had just turned to the back pages and was wondering whether Harriet would care to spend part of their summer holiday at a Bright Christian Guest House at Bognor, when the door opened and the Archdeacon came in.

He kissed Agatha in a hasty, husbandly way, which rather surprised Belinda, who had not thought that any outward signs of affection ever passed between them. Perhaps it distressed her a little, too, but he seemed so genuinely pleased to see her that she soon recovered and was listening happily to his account of how he had spent the afternoon, visiting a deathbed and then going on to see the old people in the workhouse.

'These humble people remind me of Gray's *Elegy*,' he said affectedly with his head on one side.

Neither Belinda nor Agatha had heard his conversation with Harriet, so that they listened with respectful interest while he quoted the appropriate verse. Nor were they in a hurry to be gone, as Harriet had been, and so did not say 'Oh, *quite*' when he had finished but enlarged intelligently on the charming theme. Agatha was reminded of *Piers Plowman*, Belinda of the poetry of Crabbe, which she could not remember very exactly, but she felt she had to be reminded of something out of self-defence, for Agatha had got a First and knew all about *Piers Plowman*. Indeed,

67

she seemed about to quote from it and would probably have done so had not the Archdeacon suddenly been reminded of Wordsworth and some suitable lines in *The Excursion*. Then he began to read from *The Prelude*. Belinda thought Agatha looked rather bored and fidgety, but she herself was delighted and lived happily in the past until the entry of Mr Donne brought her back into the present.

'Your sister brought me some delicious plums this afternoon,' he said, addressing Belinda, 'and some homemade cake and jelly. I'm afraid I'm getting quite spoilt.'

The Archdeacon looked envious. The plums in their garden hadn't done particularly well this year and Agatha was always too busy with parochial work to make jelly or cakes or even to ask the cook to make them.

'Ah, well, you won't always be a curate,' said Belinda indulgently.

'That doesn't follow at all,' said the Archdeacon. 'Look at Plowman and all the gifts he gets. I suppose it has something to do with celibacy.'

Agatha smiled complacently. 'Well, dear, people know that you are not in need of these things,' she said.

'I will bring you some of the plums tomorrow,' said the curate nobly.

'Now, you see, I have given Donne a chance to be unselfish,' said the Archdeacon, 'so good comes out of everything.'

Belinda was silent, wondering if by any chance there were any plums left and whether she would have the courage to bring the Archdeacon a pot of the blackberry jelly which she herself had made a week or two ago. Perhaps when Agatha went away . . . a cake, too, perhaps with coffee icing and filling and chopped nuts on the top, or a really rich fruit cake . . .

'We really must do something about the Harvest Festival,' said the Archdeacon wearily. 'I suppose I shall have to get Plowman to preach. A pity Canon Harvey is such a difficult man, he's really a better preacher.'

'Ah, yes,' Agatha nodded sympathetically.

Belinda did not join in the conversation. She remembered that the Archdeacon and Canon Harvey had a long-standing quarrel about the use of *Songs of Praise* in church, which the latter considered 'savoured of Pantheism in many instances'. They had had a heated correspondence about it in the local paper.

'Of course Plowman knows a good deal about the technical side of farming,' said the Archdeacon. 'That is some advantage.'

'Yes, indeed,' said the curate earnestly. 'He believes that digging is a kind of worship and that we get nearer to God by digging. At least, it may not be exactly that,' he stammered in confusion, 'but of course one does feel that the countryman is nearer God, in a way.'

'Nature's cathedral,' retorted the Archdeacon scornfully. 'One sees what you mean, of course.'

'I think Mr Donne was remembering the Latin *colere*, which has the double meaning of dig and worship, as in cult and agriculture,' said Agatha helpfully. 'You explained it so well in your sermon about the spiritual meaning of harvest time,' she added, turning to her husband. 'It would be nice to hear that again.'

The Archdeacon nodded and looked pleased. 'Yes, I think that may be the solution,' he said. 'I felt at the time that it was perhaps too subtle for some of the congregation.'

Belinda was silent with admiration. What a splendid wife Agatha was! She could never have dealt with him half so cleverly herself, she thought humbly. She remembered the sermon, of course, but it had been so obscure, that even she had been forced to abandon all efforts to understand it.

'Oh, Mrs Hoccleve,' burst out the curate eagerly, 'I nearly forgot to tell you, I had a pair of hand-knitted socks from Olivia Berridge. Wasn't it nice of her?'

'Yes, she mentioned you the last time I heard from her,' said Agatha thoughtfully, and then began to explain to Belinda that Olivia Berridge was a niece of hers whom Mr Donne had met when he was an undergraduate.

'We both used to sing in the Bach Choir,' explained the curate, making the acquaintance sound respectable, even dull, Belinda thought.

'She's a very clever girl,' Agatha went on, 'and she's doing some really excellent work on certain doubtful readings in *The Owl and The Nightingale*.' She sighed, and looked down at the sock she was mending. 'I envy her that opportunity.'

'Well, my dear, there is no reason why you shouldn't get down to something like that yourself,' said the Archdeacon. 'I am sure you have more time to spare than I have.'

'I do so admire people who do obscure research,' said Belinda. 'I'm sure I wish I could.'

'Of course I have done a good deal of work on Middle English texts myself in the past,' said

Agatha, smiling.

'Now, Agatha, Belinda does not wish to be forced to admire you,' said the Archdeacon. 'After all, academic research is not everything. We must remember George Herbert's lines:

A servant with this clause
Makes drudgery divine,
Who sweeps a room as for Thy laws,
Makes that and the action fine.

'Yes, they are comforting,' Belinda agreed. 'And yet,' she went on unhappily, 'I don't sweep rooms, Emily does that. The things I do seem rather useless, but I suppose it could be applied to any action of everyday life, really.'

'Oh, certainly, Miss Bede,' said Mr Donne, with curately heartiness. 'We cannot all have the same gifts,' he added, with what Belinda felt was an insufferably patronizing air.

'Olivia is a very forceful young woman,' said the Archdeacon, 'and rather a bluestocking in appearance. What do you think, Donne?'

'Well, I can't say that I've really noticed,' said the curate. 'I mean, it's what a person *is* that matters most, isn't it?'

'Ah, yes, the clergy at any rate should feel that,' said the Archdeacon sardonically. 'It might be an idea for one of your sermons, Donne. You could take the lilies of the field text and work it out quite simply. I'm not sure that I won't take it myself, though. It might be a way of reaching the evening congregations, they like something of that kind. Never waste your erudite quotations on them, they don't appreciate or understand them.'

71

The curate murmured something about not really knowing any erudite quotations, at which the Archdeacon nodded and looked satisfied.

Agatha rolled up the last pair of socks, and there was a pleasant silence, during which Belinda became rather sentimental as she contemplated the cosy domestic scene. Agatha, surrounded by the socks and her affectionate husband, dear Agatha, almost; it was very seldom that Belinda was able to think of her like that. We really ought to love one another, she thought warmly, it was a pity it was often so difficult. But as she walked home, her thoughts took a more definite and interesting turn. She began to wonder if perhaps Mr Donne loved Olivia Berridge. By the time she had reached her own house, however, she had decided that the whole idea was so upsetting that it could not possibly be so. In any case, he would not have the chance of seeing her very often, and a few pairs of socks through the post could not really do very much.

CHAPTER SEVEN

When the day came for Agatha to go away, Belinda and Harriet watched her departure out of Belinda's bedroom window. From here there was an excellent view of the vicarage drive and gate. Belinda had brought some brass with her to clean and in the intervals when she stopped her vigorous rubbing to look out of the window, was careful to display the duster in her hand. Harriet stared out quite unashamedly, with nothing in her hand to excuse her presence there. She even had a pair of binoculars, which she was now trying to focus.

The sisters had said goodbye to Agatha the day before. Belinda was sure that she would rather be alone on her last morning to say goodbye to her husband, and there were always so many last-minute things to see to that the presence of strangers could be nothing but a hindrance, she thought. She really felt quite unhappy to think of Agatha and the Archdeacon being parted, for the cosy domestic scene which she had witnessed on her last visit to the vicarage had made a deep impression, and she felt that she ought to keep reminding herself of it. Of course they did have their little differences, there was no denying that, but it was equally certain that they were devoted to each other and that Agatha was an admirable wife.

Belinda and Harriet had been at their posts by the window for about ten minutes before there was any sign of life at the vicarage. Harriet had suggested that they should be there early, as, according to her calculations, Agatha would have to start for the station at least twenty minutes before the train went at half-past eleven. To watch anyone coming or going in the village was a real delight to them, so that they had looked forward to this morning with an almost childish excitement. And yet it was understandable, for there were so many interesting things about a departure, if one could watch it without any feeling of sorrow or regret. What would Agatha wear? Would she have a great deal of luggage or just a suitcase and a hat-box? Would the Archdeacon go with her to the station in the taxi, or would he be too busy to spare the time? If he did *not* go to the station would he kiss Agatha goodbye before she got into the taxi, or would he already have done that in the house? Belinda and Harriet were busy discussing these interesting questions when Harriet gave a little cry of pleasure and amusement.

'Oh, look,' she exclaimed, 'the curate in his shirt-sleeves!'

Belinda looked. It was indeed the curate, wearing no coat and carrying a large round hat-box. As far as she could see he looked flushed and dishevelled.

'I do hope they didn't make him carry the trunk downstairs,' she said, peering anxiously through the field-glasses. 'He looks rather tired.'

The next person to appear in the drive was the Archdeacon. He was carrying a suitcase and looking round him uncertainly, as if he did not know what to do with it. But at this moment a taxi appeared, so he advanced towards it with a threatening air.

'That old car of Palmer's!' exclaimed Harriet in disgust. 'All the stuffing's coming out of the seats! I suppose the Archdeacon was too mean to order Haines.'

'Oh, Harriet, I'm sure it wasn't that,' said Belinda loyally. 'Probably Haines was engaged for this morning, and anyway, I don't think Palmer is any cheaper.'

'They've got plenty of time,' said Harriet, looking at her watch, 'but I expect the Archdeacon wants to make quite sure she doesn't miss the train. I expect they'll be glad to get away from each other for a bit,' she added.

Belinda was about to contradict her sister and remind her of what a devoted couple the

Hoccleves were, when Agatha herself appeared, carrying a fur coat over her arm and a small dressing-case.

'Oh, that's the case with gold fittings, isn't it?' said Harriet. 'I always think it must be so heavy, though. I don't like her hat very much, it makes her face look too sharp.'

Belinda suddenly felt that there was something indecent about their curiosity and turned away to clean the brass candlesticks on the mantelpiece. But nothing would move Harriet from the window. She kept up a flow of comments on Agatha's clothes, the behaviour of the Archdeacon and the curate. Belinda only hoped nobody could see her, with the field-glasses glued to her eyes. It would look so bad, somehow, though she did not doubt that others in the village were doing exactly the same thing.

Belinda went downstairs, humming *God moves in a mysterious way*, and telling herself that it was not right that she should feel relieved because Agatha was going away. Of course she was glad that Agatha was to have a well-deserved holiday and the waters would undoubtedly help her rheumatism, so there was room for gladness, but she ought not to have to tell herself this after the first thought that came into her mind had been how nice it would be to be able to ask Henry in to tea or supper without having to ask Agatha as well.

She went into the kitchen with a rather firmer step than usual and quite startled Emily, who was reading the *Daily Mirror* over her mid-morning cup of tea.

'Oh, Emily, I hoped you would have got on to the silver by now,' she said. 'Miss Harriet and I

75

have done the bedrooms'—she paused guiltily—
'and I think I will see to the lunch myself. I am
going to make a risotto out of the chicken that was
left over.'

'Yes, Miss Bede.' Emily began to assemble the
materials for silver cleaning. 'I see Mrs Hoccleve's
gone,' she remarked.

'Oh, yes, it was today she was going,' said
Belinda casually.

'I hope she won't come to any harm, you never
know with foreigners, do you?' said Emily.

'An English gentlewoman can never come to any
harm,' said Belinda, more to herself than to Emily.

'But you do hear of people having nasty things
happen to them,' persisted Emily. 'I've read it in
the papers. But of course Mrs Hoccleve's elderly,
really, isn't she, so it's different?'

Belinda was silent. She felt she could hardly
agree that Agatha was elderly when she herself
was a year older and thought of herself as only
middle-aged. And yet, middle-aged or elderly,
what was the difference really? *Calm of mind, all
passion spent* . . . she had known that before she
was thirty. 'Don't waste the Silvo like that, Emily,'
she said with unaccustomed sharpness, 'you won't
get a better polish. It's the rubbing that does it.'

The sound of heavy footsteps on the stairs told
Belinda that Harriet had finished her business
there, and as the kettle was boiling, she made a pot
of tea and took it into the dining-room.

'I think I shall see if I can alter my black coat and
make the sleeves like Agatha's,' Harriet was
saying, half to herself. 'Do you think there is
anything to let out on the seams?'

'Your coat is so nice as it is,' said Belinda

76

doubtfully, for she had had experience of Harriet's attempts at alteration. 'Altering a coat is so much more difficult than a dress.'

'Yes,' agreed Harriet gravely, 'I think you're right. I might buy some of that leopard-skin trimming though and put it on the cuffs and pockets. That would be a change, and sleeves are going to be *important* this winter, I believe.'

'Have they got Agatha away safely?' asked Belinda casually.

'Oh, yes,' said Harriet, in a more cheerful tone of voice. 'Mr Donne went in the taxi with her. I suppose he would see her off at the station. And do you *know*,' she leaned forward eagerly, 'the Archdeacon didn't even kiss her. He just waved his hand, like this.' Harriet gave a rather improbable imitation of how the Archdeacon had said goodbye to his wife.

'I expect they said their real goodbyes in the house,' said Belinda. 'After all it's rather upsetting, isn't it, a parting like that?'

'The Archdeacon didn't look in the least bit upset,' said Harriet. 'After the taxi had gone he stood in the drive grinning and rubbing his hands, looking as pleased as Punch.'

'Oh, no, Harriet, I can't believe that,' said Belinda, and so, comfortably arguing, they drank their tea and were just finishing it when there was a cry from Harriet, who pointed in the direction of the window.

'Look,' she cried, for she had been so absorbed in her task of 'strengthening' a pair of corsets with elastic thread that she had not noticed the Archdeacon creeping up the drive. Neither had Belinda, but she was less observant and sharp.

'I thought I would take you by surprise,' he said. 'I am glad to find you both engaged in the trivial round, the common task.'

Belinda was too agitated to think of any clever reply, while Harriet was bundling the corsets under a cushion in one of the armchairs. Belinda noticed to her horror that they were imperfectly hidden and planted herself firmly in front of the chair. It was too bad of Harriet to make these little embarrassments. The two cats were curled up in the basket-chair on the other side of the fire, so it was quite a problem to know where to seat the Archdeacon. But Harriet recovered her composure more quickly than Belinda, turned out the cats with a quick movement and offered him the chair.

'I'm afraid we have annoyed them,' said the Archdeacon, 'they are looking positively baleful. And yet I feel that I need rest more than they do.' He sighed and stretched out his hands to the warmth of the fire.

'We always call them the brethren dwelling in unity,' said Harriet. *'Behold how good and joyful a thing it is, brethren, to dwell together in unity,'* she quoted, as if by way of explanation. 'The psalm, you know . . .'

'Of course he knows,' said Belinda rather sharply, and yet it was odd how one sometimes felt that he might *not*. She began to wonder why he had come; it was unusual for him to call in the morning.

'I expect you know Agatha has just gone,' said the Archdeacon, in answer to her thoughts. 'Such a business getting her to the station, I really feel quite exhausted. These departures are always

78

more tiring for those who are left behind.'

'Oh, dear, we should have offered you some tea,' said Belinda reflecting that it was in fact Mr Donne who had gone to the station with Agatha. 'We had ours some time ago so it won't be very nice. I'll get Emily to make you some more.'

'Well, that is kind of you, but I had some refreshment at the vicarage,' said the Archdeacon. 'I really felt justified in having something.'

Belinda nodded sympathetically, but she could see Harriet looking scornful and so began talking quickly about the Harvest Festival and the decorations which were to be done the next day.

'We must have more corn this year,' said the Archdeacon. 'Corn is an essential part of harvest, perhaps the most important part of all.'

'Ah, yes, bread is the staff of life,' said Harriet solemnly. 'But we mustn't forget the other fruits of the earth. Ricardo Bianco has some very fine marrows and pumpkins, and bigger things really show up better.'

'The church always looks very nice,' said Belinda, fearing they were going to have an argument.

'Yes, there are always plenty of willing helpers,' said the Archdeacon complacently.

'I do hope there won't be any unpleasantness this year,' said Belinda, her face clouding. 'Last year there was the embarrassment of Miss Prior, if you remember.'

'The Embarrassment of Miss Prior,' said the Archdeacon, savouring the words. 'It sounds almost naughty, but I fear it was not. I cannot recall the circumstances.'

'Oh, I remember,' said Harriet. 'When Miss
79

Prior came to decorate it was found that somebody else had already done the lectern and she's always done it for the last twenty years or more.'

'Yes, poor little soul,' said Belinda reminiscently, 'she was rather late. She had been finishing some curtains for Lady Clara Boulding—you know, those heavy maroon velvet ones in her morning-room—and she was nearly crying. She does so enjoy doing the lectern and making a bunch of grapes hang down from the bird's mouth. Of course the only disadvantage is that they do distract the Sunday School children's attention so; last year they were very much inclined to giggle—Miss Jenner and Miss Smiley had a very difficult time with them.'

'If only they would try to teach them that it is perfectly right and fitting that we should bring the fruits of the earth into God's House at Harvest Time,' said the Archdeacon rather peevishly.

'But children don't understand things like that,' said Belinda, 'and in any case young people are so prone to giggle. I can remember I was.'

Harriet chortled reminiscently at some schoolgirl joke, but would not reveal it when asked.

Eventually the Archdeacon stood up to go and Belinda was about to hurry to the kitchen to start preparing the risotto, when Harriet pointed towards the Archdeacon's left foot and exclaimed loudly, 'Oh, you've got a hole in your sock!'

'Damn,' said the Archdeacon firmly and unmistakably. 'I suppose it was too much to hope that my clothes would be left in order.'

'I expect Agatha doesn't like darning,' said Harriet tactlessly. 'I'm not at all fond of it myself, so I can sympathize.'

80

'Oh, but a sock is liable to go into a hole at any time,' said Belinda hastily. 'It doesn't look a very big one. Perhaps it could be cobbled together . . .' she was already rummaging in her work basket for some wool of the right shade. 'I'm afraid this grey is rather too light,' she said, 'but I don't think it will show very much.'

'Oh, that doesn't matter,' said the Archdeacon impatiently. 'What a fuss it all is over such a trifling matter.'

Belinda smiled as she threaded her needle. Dear Henry, he was so inconsistent, but perhaps a hole in a sock was hardly as important as moths in a suit. 'I think it would be best if you put your foot up on this little chair,' she said, 'then I can get at your heel to mend the sock.'

The Archdeacon submitted himself to her ministrations with rather an ill will, and there was one anxious moment when Belinda inadvertantly pricked him with the needle and it seemed as if he would lose his temper.

Harriet did her best to divert him with conversation and eventually he recovered his good humour and began to ask her the origin of her elusive quotation about the Apes of Brazil. He thought that it might be Elizabethan, it reminded him of that poem with the lines about making Tullia's ape a marmoset and Leda's goose a swan.

'I don't remember anything about the Apes of Brazil,' said Belinda anxiously, for the darning of the sock was an all-engrossing occupation.

'Do you mean what I said that afternoon we met in the village?' asked Harriet. 'That's not a quotation, that's natural history.' She laughed delightedly.

81

The Archdeacon seemed surprised and Harriet began to explain.

'It's quite simple, really,' she said. 'When the Apes of Brazil beat their chests with their hands or paws, or whatever apes have, you can hear the sound two miles away.'

'Oh, Harriet,' said Belinda, as if reproving a child, 'surely not two *miles*? You must be mistaken.'

'Two miles,' said Harriet firmly. 'Father Plowman told me.'

The Archdeacon laughed scornfully at this.

'It was at Lady Clara Boulding's house,' said Harriet indignantly. 'We were having a most interesting conversation, I can't remember now what it was about.'

'I cannot imagine what the subject of it can have been,' said the Archdeacon, 'and I did not know that Plowman had ever been in Brazil.'

'You said something about sentiments to which every bosom returns an echo,' said Harriet, 'so I naturally thought of the Apes of Brazil.'

'I think the minds of the metaphysical poets must have worked something like that,' said Belinda thoughtfully. 'Donne and Abraham Cowley, perhaps.'

'Cowley was a very stupid man,' said the Archdeacon shortly. 'I cannot understand the revival of interest in his works.'

'I think the hole is mended now,' said Belinda. 'It doesn't look so bad now; of course the wool *is* just a little too light.'

'My dear Belinda, you have done it quite exquisitely,' said the Archdeacon. 'I must take care to be passing your house every time I have a hole in my sock.'

Belinda smiled and went quite pink with pleasure and confusion. She went with him to the front door and then returned to the dining-room where Harriet had collapsed heavily into a chair and was fanning herself with the parish magazine.

'Thank goodness, he's gone,' she said. 'I really don't know how Agatha manages to put up with him all the time. No wonder she's gone away.'

'Harriet, *do* speak more quietly,' said Belinda in an agitated whisper, for Emily had just come into the room to lay the table. 'I must go and start the risotto,' she said and went into the kitchen, where she walked aimlessly about in circles trying to assemble all the ingredients she needed. For somehow it was difficult to concentrate. The mending of the sock had been an upsetting and unnerving experience, and even when she had made the risotto she did not feel any pleasure at the thought of eating it.

'Nearly twenty past one!' said Harriet, as they sat down to their meal. 'The Archdeacon has delayed everything. I suppose he imagined Emily would be cooking.'

'I don't suppose he thought about it at all, men don't as a rule,' said Belinda, 'they just expect meals to appear on the table and they do.'

'Of course Emily usually does cook,' went on Harriet, 'it's only that she can't manage foreign dishes.' She took a liberal second helping of risotto. 'This is really delicious.'

'It was Ricardo's recipe,' said Belinda absently.

'We really must go and get some more blackberries soon,' said Harriet. 'Although in October the devil will be in them. You know what

83

the country people say.'

Belinda smiled.

'Mr Donne is very fond of blackberry jelly,' said Harriet. 'Apparently he very much enjoyed the apple jelly I took him. He said he really preferred it for breakfast—instead of marmalade, you know.'

'I wonder what it would be like to be turned into a pillar of salt?' said Belinda surprisingly, in a far-away voice.

'Belinda!' Harriet exclaimed in astonishment. 'Whatever made you think of that? Potiphar's wife, wasn't it, in the Old Testament somewhere?'

'I think it was Lot's wife,' said Belinda, 'but I can't remember why. I should imagine it would be very restful,' she went on, 'to have no feelings or emotions. Or perhaps,' she continued thoughtfully, 'it would have been simpler to have been born like Milton's first wife, an image of earth and phlegm.'

'Oh, Belinda, don't be disgusting!' said Harriet briskly. 'And do pass the cheese. You are hopelessly inattentive. When Mr Donne was here the other night you never passed him anything. If it hadn't been for me he would have *starved*.'

Belinda came back to everyday life again. How many curates would starve and die were it not for the Harriets of this world, she thought. 'I'm sorry, dear,' she said. 'I must try not to be so absent-minded. Today has been rather trying, hasn't it really—too much happening.'

'Yes,' agreed Harriet. 'Agatha going and the Archdeacon coming. Who knows what he may be up to now that she's gone?'

'Oh, Harriet, I wish you wouldn't talk like that,' said Belinda. 'It's really most unsuitable. And besides,' she went on, half to herself, 'what could he be up to when you come to think of it?' Her voice trailed off rather sadly, but she rose from the table briskly enough and spent the afternoon doing some useful work in the garden.

CHAPTER EIGHT

The next day Belinda had a letter from Dr Nicholas Parnell, a friend of her undergraduate days and the Librarian of her old University Library. He wrote of the successful tour which Mr Mold, the deputy Librarian, had made in Africa. 'He has penetrated the thickest jungles,' wrote Dr Parnell, 'where no white man, and certainly no deputy Librarian, has ever set foot before. The native chiefs have been remarkably generous with their gifts and Mold has collected some five thousand pounds, much of it in the form of precious stones and other rareties. I suspect that a great many of them have not the slightest idea to what they are contributing, but, where Ignorance is bliss . . .'

Belinda sighed. Dear Nicholas was really quite obsessed with the Library and its extensions. She wished he would remember that the two things which bound them together were the memory of their undergraduate days and our greater English poets. She turned to the end of the letter, where she found more cheering news. The Librarian thought he might be able to come and spend a few days with the Archdeacon while Agatha was away. Perhaps Mr Mold would come too. 'The Library can safely be left in charge of old Mr Lydgate,' he concluded. 'He is a little wandering now and is continually worrying about the pronunciation of the Russian "l". However, his duties will be light.'

How nice it would be to see dear Nicholas again, thought Belinda, eating her scrambled egg and feeling happy and proud that she, a middle-aged country spinster, should number famous librarians among her friends. At least, the Library was famous, she emended. Dear Nicholas had rather sunk into obscurity since his scholarly publications of twenty years ago, and now that he had definitely abandoned all intellectual pursuits, she assumed that no more in that line was to be expected from him. Still, *Floreat Bibliotheca*, and she was sure that under his guidance it would. And, what was perhaps even more important, the Library would be adequately heated and the material comfort of the readers considered. For who can produce a really scholarly work when he is sitting shivering in a too heavy overcoat, struggling all the time against the temptation to go out and get himself a warming cup of coffee?

The same afternoon Belinda went into the village to do a little shopping. She had to give an order at the grocer's and the butcher's, and, if there was time, she would go and choose some wool to make Ricardo Bianco a nice warm pair of socks. She wondered if he had tried taking calcium tablets for his chilblains; they were supposed to be very good.

She entered the wool shop, kept by Miss Jenner, who was also a Sunday School teacher. She always liked going to Miss Jenner's as the attractive display of different wools fired her imagination. Harriet would look splendid in a jumper of that coral pink. It would be a good idea for a Christmas present, although it was impossible to keep anything secret from Harriet owing to her insatiable curiosity. And here was an admirable clerical grey. Such nice soft wool too . . . would she ever dare to knit a pullover for the Archdeacon? It would have to be done surreptitiously and before Agatha came back. She might send it anonymously, or give it to him casually, as if it had been left over from the Christmas charity parcel. Surely that would be quite seemly, unless of course it might appear rather ill-mannered?

'This is a lovely clerical grey,' said Miss Jenner, as if sensing her thoughts. 'I've sold quite a lot of this to various ladies round here—especially in Father Plowman's parish. I was saying to the traveller only the other day that I knew this would be a popular line. He even suggested I might knit *him* a pullover'—she laughed shrilly—'the idea of it!'

Belinda smiled. She could well imagine the scene. Miss Jenner was so silly with the travellers that it was quite embarrassing to be in the shop when one of them arrived. Still, poor thing, Belinda thought, the warm tide of easy sentimentality rising up within her, it was probably the only bit of excitement in her drab life. She was getting on now, and with her sharp, foxy face and prominent teeth had obviously never been pretty. Living over the shop with her old mother must be very dull. And perhaps we are all silly over something or somebody without knowing it; perhaps her own behaviour with the Archdeacon was no less silly than Miss Jenner's with the travellers. It was rather a disquieting thought, especially when Miss Jenner, with a smirk on her face, began to tell her that eight ounces was the amount of wool that ladies usually bought.

'It will go very well with my Harris tweed costume,' said Belinda firmly. 'I think I will have *nine* ounces, in case I decide to make long sleeves.' After all, she *might* make a jumper for herself, now that she came to think of it she was certain that she would, either that or something else equally safe and dull. When we grow older we lack the fine courage of youth, and even an ordinary task like making a pullover for somebody we love or used to love seems too dangerous to be undertaken. Then Agatha might get to hear of it; that was something else to be considered. Her long, thin fingers might pick at it critically and detect a mistake in the ribbing at the Vee neck; there was often some difficulty there. Agatha was not much of a knitter herself, but she would have an unfailing eye for Belinda's little mistakes. And then the pullover might be too small, or the neck opening too tight, so that he wouldn't be able to get his head through it. Belinda went hot and cold, imagining her humiliation. She would have to practise on Harriet, whose head was fully as big as the Archdeacon's. And yet, in a way, it would be better if Harriet didn't know about it, she might so easily blurt out something . . . Obviously the enterprise was too fraught with dangers to be attempted and Belinda determined to think no more about it. *God moves in a mysterious way*, she thought, without irreverence. It was wonderful how He did, even in small things. No doubt she would know what to do with the wool as time went on.

This afternoon Belinda had naturally hoped that she might meet the Archdeacon, but it was now nearly teatime, and although she had been through the main street and all the most likely side streets, Fate had not brought them together. She decided that there was nothing for it but to go home; after all, there would be many more opportunities.

But when she had got as far as the church, she saw a familiar figure wandering about among the tombstones, with his hands clasped behind his back and an expression of melancholy on his face. It was, of course, the Archdeacon. But what was he doing in the churchyard when it was nearly tea-time? Belinda wondered. This would hardly be a suitable time to interrupt his meditations by telling him that she had had a letter from Nicholas Parnell and that she did hope they would both come to supper when he came to stay. She began to walk rather more slowly, uncertain what to do. She looked in her shopping basket to see if she had forgotten anything. She remembered now that the careful list she had made was lying on top of the bureau in the dining-room, so she could hardly expect to check things very satisfactorily. There was no reason why she should not hurry home to tea.

'These yew trees are remarkably fine,' said a voice quite close to her, 'they must be hundreds of years old.'

Belinda looked up from her basket. The Archdeacon had now come to the wall.

'Oh, good afternoon,' she said, hoping that he had not noticed her obvious reluctance to go home. 'You quite startled me. I didn't see you,' she added, hoping that she might be forgiven or at

89

least not found out, in this obvious lie.

The Archdeacon smiled. 'I was thinking out my sermon for Sunday,' he said. 'I find the atmosphere so helpful. Looking at these tombs, I am reminded of my own mortality.'

Belinda contemplated a design of cherubs' heads with a worn inscription underneath it. 'Yes, indeed,' she said, hoping that the gentle melancholy of her tone would make amends for her trite reply.

'I have lately been reading Young's *Night Thoughts*,' went on the Archdeacon, in his pulpit voice. 'There are some magnificent lines in it that I had forgotten.'

Belinda waited. She doubted now whether it would be possible to be back for tea at four o'clock. She could hardly break away when the Archdeacon was about to deliver an address on the mortality of man.

He began to quote:

> *We take no note of time*
> *But from its loss. To give it then a tongue*
> *Is wise in man. As if an angel spoke,*
> *I feel the solemn sound. If heard aright*
> *It is the knell of my departed hours . . .*

'I thought of those lines when I heard the clock strike just now,' he explained.

'It must be wonderful, and unusual too, to think of time like that,' said Belinda shyly, realizing that when she heard the clock strike her thoughts were on a much lower level. She suspected that even dear Henry was guilty of more mundane thoughts occasionally. At four o'clock in the afternoon, surely the most saintly person would think rather of tea than of his departed hours? She stood silent, looking into her basket.

'Not that Young was a great theologian, or even a great poet,' the Archdeacon went on hastily. 'Much of the *Night Thoughts* consists of platitudes expressed in that over-elaborate and turgid style, which the minor eighteenth-century poets mistakenly associated with Milton.'

'Oh, yes, the style is certainly rather flowery,' said Belinda, doing the best she could, for she was beginning to be uneasily conscious of Harriet waiting for her tea, the hot scones getting cold and Miss Beard, that excellent church worker and indefatigable gossip, passing by on the other side of the road.

'That may be, but I do find in it a little of the wonder and awe which is generally supposed to be absent from the literature of that age.' The Archdeacon stood looking at Belinda with his head on one side, as if he expected her to agree with him.

But Belinda said nothing, for she was thinking how handsome he still was. His long pointed nose only added to the general distinction of his features. There was quite a long pause until the clock struck a quarter past four.

'Tea,' said the Archdeacon, suddenly human once more. 'I'm all by myself,' he said rather pathetically. 'Won't you come and share my solitary meal? I don't know if there will be any cake,' he added doubtfully.

Belinda started. 'Oh, *no*,' she said, drawing back a little, and then remembering her manners, she added: 'Thank you very much but Harriet will be expecting me.' She did not dare to invite him to share their undoubtedly more appetizing meal and almost smiled when she pictured what Harriet's reaction would be were she to bring him home unexpectedly. All the same it would have been very nice to have had tea with him, she thought regretfully, quite like old times. Perhaps he would ask her again, though it was the kind of spontaneous invitation that comes perhaps only once in a lifetime. 'You must come to tea with us some time,' she said, doing her best to assume a light, social manner. 'I will ask Harriet what is the best day, though,' she added hastily, 'I expect you are very busy.'

'Ah, yes,' he sighed, 'nobody can possibly know how busy.'

'Then I mustn't keep you any longer,' said Belinda, moving away.

'Well, the tombs are always with us,' he replied enigmatically, raising his hat with a sweeping gesture.

Belinda could think of nothing to say to this, so she smiled and walked home very quickly. As she had expected, Harriet was waiting impatiently in the drawing-room. The tea was already in, and the hot scones stood in a little covered dish in the fireplace.

'Oh, Belinda, when *will* you learn to be punctual,' she said, in a despairing voice.

'I'm so sorry, dear,' said Belinda humbly. 'I should have been here by four, but I met the Archdeacon.' She looked about her rather helplessly for a place to put her coat. 'I'm sorry you waited tea for me.'

'Well, I was rather hungry,' said Harriet nobly,

'but having to wait will make me enjoy it all the more. What meat did you order?'

'Mutton,' said Belinda absently.

'But we haven't any red-currant jelly,' said Harriet. 'One of us will have to go out tomorrow morning and get some. Mutton's so uninteresting without it.'

Belinda sat down by the fire and began to pour out the tea.

'Where did you see the Archdeacon?' asked Harriet.

'In the churchyard,' said Belinda. 'He was walking about among the tombs.'

Harriet snorted.

'But, Harriet,' Belinda leaned forward eagerly, 'he asked me to go to tea with him, but of course I couldn't very well have gone.'

'I don't see why not,' said Harriet. 'I can't believe you didn't want to.'

'No, it wasn't exactly that,' said Belinda slowly. 'I didn't really mind one way or the other,' she lied, 'but I knew you would be expecting me back and I thought you might wonder where I was. And then Florrie and the cook might have thought it funny if I went there the minute Agatha was out of the house. You know how servants gossip, especially in a small place like this. I don't want to be silly in any way, of course there would have been nothing *in* it, but I decided it would be better if I didn't go.' She put the rest of her scone into her mouth with an air of finality.

Harriet was obviously disappointed. 'I do wish you'd gone,' she lamented. 'So little of interest happens here and one may as well make the most of life. Besides, dear,' she added gently, 'I don't think anybody would be likely to gossip about you in that old tweed coat.'

'No, you're quite right. I suppose it will have to go to Mrs Ramage next time she comes.' She got up and rang the bell for Emily to clear away the tea things. When she was going out with the tray, Emily turned to Harriet rather nervously and said, 'Excuse me, m'm, but would you mind if I just slip out to the post?'

'Oh, no, Emily,' said Harriet firmly, 'there's no need for that. I shall be writing some letters myself, so I can take yours as well. There is plenty for you to do here.'

Emily went out of the room with a sulky expression on her face, and was heard to bang the tray rather heavily on the table in the passage.

'She only wants to go and gossip with the vicarage Florrie,' said Harriet, triumphant at having frustrated her. 'And we can't have that, can we?' she said turning to Belinda for support.

But Belinda was not listening. She was wondering what they would have talked about if she *had* gone to tea, or rather what Henry would have talked about. It had started to rain outside, and the soft patter of the rain in the leaves, combined with the rapidly falling darkness, made her feel pleasantly melancholy. She wondered if Henry were looking at the twilight, missing Agatha, she thought dutifully, or even regretting that she had not stayed to tea. It *would* have been nice to go . . . Belinda put down her knitting and sat dreaming. Of course there was a certain pleasure in not doing something; it was impossible that one's high expectations should be disappointed by the reality. To Belinda's imaginative but contented mind this seemed a happy state, with no emptiness or bitterness about it. She was fortunate in needing very little to make her happy.

She was still sitting idly with her knitting in her lap, when the front door-bell rang, and Miss Liversidge and Miss Aspinall were shown into the room.

'We were just passing and thought we'd drop in,' Edith explained.

They stood in the doorway, a tall drooping figure and a short stout one, both wearing mackintoshes, and that wet-weather headgear so unbecoming to middle-aged ladies and so incongruously known as a 'pixie hood'.

'Do take off your wet things,' said Belinda rousing herself.

'You had better stay to supper,' said Harriet rather too bluntly. 'It won't be very much but we shall be having it soon.'

Why yes, it will be a good chance to repay the baked beans, thought Belinda. She wondered whether they ought perhaps to open a tin of tongue and get Emily to make a potato salad. Or would a macaroni cheese be better? With some bottled fruit and coffee to follow that should really be enough.

'I think I'll just go and tell Emily about supper,' she said.

'Oh, please don't trouble to make any difference for us,' said Connie. 'Bread and cheese or whatever you're having will do for us, won't it, Edith?'

Edith gave a short bark of laughter. 'Well, I must say that I should like to feel an effort was being made, even if only a small one,' she said in a jocular tone. 'I think we all like to feel that.'

'But we only came to see you,' said Connie. Her eyes brightened a little and she said in a low voice, 'We think we have a piece of news.'

'News? What kind of news?' asked Harriet rather sharply.

'We have heard that Mr Donne is engaged,' said Edith, in a loud triumphant tone.

'To a niece of Mrs Hoccleve's, a Miss Berry,' chimed in Connie.

'Miss Berridge, I think, if it's the niece who's doing research,' said Belinda, looking rather fearfully at her sister.

'Oh, I don't think that can be true,' declared Harriet indignantly. 'She has made him a pair of socks, but I don't think there is anything more than that between them.'

'Miss Prior told us,' persisted Edith, 'and she is usually very accurate. She has been a good deal at the vicarage lately, getting Mrs Hoccleve's clothes ready to go away. She may very well have heard something.'

'But Miss Berridge is some years older than Mr Donne,' said Harriet, equally persistent. 'It would be a most unsuitable marriage. Besides,' she added, her tone taking on a note of disgust, 'she's doing some research or something like that, isn't she, Belinda.'

'Yes, on some doubtful reading in *The Owl and the Nightingale*. It doesn't seem a very good training for a wife,' said Belinda uncertainly, thinking of Agatha and her inability to darn. 'Still, if she has knitted him a pair of socks perhaps she is not entirely lacking in the feminine arts.'

Edith gave a snort. 'I believe some of these old poems are very *coarse*, so she may not be such a bluestocking as we think.'

There was a short silence during which the front-door bell rang again and Mr Donne was shown into the room carrying a bundle of parish magazines.

'Miss Jenner couldn't manage to deliver them this month,' he explained, 'so I am doing it.'

'Just the person we wanted to see,' said Harriet. 'Now, *you* can surely tell us. Is it true that you are engaged to be married?' The words rang out as a challenge.

'I—engaged?' Mr Donne made a kind of bleating noise and a movement with his arms which scattered the parish magazines all over the floor. 'It's certainly the first I've heard of it,' he went on, recovering something of his usual manner. 'Who is the fortunate lady?'

'Miss Berridge,' said Edith Liversidge firmly.

'Miss Berridge?' he echoed in a puzzled tone. 'Well, of course, she's a very good sort, and I like her very much . . .' he hesitated, perhaps feeling that he was being ungallant.

'But you think of her more as an elder sister, I expect,' prompted Harriet with determination.

'Well, yes, I suppose I do,' he agreed gratefully. 'Anyway she's much too clever to look at anyone like me.'

'Is she beautiful?' persisted Edith.

'Well, not exactly *beautiful*,' he said, looking embarrassed, 'but very nice and so kind.'

Ah, had she been more beauteous and less kind,
She might have found me of another mind.

thought Belinda, but decided it might be better not to quote the lines.

'Well, that's that,' said Harriet. 'There is no truth in the rumour. Isn't it amazing how people will gossip?'

'I never thought there was,' said Connie to Belinda. 'I think Mr Donne will marry some pretty *young* thing.' She sighed and her eyes bulged sentimentally.

'I may not get married at all,' said Mr Donne almost defiantly. 'Many clergymen do not.'

'No, a single curate is in many ways more suitable,' said Belinda thoughtfully. 'More in the tradition, if you see what I mean. And then of course there's the celibacy of the clergy isn't there?' she added quickly.

'Is there?' said Edith scornfully. 'I thought St Paul said it was better to marry than burn.'

'Well, it is hardly a question of that,' said Belinda in a confused way. 'I mean, of burning. One would hardly expect it to be.' She felt rather annoyed with Edith, who must surely know less than anybody about what St Paul had said, for introducing this unsuitable aspect of the question.

Fortunately, Harriet, who had disappeared from the room while she was speaking, now came back with the news that supper was ready.

'You will stay, won't you, Mr Donne?' she asked, turning to him with a beaming smile. 'I'm afraid it won't be much of a meal . . .' she waved her hands deprecatingly.

Edith Liversidge moved into the dining-room with a confident step. They would all benefit from Mr Donne's presence, she knew, and noted with sardonic approval that there was a large bowl of fruit salad on the table and a jug of cream as well as a choice of cold meats.

Oh dear, thought Belinda, recognizing tomorrow's luncheon, surely the tin of tongue would have been enough?

'Let's all have a glass of sherry,' said Harriet, going over to the sideboard, where a decanter and glasses had been set out on a tray. 'After all, we *might* have been going to drink to Mr Donne's engagement.'

CHAPTER NINE

'I suppose they really *have* come,' said Harriet doubtfully. 'Emily is usually quite accurate in her information and she had this from the vicarage Florrie, who ought to know if anyone does. She told her that two gentlemen had arrived to stay at the vicarage last night, but of course we have no proof that it is Dr Parnell and Mr Mold. It might be two clergymen coming to see the Archdeacon about something.'

'Yes, I suppose it might be,' said Belinda, 'but somehow clergymen *don't* come to see him about things, do they? I don't know why.'

'They came by night,' declared Harriet, 'like Nicodemus. Isn't Mr Mold called Nicodemus?'

'Oh, *no*, Harriet, his name is Nathaniel.'

'Nathaniel Mold,' said Harriet, trying it. 'Nat Mold. I think that sounds rather common, doesn't it?'

'Well, we shall just call him Mr Mold,' said

Belinda, 'so I don't think we need worry. I believe Nicholas always calls him Nathaniel. He hates abbreviations.' She got up from the table and went to the window. 'It seems quite a nice morning after all that heavy rain,' she said. 'I think I shall go out into the village a little later on. I expect Nicholas will be taking a stroll and I am so looking forward to seeing him. Perhaps we shall meet.'

'I won't come with you,' said Harriet nobly. 'After all, he is really your friend, not mine, and I expect you will have a lot to talk about.' Privately, Harriet thought him rather a boring little man, but she hoped for great things from Mr Mold, who was reputed to be something of a 'one for the ladies'. This piece of information had also been gleaned from the vicarage Florrie, but Harriet had thought it wiser not to tell her sister. She wondered how Florrie, a plain, lumpish girl, had managed to find it out in so short a time.

Belinda was fortunate enough to come face to face with Dr Parnell before she had gone very far, and as they were just outside the Old Refectory, a tea shop run by gentlewomen, it seemed a good idea to go inside and have a cup of coffee. Dear Nicholas looked rather cold and peevish, she thought, wondering if he had had an adequate breakfast at the vicarage.

'I don't suppose you are really in need of anything,' she said, as they sat down, 'but morning coffee is a pleasant, idle habit, I always think.'

'Good morning, Miss Bede.' Mrs Wilton, a pleasant-faced woman with rather prominent teeth, and wearing a smock patterned with a herbaceous border, stood before them. She stared at Dr Parnell with frank interest and then at

100

Belinda. Nicholas Parnell was small and bearded and did not somehow look the kind of person one would marry, Belinda realized. All the same, she felt proud of his distinction and could not resist introducing him to Mrs Wilton, who was, after all, a canon's widow.

'Oh, the *Library*,' said Mrs Wilton in a reverent tone. 'My husband used to read there when he was an undergraduate. I've heard so much about it.'

'Of course we have central heating there now,' said Dr Parnell. 'There have been great improvements in the last ten years or so. We also have a Ladies' Cloakroom in the main building now,' he added, his voice rising to a clear, ringing tone. 'That is a very great convenience.' He chuckled into his beard as Mrs Wilton went away to fetch their coffee. 'I do not approve of this hushed and reverent attitude towards our great Library. After all, it is a place for human beings, isn't it?'

'Yes, I suppose it is,' said Belinda doubtfully, for she was remembering some of the strange people who used to work there in her undergraduate days, many of whom could hardly have been called human beings if one were to judge by their looks.

'These are excellent cakes,' said Dr Parnell, eating heartily, 'although I had such a late breakfast that I can hardly do them justice. I must say I was surprised that dear Henry was not up before me. I had quite expected that there would be a Daily Celebration. Now that I come to think of it, I distinctly remember seeing 'D' against the church in *Mowbray's Guide*. I hope I shall not have to write and correct them.'

'Oh, no,' said Belinda, always anxious to defend

101

the Archdeacon. 'There is always a Daily Celebration but I expect Mr Donne—he's the curate—would be taking it. Probably Henry thought it would be more courteous to breakfast with you on your first morning here.'

'Ah, Belinda, I see you have not changed. We did not breakfast until half past nine, so your argument falls to pieces. I left poor Henry in the churchyard, as I came out just now. He said the tombs put him in mind of his own mortality.'

'And did he quote Young's *Night Thoughts* to you?' asked Belinda, suddenly disloyal.

'Indeed, he did. I left him because he was so tiresomely melancholy. And then he has been trying to make me subscribe to some fund for the church roof,' said Dr Parnell.

> *. . . but perforated sore,*
> *And drill'd in holes the solid oak is found*
> *By worms voracious, eating through and*
> *through . . .*

he quoted solemnly, so that Belinda could hardly help smiling, although she knew it was very naughty of her. As they walked out of the Old Refectory towards the church she tried to remember what it was that Father Plowman had told her about the death-watch beetle and its habits, as if to make amends for her lapse. But before she had got very far, they had reached the churchyard wall and Belinda could see that the Archdeacon was sitting in his favourite seat under the yew trees. She felt a faint irritation to see him sitting there in the middle of the morning when so many people, women mostly, were going about

102

their household duties and shopping. She supposed that men would be working too, but somehow their work seemed less important and exhausting.

'What is he doing in the churchyard, I wonder?' she asked Dr Parnell, but she did not really expect him to be able to tell her. The Archdeacon's affected eighteenth-century melancholy failed to charm her this morning.

'I think he's meditating on his sermon for Sunday morning,' said Dr Parnell. 'I understand that it is to be something rather out of the ordinary.'

When the Archdeacon saw them he smiled benevolently, but at the same time condescendingly. It was as if he were letting them see how fortunate they were to be able to stroll in the village on a fine October morning, while he was condemned to sit among the tombs thinking out his sermon.

'Isn't that seat rather *damp?*' inquired Belinda sharply. 'We had some very heavy rain during the night, and you know how easily you catch cold.' She felt that as Agatha was so many miles away she was justified in adopting this almost wifely tone towards him.

He looked up irritably; Belinda had spoilt the romance of his environment. It was just the kind of remark that Agatha would make and, now that he came to think of it, he supposed the seat *was* rather damp. He felt a distinct chill striking up through his bones and began to wonder if he were perhaps catching cold. He would never have noticed it if Belinda had not put the idea into his head. He rose rather ungraciously and came towards them.

'It seems impossible to find peace and quiet anywhere,' he remarked. 'I had settled down in my study after breakfast when the girl came in with the vacuum cleaner and drove me into the churchyard. Now I am interrupted again.'

Belinda smiled at this picture. 'I'm sorry if we have disturbed you,' she said. 'I think we should really have walked past if you had not got up and come to us.'

'That would have been most unfriendly,' said the Archdeacon unreasonably. 'Besides, it is not every day that we have visitors. We should really make some effort to entertain them.'

'Belinda has been doing her best,' said Dr Parnell. 'She has given me an excellent cup of coffee and introduced me to a charming lady who showed great reverence when the Library was mentioned. It is really rather gratifying. I should be delighted to show her round,' he added. 'She would find every convenience. The next thing will be to have some kind of a restaurant where readers can take luncheon or tea together. Do you know,'—he tapped his walking stick on the ground—'I have had to have notices printed requesting readers not to *eat* in the Library? One would hardly have thought it possible.'

During this time an idea had been taking shape in Belinda's mind, and it was one which she knew her sister would approve. The talk about eating had made her think how nice it would be if they had a little supper party on Sunday evening. So, with unusual boldness, she issued the invitation, though she realized that her own rather timid way did not compare with Harriet's careless joviality.

104

'If you have no other engagement on Sunday evening,' she began, 'I was wondering if perhaps . . . I mean, would you care to come to supper at our house after Evensong? And Mr Mold too, of course.'

'That would be delightful,' said Dr Parnell. 'One feels somehow that Sunday evening should be spent *away* from a vicarage if at all possible.'

'Sunday is always a heavy day for me,' said the Archdeacon 'and this Sunday will be particularly so. I intend to preach myself both morning and evening. These people are so sunk in lethargy that they do not know their own wickedness.'

Belinda looked a little startled. 'I know,' she said inadequately. 'I mean, one is.' All the same it was uncomfortable to be reminded of one's sinfulness in the middle of a bright morning.

'Sloth and lethargy,' said Dr Parnell, with relish. 'But I take it you will accept Belinda's invitation, I know Nathaniel will want to.'

'I shall come if I possibly can,' said the Archdeacon, passing his hand over his eyes with a gesture of weariness, 'but it may be that I shall be completely exhausted by the evening.'

'But you will need a meal,' said Dr Parnell, 'and I expect Belinda will want to know the numbers. It makes some difference with the catering, the arrangement of the table and that kind of thing.'

'Ah, yes, I do not understand these mysteries,' said the Archdeacon. 'I think you can take it that I shall come,' he added, turning to Belinda with almost a smile.

'You would hardly believe what I found Henry doing when we arrived last night,' said Dr Parnell, in an easy, conversational tone.

Belinda, who was of a credulous nature, refrained from making a guess.

'Playing Patience on the floor of his study,' he went on. 'A complicated variety called Double Emperor.'

'Patience is a very intelligent relaxation,' said Belinda, her usual loyalty coming to the rescue. 'You don't realize how hard Henry works. I mean,' she added obscurely, 'there are things to do in a country parish that people don't know about unless they live in one. Your work in the Library has its fixed hours, but a clergyman is at everybody's beck and call.' Of course, she reflected sadly, people would never dare to trouble the Archdeacon with their worries; they would go hurrying along Jubilee Terrace to Mr Donne. Still, the smile that Henry gave her made her realize that being a little untruthful sometimes had its compensations.

The church clock struck half past twelve.

'Ah, lunch-time,' said the Archdeacon, and the party broke up to return to their respective houses.

When Belinda got home she found Harriet in a state of great excitement.

'Oh, Belinda,' she said, in a loud voice, 'he really is *charming*.'

As Emily was at this moment bringing in the meat, Belinda waited until they were settled at the table before she made any further inquiries.

'Harriet, I wish you *wouldn't* talk in front of Emily,' she began, but her own curiosity prevented her from saying any more. 'Who's charming?' she asked.

'Why, Mr Mold,' declared Harriet with enthusiasm. 'I saw him this morning.' Should she tell Belinda that she had seen him coming out of the Crownwheel and Pinion? she wondered. Better not, perhaps, and yet it would spoil the story to leave out such a piece of information.

'But, Harriet, how could you have seen him?' asked Belinda rather impatiently. 'I understood from Nicholas that he was tired and was spending the morning in bed.'

'Well, he must have got up because I saw him in the street,' said Harriet defiantly. She wished Belinda would not always behave quite so much like an elder sister. She decided that she would not tell her story in full. 'I spoke to him,' she declared.

Belinda was incredulous. 'But, Harriet, you don't *know* him,' she said.

'Oh, of course he didn't realize who I was,' she explained. 'I met him coming out of the Crownwheel and Pinion, and he asked me the way to the Post Office; and as I happened to be going along to buy some stamps, we walked there together.' She paused, triumphant.

Belinda put down her knife and fork in astonishment. The Crownwheel and Pinion in the morning! Surely Harriet had been mistaken? It sounded as if she had been 'picked up' by some commercial traveller. Most distasteful.

'I don't think it can have been Mr Mold,' she declared, looking very worried. 'After all, I've only met him once many years ago and you've never met him. I don't think it can have been him,' she repeated, with a puzzled frown on her face.

'It *was* Mr Mold,' said Harriet patiently. 'He said he was a stranger here, and that he had arrived last night and was staying at the vicarage.'

'Oh, well, if he said that . . .' Belinda had to

107

admit that it probably had been Mr Mold. But for a deputy librarian to go to the Crownwheel and Pinion in the morning . . . surely it was unthinkable! And yet perhaps it was not so surprising, when one came to consider it, for after all Mr Mold was not quite . . . He had started his career in the Library as a boy fetching books for readers, and although one didn't want to be snobbish and his ability had undoubtedly brought him to a distinguished position, it was certainly true that lack of breeding showed itself. Belinda could not help wishing that it had not been Harriet who had seen Mr Mold. She would be sure to tell people and the whole situation was so embarrassing. She wondered if Nicholas knew, because really he was to blame for bringing such a man to the village.

'Of course,' she said, more to herself than to Harriet, 'he may have felt ill or something. One must be careful not to judge people too hardly and, I dare say that in a town there is really no harm in a man going into a public house for a pint of beer in the morning, but these things *are* regarded rather differently in a village and I should have thought he would have realized that.'

'He certainly didn't look ill,' said Harriet, 'in fact quite the contrary. Rather a rosy complexion really and a well-built figure, not *fat*, of course . . . his suit was very well cut, a dark blue with a narrow stripe and a maroon tie. He didn't look at all flashy, though.'

'Oh, no,' said Belinda, 'one would hardly expect an official of one of the greatest libraries in England to look flashy.'

'And he had the most delightful manners,'

Harriet went on. 'He didn't try to take advantage of me in any way,' she explained.

Had she not thought it would be rather indelicate, Belinda would have laughed at this remark. The idea of anybody taking advantage of a respectable spinster, plumply attractive it must be admitted, in the main street of a respectable village in daylight, struck her as being rather ridiculous. But she thought it wiser not to let Harriet see that she was amused. Instead, she went on to tell her how she had invited the Archdeacon and his visitors to supper on Sunday evening.

Harriet was delighted. She enjoyed entertaining and often complained that they did not do enough. 'I will see if Mr Donne is free,' she said. 'I expect he would like to come.'

'Yes, if you like,' said Belinda doubtfully, 'but I had thought it would be nice to ask Ricardo, then we shall all be more of an age, as it were.'

'Oh, but I think we need youth, and Mr Donne is so amusing,' persisted Harriet.

'We shall be rather short of women of course,' said Belinda. 'I suppose we could ask Edith and Connie. I have a feeling Edith and Nicholas would get on rather well together. They are both interested in the same kind of thing.'

'What, in lavatories?' asked Harriet bluntly.

Belinda, who had been going to say 'conveniences', was forced to agree that this was what she had in mind, and told Harriet about his pride in the Ladies' Cloakroom which had recently been added to the Library.

'I should have thought he had better things to think about,' retorted Harriet, 'and we certainly don't want to encourage Edith. Mr Donne was so

109

embarrassed when she was talking like that to the Archdeacon on the morning of the garden party. And then poor Connie is so dreary, isn't she? Does it really matter if we don't have equal numbers? After all I can manage Ricardo and Mr Donne and you can have the Archdeacon and Dr Parnell.'

'Well, we shall have to think about it,' said Belinda. 'After all, Edith and Connie are always free and don't mind being asked at the last minute. The Archdeacon is preaching rather a special sermon on Sunday morning,' she added, getting up from the table, 'and he said he was preaching in the evening too and will be very tired. So I should like the supper to be particularly nice.'

'Oh, of course,' Harriet agreed, 'but whatever we give him will be better than what he would get at the vicarage. We must be careful not to have the same as we had the last time Mr Donne was here.'

'I know Henry is fond of chicken,' said Belinda thoughtfully. 'Perhaps that would be the best.'

'I really must look it up in my diary,' said Harriet, 'but I *think* we had chicken the last time Mr Donne was here.'

CHAPTER TEN

It was on the next Sunday morning that the Archdeacon preached his famous sermon on the Judgment Day.

The day had begun as other Sundays did. After breakfast Belinda had consulted with Emily about the roast beef, and together they had decided what time it ought to be put into the oven and how long it ought to stay there. The vegetables—celery and roast potatoes—were agreed upon, and the pudding—a plum tart—chosen. In addition, the chickens for the supper party were to be put on to boil and Emily was to start making the trifle if she had time. The jellies had been made on Saturday night and were now setting in the cool of the cellar. Belinda had suggested that they might have a lighter luncheon than usual, as there was so much to do, but Harriet was not going to be cheated of her Sunday roast, and had managed to persuade her sister that there would be plenty of time to get things ready in the afternoon and early evening. It was of course out of the question that either of them should attend Evensong.

At half past ten Harriet began to prepare herself for church. This morning she was taking particular care with her appearance. On ordinary Sundays she had to look nicer than Agatha, as well as wearing something that would cause Count Bianco to burst into ecstatic compliments, and she liked the curate to see that his generation still had something to learn from hers in matters of elegance and good taste. But this Sunday was a particularly important one, for Dr Parnell and Mr Mold would be among the congregation and it was most important that she should make a good impression. She could not help regretting that when she had met Mr Mold in the village and directed him to the Post Office, she had been wearing rather a countrified tweed coat, as was perhaps only to be expected on a weekday morning in a country village. This morning she was determined to make amends for this. Mr Mold would hardly recognize the plump woman he had met outside the Crownwheel and Pinion in the elegant creature he was to see this morning. Once or twice, though, she felt a twinge of anxiety. Supposing he were not there?

'Belinda,' she called down the stairs, 'Mr Mold isn't a Roman Catholic or a Methodist, is he?'

'No, I don't think so,' Belinda called back, wondering why her sister should want to know. Perhaps Harriet had some doctrinal difficulty to be solved, although she had never before betrayed any interest in that direction. The Church of England had been good enough for a long line of dear curates; it would have been presumptuous of her to attempt to go further than that.

'What I meant, was, will he be in church this morning?' Harriet explained.

'Oh, surely,' said Belinda. 'I expect everyone will want to hear the special sermon.'

Harriet snorted, as if expressing her contempt for anyone who would go to church to hear the Archdeacon preach.

'Henry is very particular about the observance of Sunday,' Belinda went on. 'I'm sure he wouldn't like anyone staying at the vicarage not to attend Divine Service.'

Harriet, who had got to the stage of arranging the veil on her hat, was too preoccupied to make any answer, but she could not help wondering if Belinda had forgotten one occasion when the Archdeacon himself had not been in church, and had later been seen in the vicarage garden, obviously in excellent health.

By ten minutes to eleven Harriet was ready, and waiting impatiently in the hall.

'Belinda!' she called in an agitated voice. 'If you

don't hurry up somebody might take our pew.'

Belinda reflected unhappily that the church was never likely to be full enough for that to happen, unless there was a bishop or somebody very special preaching, like that time when, she could only imagine through some mistake, they had had a handsome Brother from a religious community, obviously intended for Father Plowman's church. She looked quickly in her bag to see if she had a half-crown and a clean handkerchief, picked up her prayer book, and hurried downstairs.

By this time Harriet was halfway out of the gate. Belinda received her scolding meekly and was still silent when Harriet, quite kindly of course, began to criticize the clothes she was wearing.

'You ought to have tied your scarf in a bow,' she said, 'it's much smarter, and you know that hats are turning *up* at the back this winter, don't you?'

'Yes, dear,' said Belinda. 'I like yours very much, but I don't think I could wear one like that myself.'

'Oh, it's quite easy,' said Harriet airily, tipping her hat forward to an angle which Belinda considered a little too rakish for church, 'but you'd have to have your hair curled up at the back,' she added.

'Yes, I know,' said Belinda hopelessly, looking at Harriet's carefully arranged ringlets. But I doubt whether Henry would like me any better, she thought.

This worldly conversation had carried them almost to the vicarage. There was as yet no sign of the important visitors. Harriet looked in at the gate rather anxiously; of course it was not quite five minutes to eleven, there was plenty of time for them to appear. It would perhaps be better to be

113

settled in their own pew before they arrived. She hurried Belinda into the church.

When they were inside Belinda knelt down hastily to say a prayer, but Harriet waited until she had arranged her bag and umbrella, removed her gloves and loosened her silver-fox fur. The next moment Belinda found herself being nudged by her sister, who whispered rather loudly, 'Here they come, they're going to sit by Ricardo.'

When they were sitting down again, Harriet assured Belinda triumphantly that she had not been mistaken, it *had* been Mr Mold whom she had seen in the village. It was rather difficult to study them at all intently, because they were sitting behind Harriet and Belinda, but it was possible to do it not too obviously by putting your umbrella in the stand behind and taking some time in doing it. When Harriet had gone through this process, she was able to inform Belinda that Dr Parnell was wearing a dark tie and that Mr Mold had on the same suit she had seen him in before.

The service began quite uneventfully with one of the usual morning hymns, *New every morning is the love*. As they sang, Belinda noticed that the Archdeacon was not joining with them, but looking rather sternly round the church. As she did not want to catch his eye, Belinda looked down at her prayer book and concentrated on Keble's fine lines

Through sleep and darkness safely brought,
Restored to life, and power and thought.

Not that she ever thought of herself as having much *power*, but she was certainly alive and might be considered capable of a small amount of

114

thought. She could at least thank God for that. The curate was joining heartily in the singing and Belinda hoped he was saving enough voice to read the lessons.

Obviously the Archdeacon was out to impress his visitors, for the *Te Deum* and the *Benedictus* were sung to elaborate, unfamiliar settings, which the congregation could not attempt and which seemed rather beyond the choir at some points. The Archdeacon himself read the first lesson and the curate the second. The Archdeacon also intoned many of the prayers and his voice went up and down in the oddest way. Of course the voice should go up or down, Belinda couldn't quite remember which, at the end of a line, but there seemed to be something wrong somewhere and so much disturbance was caused among the choir boys that Mr Gibson, the organist, had to hurry out of his place to control them.

Belinda thought that as the Archdeacon was going to preach, he was perhaps doing too much of the service himself, and what with the curious intoning and the curate's church voice, which was like nothing so much as a bleating sheep's, it was difficult for Belinda to keep from smiling. And even she was forced to admit to herself that they were getting a little too much for their money, when she realized that they were going to have the Litany.

Just before he went to the Litany desk, the Archdeacon glanced round the congregation with what appeared to be a look of malicious amusement on his face. At least, that was how it must have seemed to most people, but perhaps it could hardly have been amusement. Indulgence for his sinful flock was more likely and certainly more fitting. Everyone knelt down rather angrily. They had had the Litany last Sunday and the Archdeacon never made any attempt to shorten it. As he could not sing, he made up for it by making his voice heard as much as possible in other ways.

Belinda was trying hard to concentrate on her sins, but somehow the atmosphere was not very suitable this morning and she was at last forced to give it up. Staring at the Archdeacon's back, she reflected that he was still very handsome. Perhaps he would read aloud to them when he came to supper tonight, though, as she would be the only person who wanted to listen, it might be rather difficult to arrange. Harriet could play the piano and the curate might be asked to sing, but the main entertainment of the evening would be the conversation. Dear Nicholas was so delightfully witty and Mr Mold would no doubt be able to tell them many interesting things about the Library. By the time the Archdeacon had ascended the pulpit steps, Belinda had forgotten all about the special sermon, and settled herself comfortably in her pew, as did the rest of the congregation, having just sung with great vigour that the world was very evil.

The text was given out, quite a usual one from the Revelation. *And I saw a new heaven and a new earth, for the first heaven and the first earth were passed away.*

Harriet looked at her watch. She supposed they would have to endure the Archdeacon for at least twenty minutes, possibly twenty-five minutes or even half an hour. She sighed and tried to listen to what he was saying. It was some consolation that

116

he was preaching a sermon of his own composition instead of one of those tedious literary things that Belinda said he read so magnificently.

'We are apt to accept this vision of the new heaven and the new earth with too much complacency,' he declared.

Oh, well, thought Harriet, clergymen are always saying things like that.

'But do we realize all that must happen before we can hope to share in this bliss? If indeed, we are found worthy. I say again, do we realize? Have we any idea at all?' The Archdeacon paused impressively and peered at his congregation; a harmless enough collection of people—old Mrs Prior and her daughter, Miss Jenner, Miss Beard and Miss Smiley in front with the children, ever watchful to frown on giggles or fidgets—the Bank Manager, who sometimes read the lessons—the Misses Bede and the guests from the vicarage— Count Bianco—Miss Liversidge and Miss Aspinall—of course they did not realize but he was going to tell them. 'The *Judgment Day*,' he almost shouted, so loudly that Harriet had to take out her handkerchief to stifle her inappropriate amusement, and old Mrs Prior let out a kind of moan. 'That day may be soon,' he went on, 'it may even be *tomorrow*.'

The congregation shifted awkwardly in their seats. It was uncomfortable to be reminded that the Judgment Day might be tomorrow.

'*Dies Irae*,' he continued, lingering on the words with enjoyment. Belinda saw Edith Liversidge purse her lips disapprovingly at this Romish expression. 'Day of Wrath,' he translated. 'And what a terrible day that will be!'

117

The congregation, still rather uneasy and disturbed, reminded themselves that of course such a thing couldn't *really* happen. Why, scientists told us that it would take millions of years for the sun to move sufficiently far away from the earth for life to become extinct. At least it was perhaps not exactly that, but something very like it. They knew enough to realize that the Archdeacon was being ridiculous and that the Judgment Day could not possibly be tomorrow. When the first uncomfortable shock had passed they were able to laugh at themselves. How could they have been so silly as to be alarmed!

But even as they were thinking thus, the relentless voice from the pulpit was pouring scorn on those scientists who thought they knew how the world had begun and how it would end. How *could* they know? These matters were incomprehensible mysteries known to God alone. The Judgment Day was as likely to be tomorrow as at any time in the far distant future. The world was indeed very evil, as they had just been singing in that fine hymn translated from the Latin, the times were waxing late. All through our literature poets had been haunted by the idea of the Last Day and what it would be like . . .

The congregation suddenly relaxed. It was just going to be one of the Archdeacon's usual sermons after all. There had been no need for those uncomfortable fears. They settled down again, now completely reassured, and prepared themselves for a long string of quotations, joined together by a few explanations from the Archdeacon.

He began at the seventeenth century. Belinda

118

reflected that if he had gone back any further, the sermon would have assumed Elizabethan proportions. As it was, it promised to be longer than usual. She listened admiringly. The Archdeacon was quoting Thomas Flatman's lines written in 1659, to show how poets of the latter half of that century had imagined that the Judgment Day was near.

> 'Tis not far off; methinks I see
> Among the stars some dimmer be;
> Some tremble as their lamps did fear
> A neighbouring extinguisher . . .

And curiously enough one of the oldest inhabitants of the parish had remarked to him only the other day that the stars did not seem to be as bright as they were when he was a boy. It was very significant. The Archdeacon liked the sound of his own voice and so did Belinda, and she was delighted to hear him read about thirty more lines of Flatman's poem.

Those of the congregation who were still listening—Harriet's attention had long since wandered—smiled complacently. That had been in 1659, they thought, and nothing had come of this man's noticing that some of the stars were dimmer. Why even the Archdeacon himself was forced to admit it! 1659. 1660. What had happened in 1660? His hearers resented this history lesson. The Restoration. Everyone knew that. But here was the Archdeacon trying to tell them that the Restoration was itself a kind of Judgment Day.

Belinda tried hard to follow, but she found this point rather obscure. She was frowning slightly

119

with the effort of concentration. Harriet was looking at the curate, but he had sunk so deeply into his stall that very little of him was visible. By looking out of the corner of her left eye and turning her head slightly, she could see Dr Parnell and Mr Mold. Mr Mold was looking at his watch and Dr Parnell appeared to be smiling at some private joke. Count Bianco, sitting in front of Dr Parnell, had long ago given up any attempt to follow the sermon. A Roman Catholic by upbringing, he still found the service confusing and only attended the Archdeacon's church because he felt it might bring him nearer to Harriet. This morning she had looked in his direction; she had distinctly turned her head. Could it be that she was looking at *him*?

When the Archdeacon reached the eighteenth century, the going was a little easier. Several people smiled at the lines he quoted from Blair's poem *The Grave*:

*When the dread trumpet sounds, the slumb'ring
    dust,
Not unattentive to the call shall wake,
And ev'ry joint possess its proper place,
With a new elegance of form unknown
To its first state. Nor shall the conscious soul
Mistake his partner . . .*

Belinda liked this very much, but she was uneasily conscious that the Archdeacon had already been preaching for nearly half an hour, and she began to worry about the beef. It would be roasted to a cinder by now, unless Emily had had the sense to turn down the oven. Harriet did so like it underdone, and they were usually well out of church and sitting down to their meal by half past twelve. And Henry had only got as far as the eighteenth century without yet having mentioned Edward Young, who was sure to be brought into the sermon somehow. She had rather lost the thread of what he was saying now, but suddenly felt herself on safer ground when she heard him mention the *Night Thoughts*. He seemed to be implying that each person listening to him this morning was little better than the unknown Lorenzo, for whose edification the poem had been written. Even Belinda thought the Archdeacon was going a little too far when he likened his congregation to such as *'call aloud for ev'ry bauble drivel'd o'er by sense'*. Whatever it might mean it certainly sounded abusive. He concluded his reading from Young by flinging a challenge at them.

> *. . . Say dreamers of gay dreams,*
> *How will you weather an eternal night,*
> *Where such expedients fail?*

He paused dramatically and the sermon was at an end. There was quite a stir in the congregation, for some of them had been dreaming gay dreams most of the morning, although many of them had given the sermon a chance, and had only allowed their thoughts to wander when it had passed beyond their comprehension. They now fidgeted angrily in bags and pockets for their collect-money. One or two even let the plate pass them, waving it on with an angry gesture.

Belinda soon recovered from her first feeling of

121

shocked surprise. Of course dear Henry had not really meant to insult them. He had obviously been carried away by the fine poetry, and naturally he must have meant to include himself among those he condemned. It had really been one of the finest sermons she had ever heard him preach, she told herself loyally, even if the ending had been rather sudden and unusual. It didn't do people any harm to hear the truth occasionally. We were all inclined to get too complacent sometimes. She thought rather vaguely of great preachers like Savonarola, Donne and John Wesley. No doubt they had not spared the feelings of their hearers either, but as she was unable to think of anything that any one of them had said, she could not be absolutely sure. As they were singing the last hymn *Ye servants of the Lord*, Belinda tried to think of some intelligent criticisms, for she did not want her praise of dear Henry to be lacking in discernment. He might welcome intelligent criticism, she thought, knowing perfectly well that he would not. Perhaps there had been rather too many literary quotations, and she had the feeling that it was not quite the thing to read bits of Restoration drama in church . . . but it had certainly been a fine and unusual sermon. She could not help wondering whether he would continue it this evening, going through the Victorians and the modern poets and so bringing it up to date. But that would hardly be suitable for the evening congregation, who, as he had admitted himself, liked simpler stuff.

As they came out of church they passed the time of day with Dr Parnell and Mr Mold, but Belinda hurried Harriet away before they could get involved in conversation. Mr Mold's manner seemed very free and he had looked almost as if he were going to *wink* at Harriet. Ricardo, who was hovering hopefully by a tomb-stone, saw her whisked away before he could do more than bow and say good morning. But he comforted himself with the prospect of seeing her that evening.

'I was sorry not to stop and talk to Ricardo,' said Belinda, 'but we are so late as it is.'

'Yes,' said Harriet, 'I expect many people's Sunday dinner will be ruined. I wonder what they are having at the vicarage?'

'I think they are having duck,' said Belinda. 'At least, I saw one in Hartnell's on Saturday which was labelled for the vicarage. And of course,' she said thoughtfully, as she watched her sister carve the over-cooked beef, 'duck needs to be *very* well done, doesn't it? It can't really be cooked too much.'

CHAPTER ELEVEN

The guests were due to arrive at about eight o'clock, by which time Evensong would be over. Both Belinda and Harriet had of course been much too busy with their preparations to attend it. Belinda had felt very much tempted, indeed, the thought of missing one of the Archdeacon's sermons was almost unbearable, but she consoled herself with the reflection that looking after his material welfare was just as important as her own spiritual welfare, if such it could be called, and that she was making the sacrifice in a good cause.

A very nice supper had been prepared. It had to

123

be so, for not only must the Archdeacon be pleased, but Harriet had thought the curate needed feeding up as he had been looking especially thin and pale lately. She could only hope it was nothing to do with that Miss Berridge. There were to be cold chickens with ham and tongue and various salads, followed by trifles, jellies, fruit and Stilton cheese. An extra leaf had been put in the dining-room table as, much against Harriet's will, Belinda had decided to invite Miss Liversidge and Miss Aspinall. She really thought that five men and two women was a little disproportionate and such a party might give rise to talk. Emily would think it so funny. It was rather an undertaking to have seven people to supper, but as most of the food was cold and could be prepared well in advance there was no reason why everything should not go very well.

Harriet was a little inclined to worry about what they should drink. Mr Mold would be used to living in style, she thought, and would surely expect whisky or gin.

'But we have a very good sherry,' said Belinda. 'I am sure that is quite correct, and there will be the hock and afterwards port.' Whisky was to Belinda more a medicine than a drink, something one took for a cold with hot milk or lemon. It was not at all suitable for a Sunday evening supper party at which there were to be clergymen and ladies present.

'We must be sure that the hock *is chilled* enough,' said Harriet. 'Not iced, of course that would be a serious error; I shouldn't like Mr Mold to think that we didn't know about wine.'

'Nicholas is a great connoisseur,' said Belinda. 'It

124

seems right that a librarian should be, I think. Good wine and old books seem to go together.'

'And of course the Archdeacon likes a drop,' said Harriet rather vulgarly. 'We shall have to watch him. I don't suppose Agatha lets him have much. Good heavens, it's nearly seven o'clock. We must go and change.'

Harriet was determined that this evening should see the climax of her elegance and only lamented the fact that she could not wear full evening dress. Still, her new brown velvet would be magnificent with her gold necklace and long ear-rings. Belinda had decided to wear her blue chiffon. Henry had once said that he liked her in pale colours, and although that had been over thirty years ago it was possible that he still might. Her crystal beads and ear-rings went quite well with it, and when she had put on a little rouge the whole effect was rather pleasing. She went into the bathroom where Harriet was splashing about in the bath like a plump porpoise. Her curls were protected by a round cap of green oilskin and the room was filled with the exotic scent of bath salts.

Harriet looked at Belinda critically. 'Yes, you look very nice,' she said, 'but I think I should use some more lipstick if I were you. Artificial light is apt to make one look paler.'

'Oh, no, Harriet, I don't think I can use any more,' said Belinda. 'I shouldn't really feel natural if I did. *Thou art not fair for all thy red and white,*' she quoted vaguely, leaving Harriet to wallow in her bath.

At five minutes to eight Belinda was downstairs in the drawing-room, waiting for somebody to arrive. She was sitting in a chair by the fire with a

125

book on her knee, which she was not reading. It was something by an old friend of Harriet's—a former curate—Theodore Grote, now Bishop of Mbawawa in Africa. Dear Theo, he had certainly done splendid work among the natives, at least, that was what everyone said, although nobody seemed to know exactly what it was that he had done. Certainly they still *looked* very heathen, grinning away in their leafy dress. But perhaps that was before he converted them. She opened the book with a view to finding out, but she could not settle to reading and walked restlessly round the room, moving the flowers, rearranging the cushions and altering the position of chairs. She brought out a photograph of Nicholas Parnell in his academic robes and put it on the mantelpiece; she also displayed on a small table a little pamphlet he had written about central heating in libraries. It was prettily bound and had a picture of a phoenix on the cover with a Greek inscription underneath it. Something about Prometheus, Harriet had said, for Belinda was like Shakespeare in having little Latin and no Greek.

At eight o'clock the bell rang. Men's voices were heard in the hall and a minute or two later Emily showed the Archdeacon, Dr Parnell, Mr Mold and the curate into the room. Belinda shook hands with them rather formally. The Archdeacon advanced towards an armchair by the fire and sank down into it rather dramatically, as if exhausted. Dr Parnell took up his own pamphlet and said that he was glad to find somebody who had cut its beautiful pages.

'I'm afraid you're hardly a best seller,' said Mr Mold jovially. 'Nor even as much ordered in the

Library as Rochester's poems,' he added.

Belinda frowned and looked embarrassed when the curate asked, with his usual eager interest, what poems those were.

'I am afraid they are rather *naughty*,' said Dr Parnell. 'We have had to lock them away in a special place, together with other books of a similar nature. All the same, they are quite often asked for by our readers.'

'Oh, well, I suppose people have to study them,' said Belinda, handing round cigarettes and wondering how she could change the subject.

'We should not like to think that they ordered them for any other reason,' said Dr Parnell, chuckling and rubbing his hands in front of the fire.

Belinda was greatly relieved when Miss Liversidge and Miss Aspinall arrived and she was able to introduce them. She was so afraid that Nicholas and Edith would discover their common interest in sanitary arrangements too soon, that she resolutely kept them apart. It was all very difficult and she wished Harriet would hurry up and come in. Only the curate was making what Belinda considered to be suitable conversation for the awkward interval between arriving and sitting down to eat.

'Do you know,' he was saying eagerly, 'there was quite a *nip* in the air this evening? I shouldn't be surprised if we had frost.'

'And the later the frost the harder the winter,' said a cheerful voice in the background. 'I do hope you're all wearing warm underclothes.'

It was Harriet, ready far sooner than Belinda had hoped was possible, looking splendid too, in her

127

brown velvet and gold ornaments.

The curate laughed heartily and assured her that he had his on.

Harriet was in excellent form and soon had everybody laughing, except for the Archdeacon, who went on reclining in the armchair, not speaking.

'Well, what did you preach about this evening?' asked Harriet. 'I haven't heard any comments on the sermon yet.'

The Archdeacon roused himself. 'It was a continuation of this morning's, brought up to date as it were,' he explained.

'Oh, it was beautiful,' gushed Connie Aspinall, 'I did so enjoy it.'

The Archdeacon looked pleased. 'I had feared it might be rather too obscure,' he said. 'Eliot is not an easy poet.'

Belinda gasped. Eliot! And for the evening congregation! But it must have been magnificent to hear him reading Eliot. 'Perhaps you will give the sermon again,' she suggested timidly, 'for the benefit of those who were not at Evensong.'

'Perhaps I will,' said the Archdeacon, 'perhaps I will.' He paused. 'I have been considering giving a course of sermons on Dante,' he mused. 'Not of course in the original—Carey's translation, perhaps.'

'It would be a fine and unusual subject,' said Belinda doubtfully.

'Well, you can count me out,' said Edith bluntly. 'I couldn't make much of the sermon this morning. Too full of quotations, like *Hamlet*.' She gave her short barking laugh.

'I think people prefer the more obvious aspects

of the Christian teaching,' said Nicholas regretfully. 'I mean, I am afraid that they do. Simple sentiments in intelligible prose. A great pity really. I can see how it limits the scope of the more enterprising clergy.'

'*Sentiments to which every bosom returns an echo,*' said the Archdeacon. 'Yes, one appreciates that, and yet, why shouldn't Eliot express those sentiments?'

'Do the bosoms of people nowadays return any echo?' said Mr Mold. 'One wonders really.'

'Well, if they do, it certainly isn't as loud as the echo made by the Apes of Brazil,' chortled Harriet, and in response to a very pressing appeal by Mr Mold, she began to explain it all over again.

'Can the sound really be heard two *miles* away?' said Connie, whose voice held just the same note of rapt awe as when she had praised the Archdeacon's sermon. 'Isn't that wonderful?'

The Archdeacon looked rather annoyed. 'Oh, it is nothing very unusual,' he said shortly, so that Belinda began to wonder whether he was about to embark on some tale of his own. But he lapsed into silence again, so that she was forced to continue the conversation with a bright and rather insincere remark about Agatha, and what a pity it was that she was not with them that evening.

'I had a postcard from her yesterday,' said the Archdeacon. 'She says she is getting on quite well speaking Anglo-Saxon and Old High German in the shops.'

'Ah, well, Agatha is so clever,' said Belinda, without bitterness. 'I'm afraid I've forgotten all my Anglo-Saxon. But surely the vocabulary is rather limited?'

'Yes, quite ridiculous,' said Edith shortly. 'Like trying to talk Latin in Italy.'

'Why, Ricardo isn't here yet,' said Belinda. 'What do you say to a glass of sherry while we are waiting?'

'I say yes,' said Mr Mold promptly.

'Yes *please*, Nathaniel,' Dr Parnell reminded him. 'We should not like it to be thought that an official of our great Library was lacking in manners.'

'I feel that I have been lacking in manners for not offering it sooner,' said Belinda quite sincerely, thus taking upon herself the blame for all the little frictions of the evening. But it was so obvious that women should take the blame, it was both the better and the easier part, and just as she was pouring out the sherry, Ricardo arrived, with such profuse and gallant apologies for being late that everyone was put into a good humour. He was a little encumbered by a magnificent pot of chrysanthemums, which he presented with a ceremonious gesture.

Shortly after this they went into supper, Edith and Harriet followed by Mr Mold and the curate, making for the dining-room with what Belinda considered indecent haste. But even those who followed more slowly moved with confident anticipation. Belinda had taken care to arrange the table so that Harriet should sit between Ricardo and Mr Mold, when she might see how superior dear Ricardo was. Belinda herself sat by the Archdeacon and Dr Parnell, while Miss Liversidge and Miss Aspinall were fitted in where there happened to be spaces.

'Why, the table is groaning!' exclaimed Dr

130

Parnell. 'I like that expression so much, but one is hardly ever justified in using it or even expecting it. Certainly not at Sunday supper.'

Belinda looked pleased. 'I hope everything will be nice,' she said. 'I never see why Sunday supper should be the dreary meal it usually is. I mean,' she added hastily, remembering that they had had just such a dreary Sunday supper at the vicarage a few weeks ago, 'that it can sometimes be.'

'We always have cold meat with beetroot and no potatoes,' said the Archdeacon, as if reading her thoughts. 'Nothing could be more unappetizing.'

'Of course the servants are often out on Sunday evening,' said the curate, 'and one likes to feel that they are having an easier time.'

'I don't feel that at all,' said the Archdeacon. 'I like to feel that somebody has taken a little trouble in preparing a meal for me. I think we deserve it after the labour of Sunday.'

'Especially after that magnificent sermon this morning,' murmured Belinda loyally, giving him some of the best of the chicken.

'All that reading must be very tiring,' said Dr Parnell spitefully.

'It was some very fine poetry,' said Ricardo vaguely, for he had not grasped much of the sermon apart from the bare fact that it was supposed to be about the Judgment Day.

'We certainly thought it magnificent, didn't we, Harriet?' said Belinda, turning towards her sister rather urgently. It was tactless of Harriet not to have made any comment. But then she herself was rather to blame for introducing the subject when they had already discussed it once. It was a pity that her loyalty had got the better of her.

131

'Oh, splendid,' said Harriet, rather too enthusiastically. 'But of course I'm *not* a theologian,' she added, with a brilliant smile.

Mr Mold laughed at this and so did Dr Parnell, but the Archdeacon looked rather annoyed.

'Few of us are true theologians,' said the curate sententiously. 'But after all, the real knowledge comes from within and not from books.'

Belinda looked at him rather apprehensively. She hoped the wine wasn't beginning to have its effect on him. White wine wasn't really intoxicating and he had only had one glass of sherry.

'That is rather a disconcerting thought,' said Dr Parnell. 'You are preaching sedition. I maintain that the true knowledge comes from *books*. It would be a poor prospect for me and for Nathaniel if everybody thought as you do.'

'Ah, but it is true what Mr Donne says,' said Ricardo thoughtfully. 'My dear friend John Akenside used to say that he learned more about the political situation in central Europe in those quiet moments with a glass of wine at a café table than by all his talks with Pribitchevitch's brother.'

'Oh, yes, I can believe that,' said Edith Liversidge, 'John liked his glass of wine.'

'But surely the intrigues of Balkan politics can hardly be compared with the true knowledge that comes from within?' Dr Parnell protested. 'I hardly think it is the same thing.'

Belinda too, thought Ricardo's remarks hardly relevant, but one could not argue the point. Perhaps it was a mistake to have any kind of serious conversation when eating, or even anywhere at all in mixed company. Men took themselves so seriously and seemed to insist on arguing even the most trivial points. So, at the risk of seeming frivolous, she turned the conversation to something lighter.

'I can never think of Belgrade without thinking of the public baths,' she said.

Mr Mold looked across the table expectantly. Perhaps this would be more amusing than the knowledge that comes from within.

'Why does it remind you of public baths?' said the Archdeacon. 'It seems most unlikely.'

'Oh, well,' said Belinda, who hadn't really a story to tell, 'I once heard somebody describing them and I thought it was rather funny. A lot of old men all swimming about in a pool of hot water,' she concluded weakly, hoping that somebody would laugh.

Most of them did, especially the Archdeacon, who seemed to be in a good temper again.

'I never heard of there being any hot springs in Belgrade,' said Ricardo seriously.

'Oh, I expect the water was artificially heated,' explained the curate, turning earnestly to Belinda for further information on this interesting point.

Belinda felt rather flustered at the interest which everyone was taking in her silly little story. 'I don't really know,' she said. 'I've never been to Belgrade myself, and even if I had I don't suppose I should have visited the public baths.'

'Not the ones with the old men in them, we hope,' said Mr Mold, with almost a wink.

Belinda was rather taken aback. She didn't think she liked Mr Mold very much. Of course one didn't want to be snobbish, but it really was true that low origin always betrayed itself somewhere.

'Oh, Belinda never remembers where she's been,' said Harriet, hardly improving the situation. 'Now, Mr Mold, do have some more trifle,' she said, favouring him with a brilliant smile.

'Perhaps I may have some too,' said the Archdeacon. 'It really is delicious. I don't know when I've tasted anything so good.'

But Belinda hardly noticed his praise. She was thinking indignantly that Nicholas had always encouraged Mr Mold too much as a boy, although one would have thought that moving in a cultured intellectual society would have cured him of any tendency to make jokes not quite in the best of taste. And yet, she thought doubtfully, the Library, great though it was, did not always attract to it cultured and intellectual persons. Nicholas himself, obsessed with central heating and conveniences, was perhaps not the best influence for a weak character like Mr Mold. Belinda began to wish that she were in Karlsbad with dear Agatha, helping her to get cured of her rheumatism. She imagined herself in the pump-room, if there was one, drinking unpleasant but salutary waters, and making conversation with elderly people. Perhaps taking a gentle walk in the cool of the evening with an old clergyman or a retired general . . .

All around her the conversation buzzed pleasantly. Mr Mold's little lapse was quite forgotten, if indeed it had ever been noticed by anyone except Belinda. Harriet was asking Ricardo if it was true that the fleas on the Lido were so wonderful. She had heard that they bounced balls and drew little golden carriages.

'Indeed, they are,' said Ricardo gravely. 'I have

134

seen them myself.'

The curate leaned forward eagerly. 'It is wonderful what things animals and even insects can be made to do if they are trained with kindness,' he said, his face aglow with interest.

Everyone agreed with this very just remark. Dr Parnell even went so far as to observe that it was also true of people.

'I should love to go to Venice,' said Belinda. 'I think there is something very special about Italy. It is so rich in literary associations.'

'Ah . . .' Ricardo put down his spoon and was obviously on the point of bursting into a flow of Dante, but the Archdeacon was too quick for him and got in first with Byron.

I stood in Venice on the Bridge of Sighs
A palace and a prison on each hand:

he quoted, and remarked that he had thought of visiting Italy in the spring, but that of course it was almost impossible for him to take a holiday however much he might need it.

'Oh, but I don't see why you shouldn't,' said Harriet, loudly and tactlessly. 'It isn't as if you had a frightful lot to do, and I'm sure Mr Donne could manage perfectly well when you were away.'

There was an uncomfortable silence.

'You know, you really should take a holiday,' said Edith Liversidge. 'A change does everyone good. Everyone would benefit.'

'You would feel you were doing good to others as well as yourself,' said Dr Parnell, 'so you would have a double satisfaction.'

'I doubt whether I could allow myself that

luxury,' said the Archdeacon quite good humouredly. 'Of course a change can sometimes be a good thing. I have often wondered whether I ought to have a town parish. There is more scope for preaching.'

'Oh, yes,' Connie Aspinall broke in eagerly. 'I remember when Canon Kendrick was rector of St Ermin's there wasn't a vacant seat at Evensong—you had to be there half an hour before it started. He said some very shocking things.'

'Well, of course people like that,' said Dr Parnell. 'Kendrick was a contemporary of mine. He got a very poor degree, I believe, but he found out what his line was and made a success of it.'

'What a cynical way to talk,' said Harriet indignantly. 'He was probably a very sincere man.'

'Oh, he was,' said Connie, 'but I suppose he thought it his duty to say those things, unpleasant though they were.'

'Yes, there is evil even in Belgravia,' said Dr Parnell.

'There is evil everywhere,' said the curate.

Belinda looked around her uncomfortably as if expecting to find the devil sitting at the table, but by the time they were drinking their coffee in the drawing-room that solemn subject had somehow been forgotten and Ricardo, talking about the picturesque costume of the ancient Etruscans, was the centre of the little group. Belinda marvelled at the way conversation rushed from one subject to another with such bewildering speed, but decided that this was one which could give offence to nobody and was therefore to be encouraged. So she appeared interested although she knew nothing whatever about the ancient Etruscans. It was hardly the kind of thing one would know about, unless one had had the advantage of a classical education, as Nicholas and Ricardo had.

'Was their dress anything like that of the Germanic tribes?' she asked. 'I mean the ones Tacitus described in his *Germania*,' she added vaguely, for it was a long time since she had taken her first University examination in which it had been one of the set books.

Ricardo paused and looked thoughtful, but before he had time to answer, Harriet let out a cry of joy, as if she had suddenly come upon something which she had long ago given up for lost.

Locupletissimi veste distinguuntur, non fluitante . . .

she paused appealingly, and waved her plump hands about, searching for the rest of the quotation. While she did so, Belinda and Dr Parnell began to laugh, the curate and Miss Aspinall looked amazed and expectant, while the Archdeacon smiled a little doubtfully, for he was not a very good Latinist, nor had he known his Tacitus very well as an undergraduate. Mr Mold looked frankly bored, although he could not help thinking that Harriet looked very attractive, waving her hands about in the air.

Ricardo was frowning, but only for a moment. How terrible it would be if he were to fail her! He cleared his throat . . .

non fluitante sed stricto et singulos artus exprimente,

he recited.

137

Really, reflected Belinda, Ricardo's faculty for quoting Tacitus is quite frightening!

'I suppose *veste* means vest,' said the curate earnestly, with an expression of painful intelligence on his face.

'Hardly in the modern sense, perhaps,' said Ricardo thoughtfully, 'although it was a tight-fitting garment, as you hear from the description.'

'More like men's long pants,' said Edith Liversidge bluntly. 'They must have looked rather comic.'

'Yes, it is strange that the rich men should have been distinguished by the wearing of underclothes,' said Belinda thinking that the conversation was getting more than usually silly. She was herself smiling, as she could not help thinking of the curate's combinations. It was a good thing, she felt, when Ricardo suggested that Harriet might honour them by playing something on the piano.

'How very talented your sister must be,' said Mr Mold, who was sitting on the sofa by Belinda. 'She would be an asset to any household,' he declared pompously.

Belinda tried to think of something to say which would put him off, but could think of nothing without being disloyal to her sister. Certainly she looked very splendid sitting at the piano; it was not surprising that he should admire her.

The first chords of *The Harmonious Blacksmith* jangled forth. Belinda wondered why Harriet had chosen this particular piece, and began to be a little anxious about the later variations, which she knew were rather tricky. But Harriet avoided this difficulty by playing only the first two variations.

138

'I don't want to bore you with the whole lot,' she said, and broke into a gay Chopin mazurka.

There was now an atmosphere of peace and contentment in the room. Everyone had eaten well, there was a good fire and comfortable chairs. The Archdeacon, in the best chair, was nodding now. Miss Aspinall had found a polite listener in the curate, who was asking her just the kind of questions she liked about the past glories of her life in Belgrave Square. Dr Parnell and Miss Liversidge were talking, but in a low voice, about the 'improvements' in the Library and what further ones could conveniently be made. Ricardo and Mr Mold were both admiring Harriet and vying for her attention. Only Belinda was unoccupied, but she was quite happy in the knowledge that the party had really been quite successful. Of course, if the Archdeacon had not been asleep, she could have had some conversation with him, but it was nice to know that he felt really at home, and she would not for the world have had him any different.

CHAPTER TWELVE

The next day Harriet could talk of nothing but Mr Mold. At breakfast she declared that he was remarkably young-looking for his age.

'I suppose he must be in the early fifties, but that's really the Prime of Life, isn't it?' she said to Belinda, who had not so far contributed anything to her sister's eulogy apart from the observation that he certainly had rather a high colour. Harriet repeated 'the Prime of Life', and went on eating her sausage.

'Yes, I suppose he is,' agreed Belinda, but rather doubtfully, for she was not really sure what the Prime of Life was. She had always thought that her own prime was twenty-five, so that by her reckoning Mr Mold must be nearly thirty years past it. 'Personally he isn't a type that appeals to me very much,' she added, remembering the joke about the public baths in Belgrade.

'Oh, I know he isn't always quoting Gray's *Elegy*,' said Harriet pointedly, 'but he's so amusing, such a Man of the World,' she added naively. 'I wonder how long he will be staying?'

'I expect he will have to get back to the Library soon,' said Belinda. 'Old Mr Lydgate is in charge now, but I should think he is hardly up to the work really, though,' she added irrelevantly, 'he had some very interesting experiences in Ethopia.'

With that she went upstairs, thinking that it would really be a good thing when both the Librarian and Mr Mold went back. Although it was nice seeing different people, especially if they were old friends as dear Nicholas was, Belinda found it rather unsettling. The effort of trying to talk to so many people last night and keep them at peace with each other had quite exhausted her. But there was some satisfaction mixed with her tiredness, for she felt it had been quite a successful party. Edith and Connie had obviously enjoyed both the food and the company, and as inviting them had been something in the nature of a duty, one could feel special satisfaction there. Nicholas and Edith had had a very full conversation about conveniences and he had invited her to come for a personally

140

conducted tour of the Library, where her advice on certain points would be much valued. The curate, Count Bianco and Mr Mold had seemed quite happy, though perhaps the word was scarcely applicable to the Count, who preferred his gentle state of melancholy which must have been enriched by Harriet's attentions to Mr Mold and the curate. Belinda's only fear was that the Archdeacon had been bored, though she had decided that his going to sleep showed rather that he felt at home in her house and she was determined to go on thinking so. As she dusted her dressing-table, she broke into Addison's noble hymn, *The spacious firmament on high.*

In Reason's ear they all rejoice . . . How admirable that was! Belinda began to think rather confusedly about the eighteenth century, and what in her undergraduate essays she had called its 'Rationalism'. Had not her favourite, Young, said something about his heart becoming the convert of his head? How useful that must have been! Belinda began to look back on her own life and came to the regretful conclusion that she had admired the great eighteenth-century poet without really taking his advice. She comforted herself by reflecting that it was now too late to do anything about it, but as she opened a drawer she came upon some skeins of grey wool, the wool she had bought to knit the Archdeacon a pullover. She knew now that she would never do it. She would make a jumper for herself, safe, dull and rather too thick. Surely this was proof that her heart had now become the convert of her head? Or was it just fear of Agatha?

She shut the drawer and turned her attention to

141

other work, preparing to live this day as if her last. As it was a nice bright morning, she felt that it would be a good opportunity to do some gardening, and later, if she had time, she might write a letter to poor Agatha, who was probably feeling rather lonely all by herself in Karlsbad. It was quite a luxury to be able to think of her as 'poor Agatha'; it showed that absence could do more than just make the heart grow fonder.

Belinda went downstairs and put on her galoshes and an old mackintosh. She decided to put some bulbs in the beds in the front garden and then move round to the back. If people came to the door it was more likely that they would come later, and by then she would be out of sight. She began to plant tulip bulbs in between the wall-flower plants. They would make a pretty show in the late spring. She noticed how splendidly the aubretias had done; they were spreading so much that they would soon have to be divided. Belinda remembered when she had put them in as little cuttings. They had had a particularly hard winter that year, so that she had been afraid the frost would kill them. But they had all lived and flourished. How wonderful it was, when one came to think of it, what a lot of hardships plants could stand! And people too. Here Belinda realised how well her own heart, broken at twenty-five, had mended with the passing of the years. Perhaps the slave had grown to love its chains, or whatever it was that the dear Earl of Rochester had said on that subject. Belinda was sure that our greater English poets had written much about unhappy lovers *not* dying of grief, although it was of course more romantic when they did. But there was always hope springing eternal in the human breast, which kept one alive, often unhappily . . . it would be an interesting subject on which to read a paper to the Literary Society, which the Archdeacon was always threatening to start in the village. Belinda began to collect material in her mind and then imagined the typical audience of clergy and female church workers, most of them unmarried. Perhaps after all it would hardly be suitable. She must consider, too, what was fitting to her *own* years and position.

By this time she had planted most of the bulbs, and her back was aching. She stood up to rest herself, and looked idly over the wall. The road was deserted and there was no sign of life at the vicarage, but of course it was barely half past ten, and in the village the best people did not appear till later, when they would start out to do their shopping or to meet a friend at the Old Refectory for coffee. Belinda leaned her arms on the wall, apparently lost in thought. It did not occur to her that she would look odd to anyone passing by. Absent-mindedly she scraped the moss off the wall with a trowel. She would rest for a few minutes and then put some scyllas in the rockery. It was nice to think that she had the whole morning before her. She must go into the cellar and see if the bulbs she had planted in bowls were showing any shoots yet. It would be fatal if they were left in the darkness too long . . .

She looked up from the moss and glanced in the direction of the vicarage, to see if anything had happened since she last looked. In the next instant she knew that a great deal had happened. Mr Mold had come out of the gate and was walking rapidly towards her.

He must be coming *here*, thought Belinda, in a flurry of agitation. For some seconds she wondered whether she ought to go and warn Harriet, but even now she could hear his step on the pavement. How quickly he walked! It would be as much as Belinda could do to hide herself before he came through the gate and walked up the drive.

She looked around frantically. There was no time to run back to the house, as he would see her, and even if he did not recognize her in her gardening clothes it would look so conspicuous. So Belinda concealed herself as best she could behind a large rhododendron bush, which grew on one side of the little drive leading up to the front door. She was fully aware how foolish she would feel if she were discovered in this undignified crouching position, but she could not imagine that Mr Mold would take the trouble to penetrate the thickness of the bush before he rang the bell and announced himself. She wished he would hurry, for it was very uncomfortable behind the bush and rather dirty. Also, Belinda felt like laughing and it would indeed be terrible if Mr Mold were startled on the doorstep by a sudden burst of laughter coming out of a bush.

The crunching of the gravel told Belinda that her ordeal was nearly over. From her hiding-place she could observe him quite well, and she noticed that he looked unusually smart. He seemed to be dressed all in grey and carried very new gloves and a walking-stick. Belinda could not see whether he had a flower in his buttonhole or not, but she thought it was not unlikely.

When he was safely in the house, Belinda took

the opportunity to run as fast as she could into the back garden, where she arrived rather out of breath. She sat down on an upturned box in the toolshed and began to consider the situation.

What could bring him to their house so early in the day? It seemed unlikely that he was the kind of person who would call to thank them for the supper party. It was more probable that he had come to demand a subscription for the Library extensions. It might be that he was calling on several people for this purpose and had come to their house first because it was nearest. Belinda hoped Harriet was not going to be disappointed. She seemed to have taken quite a fancy to Mr Mold, and it would be so unfortunate if she got any *ideas* about him. For Belinda was sure that if Mr Mold ever did decide to marry he would choose for his bride some pretty, helpless young woman, perhaps a reader in the Library, who asked him in appealing tones where she could find the *Dictionary of National Biography*. In any case, he was certainly not good enough for Harriet, who would soon tire of his florid complexion and facetious humour. Also, he was not really a gentleman; that seemed to matter a great deal. All the same, it would be interesting to know why he had called.

Harriet, who had been sitting over the fire in the dining-room at her usual task of 'strengthening corsets' with elastic thread, had not been so slow in finding an answer to this important question. It was quite obvious that he had come to see *her*. She had no time to go into this question more deeply, for almost immediately after she had heard the front-door bell, Emily had come into the dining-room and announced Mr Nathaniel Mold.

'Tell him I shall be with him in a minute,' said Harriet, rolling up the corsets and putting them under a cushion. It would never do for him to see her with her face all flushed and shining from sitting over the fire. 'Oh, and Emily, I hope you have switched on the electric fire in the drawing-room?'

Five minutes later she walked down the stairs looking considerably more elegant, her face rather heavily powdered and her hair neatly arranged. There was no need to hurry, she decided, as she paused for a moment in the hall to take a final look at herself in the mirror.

She opened the drawing-room door quietly. Mr Mold was standing with his back to her. At Harriet's entry he turned round, rather startled. He was holding in his hand a copy of *Stitchcraft*, in which he had been reading how to make a table runner. It is always difficult to know how one ought to be occupied when waiting for a lady in her drawing-room, and he had resisted the temptation to probe into the pigeon holes of the large desk, which stood invitingly open. *Stitchcraft* was dull but safe, he felt.

'Good morning,' said Harriet, advancing towards him with hands outstretched in welcome and a brilliant smile on her face. 'I'm so sorry to have kept you waiting. I'm afraid you didn't find anything very interesting to read, but it must be a change for you to look at a frivolous feminine paper.'

'A very pleasant one,' he said gallantly, 'but of course we do take all these papers in the Library. I was in charge of cataloguing them at one time. I learnt quite a lot about needlework and beauty culture.'

'How wonderful—to think that these papers are preserved,' said Harriet, laughing. 'But I suppose you would be much too important to have anything to do with them now.'

'Oh, no!' Mr Mold smiled and laughed and looked generally rather coltish.

'Do sit down,' said Harriet, sinking into the softness of the sofa. 'It's very nice of you to have called,' she went on, hoping that he would soon give her some clue as to why he had come.

She was even more handsome in daylight than she had been in the evening, he decided, which was indeed very surprising. He had almost expected to be disappointed at their second meeting and had planned an alternate course of action should this happen.

'It is a very great pleasure to see you again,' he said rather stiffly. 'I felt I wanted to call and thank you and your sister for the very delightful party last night. I enjoyed it immensely.'

'Oh, I'm afraid my sister is out in the garden,' said Harriet, half rising, 'but I'm sure she would like to see you.'

'Oh, well perhaps you could convey my thanks to her. I expect she is busy and I shouldn't like to bother her,' said Mr Mold quickly. He had not been at all taken with the sister, and the last thing he wanted was to have to sit making conversation with her.

There was quite a long pause. Mr Mold began to feel rather uncomfortable. This was not at all his usual style. Perhaps it would have been better if he'd had a whisky before he came out, though half past ten was a little early even for him. Still, it might have given him courage, though he could not help feeling that he might be more successful if there were a certain diffidence or nervousness about his bearing. He could not draw upon his experience in such matters because he had never before proposed marriage to anyone. His intrigues had been mostly with the kind of women who would hardly make suitable wives for the deputy Librarian of one of England's greatest libraries; nor had they ever been considered as such.

What *is* the matter with him? Harriet was wondering. He was not at all like his usual self, in fact he seemed quite nervous, almost like poor Ricardo when he was about to propose to her. She determined to put him at his ease, so she said in a light joking way, 'Now, I do hope you haven't come to say goodbye. It will be very naughty of you to run off and leave us so soon.' She found this way of talking very good with curates and it certainly seemed to make Mr Mold less shy.

'Unfortunately my work demands that I should go back this afternoon, or tomorrow at the latest,' he said, gaining courage from her manner. 'But before I went I hoped I should be able to have a talk with you.' He looked at her plump, handsome profile expectantly.

Very much what I expected, thought Harriet complacently, but she was pleased and flattered to discover that she had been right. It was gratifying to feel that such a Man of the World as Mr Mold obviously was should want to marry her. But should she accept him? When it came to the point, Harriet found herself surprisingly undecided, considering how well she had spoken of Mr Mold to Belinda. She began to see that there were many reasons why she should refuse his offer when it came. To begin with she had known him for such a short time; indeed, this morning was only their third meeting. Harriet was not the kind of person to believe with Marlowe that

Where both deliberate, the love is slight:
Whoever loved, that loved not at first sight?

Obviously that was quite ridiculous. How could one possibly know all the things that had to be known about a person at first sight? Belinda had said she believed Mr Mold had a very nice house, but then poor Belinda was so vague, and for all that the house might be semi-detached and not at all in an advantageous position. If Mr Mold were very much in love with her it might be unkind to hurt his feelings—Harriet did not stop to consider how many times she must have hurt the feelings of her faithful admirer Count Bianco—but a smart and floridly handsome admirer in the Prime of Life would be much more acceptable to her than a husband of the same description. In her girlhood imaginings Harriet had always visualized a tall, pale man for her husband, hence her partiality for the clergy. People of Mr Mold's type could never look well in a pulpit. And finally, who would change a comfortable life of spinsterhood in a country parish, which always had its pale curate to be cherished, for the unknown trials of matrimony? Harriet remembered Belinda once saying something about people preferring to bear those ills they had, rather than flying to others that they knew not of, or something like that. It had been quite one of Belinda's most sensible observations.

Thus Harriet's mind was practically made up to refuse Mr Mold's offer when it came. In the meantime, she waited for him to declare himself. He was nearly as slow as poor Ricardo, who always took so long to come to the point that Harriet sometimes found herself helping him out.

There was a pause. Harriet sighed. Perhaps even Mr Mold needed to be helped a little; she had thought he might be better at coming to the point than Ricardo.

'How I envy you living in that lovely town,' she said, looking at him rather intensely. 'Your house is in the Woodbury road, isn't it? I always think that's the very nicest part.'

'Yes, it is pleasant. My house is on a corner, so it has a rather larger garden than the others.' Again there was a short pause, then Mr Mold burst out with rather forced joviality, 'You know, I feel that you and I have so much in common . . .'

Harriet said nothing. She was going rapidly over her own interests and comparing them with those that Mr Mold might be supposed to have. A certain standard of living, comfort, good food, all these they might share, but as before her mind went back to what was undoubtedly her greatest interest—curates. Perhaps she did not define it in that one simple word, but the idea was there, and with it the suspicion that Mr Mold was the kind of person who was not entirely at his ease with the clergy.

Encouraged by her silence Mr Mold went on: 'What I mean to say is, that I think we should be very happy if we married. My house is large and comfortable and my financial position is sound . . . and,' he added, rather as an afterthought, 'I loved you the moment I saw you.'

Harriet almost laughed when she remembered their first meeting in the village, when she had been wearing that awful old tweed coat, too! It was really amazing how blind love made people. Nevertheless, she was disappointed. Proposals from Ricardo several times a year had accustomed her to passionate pleadings, interspersed with fine phrases from the greater Italian poets. Besides, Ricardo never proposed sitting down. Always standing or even kneeling, indeed, his courtly manners had often caused Harriet some amusement. Compared with Ricardo, Mr Mold sounded so prosaic and casual. He didn't sound as if he really *cared* at all. She glanced at him hastily; little beads of sweat were glistening on his forehead and his face was crimson. Harriet could not help remembering that Ricardo always looked pale, and although these differences were rather trivial, they seemed somehow to add themselves to the list of reasons why she should not accept Mr Mold's proposal.

'Dear Mr Mold,' she began, not quite as certain of herself as usual, for she was not yet used to rejecting him, and did not know how he would take it. 'It is really charming of you to say such kind things, and I am deeply honoured by your proposal, but I feel I cannot accept it. It would not be fair to *you*,' she added hastily, not wishing to appear unkind.

Mr Mold looked genuinely disappointed. 'Of course I know this must be a shock to you,' he ventured. 'Perhaps you would like to wait a few days and decide after thinking it over?'

But Harriet didn't think she would like to do that. Thinking things over was so tiring, and really there was nothing to think about. The more she considered it, the less attractive the prospect of this marriage seemed to be. He had been so jolly last night, that was what she had liked. Perhaps that was because he had been a little drunk? And somehow he didn't look so handsome at close quarters. Was it possible that he was just *past* the Prime of Life? she wondered.

So she smiled at him very charmingly and repeated that although she was flattered and deeply touched by his proposal she thought it would be kinder to give him his answer now.

'I'm afraid my sister and I are *very* confirmed spinsters,' she added, in a lighter vein.

Mr Mold felt like saying that he had not intended to marry her sister as well, for he was now annoyed rather than hurt at her refusal, and did not consider that she had sufficiently realized the compliment he had paid her in asking her to be his wife. He muttered something about it being a great pity, and then Harriet said she hoped that he would have a pleasant journey back; the afternoon train was a very convenient one and she believed there was a restaurant car on it. Dr Parnell would be staying a little longer, perhaps? It was such a real pleasure for them to see visitors as they lived such uneventful lives in this quiet village. She did hope that Mr Mold would come and see them again next time he was in the neighbourhood.

As he stood on the front doorstep, Mr Mold extended a cordial invitation to her to come and visit him some time. 'You'll always find me in the

Library,' he added jovially, almost his old self again.

'Reading *Stitchcraft*, I suppose,' said Harriet, on a teasing note.

As he went out of the gate, he even waved one of his new gloves at her. Perhaps after all the Librarian was right when he said that marriage was a tiresome business and that he and Mold were lucky not to have been caught. He looked at his watch. There would be plenty of time for a chat with the landlord of the Crownwheel and Pinion before lunch. Marriage might put a stop to all that kind of thing.

While Mr Mold's proposal was being rejected in the drawing-room, Belinda was in the dining-room, writing a letter to Agatha. 'We have had remarkably mild weather lately,' she wrote, 'and I have been able to do a lot of gardening, in fact I have just been putting in the last of the bulbs. I have noticed your pink chrysanthemums showing buds, which is very early for them, isn't it?

'The Archdeacon preached a very fine sermon on Sunday, about the Judgment Day. We were all very much impressed by it. You will be glad to hear that he is looking well and has a good appetite.'

Here Belinda paused and laid down her pen. Was this last sentence perhaps a little presumptuous? Ought an archdeacon to be looking well and eating with a good appetite when his wife was away? And ought Belinda to write as if she knew about his appetite?

She turned to the letter again and added 'as far as I know' to the sentence about the appetite.

'It was so nice to see Nicholas Parnell again, and I think he enjoys coming here for a quiet holiday.

He brought the deputy Librarian, Mr Mold, with him. I don't know whether you have met him? Personally, his type does not appeal to me very much. He is supposed to be a great ladies' man, and is too fond of making jokes not always in the best of taste. Harriet saw him coming out of the Crownwheel and Pinion in the morning, which I thought a pity.'

Here Belinda laid down her pen again. Was she being quite fair to Mr Mold? She had allowed herself to get so carried away by her own feelings about him that she had rather forgotten she was writing to Agatha, in whom she did not normally confide.

'Still, I daresay he is a very nice man,' she went on, 'when one really knows him.'

This last sentence reminded Belinda that he had now been closeted in the drawing-room with Harriet for some considerable time. Belinda had not yet been able to decide why he had come, indeed, she had rather forgotten about the whole thing. Nothing was further from her mind than a proposal of marriage, and had she known what was going on, she would probably have rushed into the drawing-room, even if she had still been wearing her old gardening mackintosh and galoshes, and tried her best to stop it, for one was never quite sure what Harriet would do. Especially after her apparent admiration of Mr Mold and her continual harping on the Prime of Life. Belinda went so far as to go into the hall, but could not bring herself to listen at the drawing-room door. From where she stood she could hear a low murmur of voices. It was no use being impatient, and the last thing she wanted was to see Mr Mold

154

herself, so she went back to her letter. Writing to Agatha was not easy, more of a duty than a pleasure, but Belinda felt that she might like to hear some of the details of the parish life which the Archdeacon probably would not give her, so she wrote about the autumn leaves and berries they had used to decorate the church, the organist's illness and Miss Smiley's brave attempt to play at Evensong, the success of the Scouts' Jumble Sale and other homely matters.

At last she heard the sound of a door opening, then conversation and laughter. Harriet and Mr Mold had come out of the drawing-room. Belinda waited until she judged him safely out of the front door and then went eagerly into the hall to hear the result of his visit.

She found Harriet standing in front of the mirror, rubbing her hands together and looking pleased with herself. Her face was rather red and she looked more elegant than was usual at such an early hour of the day.

'Well,' she said, with a hint of triumph in her voice, 'that's that.'

'Yes,' said Belinda, 'but what? I hope you didn't promise him anything for the Library Extension Fund. There are far more deserving causes in the parish.'

'But, Belinda, surely you guessed why he had come?' said Harriet patiently, for really her sister was very stupid. 'He came to ask me to marry him,' she declared, smiling.

'Oh, *Harriet* . . .' Belinda was quite speechless. She might have known that something dreadful like this would happen. As if he would bother to come and ask for a subscription to the Library funds! Her supposition seemed very vain and feeble now. Still, as Belinda would not have to live with them, perhaps she need not see very much of her over-jovial brother-in-law—that would be some consolation, though it would hardly make up for the loss of her sister. Of course, she supposed, she could always have a companion to live with her, some deserving poor relation like Connie Aspinall, or she might advertise in the *Church Times*; somebody with literary interests and fond of gardening, a churchwoman, of course. Belinda shuddered as she thought of the applications and the task of interviewing them; she was sure she would never have the strength to reject anyone, however unsuitable. Perhaps, after all, it would be better to live alone.

'Of course, I couldn't accept him,' said Harriet, rather loudly, for she had expected Belinda to show real interest, instead of just standing and staring at the floor.

The look of relief that brightened Belinda's face was pathetic in its intensity.

'Oh, *Harriet* . . .' again she was speechless. However could she have thought for a moment that her sister would do such a thing?

'Indeed I couldn't,' said Harriet calmly. 'Why I hardly know him, and you remember what Shakespeare said about when lovely woman stoops to folly . . .' she made a significant gesture with her hand.

Belinda frowned. 'I don't think it was *Shakespeare*, dear,' she said absently. 'I must ask Henry. I have an idea it may be Pope.' But what did it matter? Belinda was so overcome with joy and relief at Harriet's news that she kissed her impulsively and suggested that they should have some meringues for tea, as Harriet was so fond of them.

Together they went into the dining-room, where Harriet with many ludicrous and exaggerated imitations, gave a demonstration of how Mr Mold had proposed to her.

'Oh, Harriet, you mustn't be so unkind!' protested Belinda, in the intervals of laughing, for her sister was really much funnier than Mr Mold could possibly have been. They laughed even more when the corsets were discovered under a cushion.

'Just imagine if Emily had brought him in here and he had discovered them while he was waiting. Or if the Archdeacon had when he came the other day,' chortled Harriet.

'Oh, Harriet,' said Belinda faintly. There was a vulgar, music-hall touch about it all that one could associate with Mr Mold but hardly with the Archdeacon.

'I expect he's consoling himself in the Crownwheel and Pinion,' said Harriet, 'so we needn't really pity him.'

She was perfectly right; so much so that, when he arrived at the vicarage rather late for lunch, Dr Parnell was constrained to whisper to his friend the Archdeacon, 'I fear poor Nathaniel is not entirely sober.'

CHAPTER THIRTEEN

As Mr Mold settled himself comfortably in his first-class corner seat he decided that he had probably had a lucky escape. And indeed, he reflected, *Love is only one of many passions and it has no great influence on the sum of life*, as the Librarian was so fond of quoting.

A few days later Belinda and Harriet were invited to tea at the vicarage. It was hardly surprising that Mr Mold's proposal, which appeared to be known to the Archdeacon and Dr Parnell, should be the chief topic of conversation.

Dr Parnell was inclined to think it a pity that Harriet had refused his colleague, for although he had always been of the opinion that it must be very tiresome to be married, he did not deny that it was an interesting state. Indeed, he often regretted that the Archdeacon was the only one of his friends who had a wife. As a young man Dr Parnell had looked forward to the time when Belinda would come to him for advice on the trials of matrimony. In those days he had hoped that she might marry the Archdeacon, and was almost as disappointed as she had been at her failure to captivate him. He had never liked Agatha, but he could not help admiring her skill, and when by her powers her husband was raised to the dignity of archdeacon, Mr Parnell, as he then was, had aptly remarked that Henry was indeed fortunate in having won the love of a good woman. Nevertheless, he considered himself almost equally fortunate in *not* having done so, and often used to remark to John Akenside that he did not think poor Henry was quite as *free* as he had been.

But there was no denying that Harriet and Mr Mold would have made an admirable couple. They had both reached an age when temperament and character were settled, and instead of one dominating the other they would have been able to live in comfortable harmony. Besides, there would be plenty of money, so that if there had been love, which Dr Parnell rather doubted, it would have been less likely to fly out of the window, as he had been told it did when poverty came in at the door.

Sitting round the fire in the Archdeacon's study, they considered the problem.

'Of course I never advise anyone to enter into that state without long and careful thought,' said Dr Parnell, 'but I should be the last to admit impediments to the marriage of true minds, and it seems to me that you and Nathaniel have a great many tastes in common.'

Harriet denied this indignantly: perhaps she was still thinking of curates. 'The only thing we have in common is a love of good food,' she said, thinking that Dr Parnell was being more than usually interfering. 'I could never marry Mr Mold.'

'But surely liking the same things for dinner is one of the deepest and most lasting things you could possibly have in common with anyone,' argued Dr Parnell. 'After all, the emotions of the heart are very transitory, or so I believe; I should think it makes one much happier to be well-fed than well-loved.'

Belinda did not trouble to contradict this statement, romantic and sentimental though she was. She was feeling much too happy and peaceful

159

to indulge in any argument. For here she was sitting on the sofa with the person she had loved well and faithfully for thirty years, and whom she still saw as the beautiful young man he had been then, although he was now married and an archdeacon. And as if this were not enough, had she not just escaped having a brother-in-law who was not really a gentleman, and made jokes not always in the best of taste? When one reached middle age it was even more true that all change is of itself an evil and ought not to be hazarded but for evident advantage. She smiled at Dr Parnell indulgently, but said nothing. The Archdeacon in his turn smiled affectionately at her, and thought what a nice peaceful creature she was, so different from his own admirable wife, with her busy schemes for his preferment.

Dr Parnell was still regretting Harriet's hasty action, and suggested that she might write Mr Mold a letter giving him some *hope* for he had heard that even hope was better than nothing.

But Harriet, who knew she was being teased, merely listened with a smile on her face and said with dignity that she believed she could do a great deal better for herself. She looked at the three of them rather mysteriously, and Belinda wondered whether she could be making plans to captivate Dr Parnell.

'You would have kept poor Nathaniel out of mischief,' he said, still harping on the same subject.

'I daresay,' remarked Harriet, 'and I expect he needs it. Do you know,' she leaned forward confidentially, 'I believe he *drinks* . . .' she said, pronouncing this last word in a suitably hushed

160

whisper.

'Oh, Harriet,' protested Belinda, for she could now afford to feel kindly towards Mr Mold, 'I don't think you should say that. We all like to take something occasionally, a drink can be a great comfort at times.'

'I am glad to hear that you are so broad-minded,' said the Archdeacon. 'I remember Agatha being quite shocked when I said something of the kind to the Mothers' Union once.'

'Well, I suppose it is a dangerous thing to say,' said Dr Parnell. 'They might abuse the comfort of drink.'

'Whereas *we* know how to be moderate,' said Harriet primly.

'I cannot imagine Agatha taking too much,' said Dr Parnell. He chuckled. 'No, I'm afraid I can't.'

Belinda gave him a shocked glance. 'Have you heard from Agatha again?' she asked the Archdeacon brightly.

'Yes, as a matter of fact I had a letter by the lunch-time post,' he said. 'You can read it if you want to,' he added, taking a letter out of his pocket and handing it to her.

Belinda took the letter rather gingerly, thinking it odd that he should hand it to her so willingly. But when she came to read Agatha's neat handwriting, she saw that the letter contained nothing private. It seemed to be a long list of things he must not forget to do. It was admirably practical, but unromantic. And yet, after so many years of being married to a charming but difficult man like the Archdeacon, perhaps it was rather too much to expect that Agatha should dwell on the desolation of life without him. All the same,

161

Belinda could not help remembering her own letters, and she was sure that even now she could have found something a little more *tender* to write about than Florrie's and cook's wages and the Mothers' Union tea. She was just going to hand the letter back when she noticed that there was a postscript over the page.

'I forgot to tell you that among the people staying here is the Bishop of Mbawawa. I believe the Bedes know him. He is a delightful man, so friendly, and he tells many interesting stories about the splendid work he has been doing among the natives. I am trying to persuade him to come home with me, as I am sure everyone would be interested to meet him.'

Belinda stopped short in amazement as she read these words. 'Harriet,' she said, '*who* do you think is there?'

Harriet, who was quietly enjoying a substantial tea, looked up and asked who was where.

'In Karlsbad,' said Belinda.

'I don't know,' she said, not very interested. 'It's the sort of place where King Edward VII might be, only of course it could hardly be him.'

'It's an old friend of yours,' said Belinda.

'Is he an old friend?' asked the Archdeacon.

'I should like to number bishops among my friends,' said Dr Parnell.

Harriet seemed to brighten up at this. 'Bishops? Well, of course I know quite a number,' she mused. This was not really surprising, for after all every bishop has once been a curate. 'It couldn't be Willie Amery, I suppose or Oliver Opobo and Calabar—isn't that a lovely title?—no, he's in Nigeria, I believe. Of course it might be Theo

Grote, Theodore Mbawawa, as he signs himself,' she smiled to herself. '*That* would be the nicest of all.'

'Yes, Harriet, it's Theo Grote,' said Belinda. 'I knew you would be interested to hear that.'

'Oh *ho*,' said Dr Parnell, seeing that Harriet had gone quite pink in the face. 'I believe we are going to see some old broth being warmed up. I like to see that.'

'Agatha talks of bringing him to stay here,' said the Archdeacon distastefully. He disliked other members of his calling.

Clean sheets on the spare bed and a tin of biscuits on the little table in case he should feel hungry in the night, thought Belinda irrelevantly.

'He must be about fifty-seven or fifty-eight,' said Harriet, who seemed to have been doing a little calculation. 'It *will* be nice to see dear Theo again.'

'On the threshold of sixty,' mused Dr Parnell. 'That's a good age for a man to marry. He needs a woman to help him into his grave.'

'But that's just the Prime of Life,' said Harriet indignantly. 'I'm sure we shan't find Theo at all *doddery*.'

Belinda began to suspect that Harriet regarded the Bishop as a possible husband. She had certainly been very much in love with him when she was a schoolgirl and he a willowy curate in the early twenties. Belinda had often thought that the reason why Harriet made so much of Mr Donne was because he reminded her of dear Theo Grote. And then Belinda had often heard her say that a bishop needed a wife to help him with certain intimate problems in his diocese, things which a woman could deal with better than a man. It

163

seemed a little hard, Belinda thought, that this new menace should appear, just when she was so relieved at having escaped Mr Mold, but she would just have to leave Harriet to her schemes. Belinda trembled for the unmarried Bishop of Mbawawa if he did not feel inclined to enter into that blessed state.

'Shall I read aloud to you?' suggested the Archdeacon hopefully. He went over to the bookshelves and invited requests for what anyone would like. But Dr Parnell suddenly got up from his chair and announced that he thought he had better do his packing. It was so tiresome to have a rush at the last minute. Harriet, too, had suddenly remembered that she was to deliver some parish magazines and was already halfway out of the door, thanking the Archdeacon for a delightful tea party, and inviting him to drop in at four o'clock any afternoon. She and Dr Parnell hurried out of the room together, the latter remarking that he wondered Henry could spare the time from his parochial duties to listen to the sound of his own voice.

'We should all have time to improve our minds,' said Belinda smiling happily.

The Archdeacon turned towards her with a volume of Spenser in his hand. 'I think it would be pleasant to have something from the *Faerie Queene*,' he declared.

The clock struck half past five. Belinda settled herself comfortably in her chair. She felt rather drowsy and the *Faerie Queene* was such a soothing poem. It just went on and on.

At six o'clock the Archdeacon suggested a little Wordsworth. Belinda agreed that this would be very nice. She had always been so fond of *The Prelude*.

At half past six Belinda began to murmur something about being sure that she was disturbing the Archdeacon, who must have a great deal to do.

Well, yes, he supposed that she *was* disturbing him really, but it was very pleasant to be disturbed occasionally, especially when there were so many tiresome things to do.

'Do you know,' he said suddenly, with the air of one who has made an important discovery, 'this reminds me of the old days. I used to read aloud to you then. Does it remind you?'

Belinda was speechless, as she considered this proof of man's oddness. Whatever did he imagine that it reminded her of? 'Oh, yes, it's quite like the old days,' she said at last, and then tried to think of something more intelligent to continue the conversation.

Silences were awkward things, especially when one's mind was only too apt to wander back into the past and remember it so vividly that it became more real than the present. Unless she fixed her attention on something definite, she might find herself saying the wrong thing. Her eyes lighted on a set of Bible commentaries. Well, nobody could expect her to talk about them. She must try again. The mantelpiece is dusty, she thought. Florrie needs keeping up to the mark, and I don't believe she's used the Hoover on this carpet since Agatha went away. Agatha. There was something definite. There was nothing vague or nebulous about an archdeacon's wife, even when she wasn't there. I loved you more than Agatha

165

did, thought Belinda, but all I can do now is to keep silent. I can't even speak to Florrie about the dusty mantelpiece, because it's nothing to do with me. It never was and it never will be.

'Florrie never bothers to dust my study when Agatha's away,' said the Archdeacon, seeing where Belinda was looking.

'No, things always go wrong in a house when there's no woman at the head of things,' agreed Belinda. 'I mean, it's different when Agatha's away.'

The Archdeacon sighed. 'Yes, it is different,' he agreed. 'But there it is. We can't alter things, can we?'

Belinda did not know what to say to this, as she was not quite sure what he meant. She was just wondering what would happen if she led the conversation round to more personal things than dusty mantelpieces, when the door opened and in came Dr Parnell, complaining that he was hungry and asking if they were never going to have anything to eat.

'Why, yes, it must be nearly supper-time,' said Belinda, starting to put on her gloves. 'I must go.'

'Oh, but I insist that you stay,' protested the Archdeacon.

'I really couldn't,' said Belinda mechanically. 'Harriet will be expecting me.'

'Please, dear Belinda,' he said coaxingly. 'You know I asked you to tea the other day and you wouldn't come. The least you can do is to stay now. For the sake of old times,' he added, with uncharacteristic heartiness.

'Really, Henry, I think you might have put it better,' said Dr Parnell. 'I should hardly imagine

166

that poor Belinda can really wish to be reminded of old times.'

But Belinda only smiled. 'All right, I will stay,' she said.

'I shall never understand women,' said Dr Parnell complacently.

CHAPTER FOURTEEN

Belinda arrived home that evening feeling very happy. It had been so nice having supper at the vicarage without the restraining presence of Agatha, the efficient wife and good philologist. During those few hours Belinda had almost imagined herself back in her youth. As she had listened to the Archdeacon giving a short dissertation on the Beast Fable in the Middle Ages, she had found herself looking at her watch and thinking that she would have to be back at her college by half past ten if she did not want the Principal to ask any awkward questions. When the Archdeacon had gone on to discuss the sources of his Judgment Day sermon, she had realized regretfully that the Principal of whom she had stood in awe had been in her grave at least ten years.

It was not until she reached her own front door that Belinda began to feel a little uneasy, and wonder if it had been quite the thing for her to spend a whole evening at the vicarage without Agatha or Harriet to chaperone her. For although Dr Parnell had been there, he wasn't quite the same as some respectable middle-aged woman.

And yet why should not she be allowed her occasional joys, such very mild ones, which were mostly remembrance of things past?

Sound of hearty laughter came from the drawing-room. The curate was there. Perhaps he had dropped in after Evensong, as Harriet had so often told him to, and had stayed to supper. Belinda was glad that he was there, as his presence would save her a little from Harriet's ruthless cross-examination, which was bound to come sooner or later.

Belinda went upstairs to take off her hat and coat and then into the middle of the cheerful noise.

Harriet and the curate were sitting on the sofa, deeply engrossed in a book. The curate leaped up and expressed himself delighted to see her. Belinda thought it a little unnecessary of him to welcome her to her own house, but she said nothing.

'I suppose you've had supper?' asked Harriet.

'Yes,' said Belinda, 'I stayed at the vicarage. I hope you didn't wait for me?'

'Oh, no,' said Harriet, 'in fact I didn't expect you back even as soon as *this*.'

Belinda laughed rather uncomfortably. 'What are you reading?' she asked, hoping to change the subject.

'We were reading Catullus. I really don't know how we got on to it,' said Harriet merrily. 'Mr Donne's so good at Latin but of course it's quite thirty years since I read a *word* of it.'

'Oh, come,' said the curate playfully. 'I can't believe that.'

Belinda took up her knitting. She remembered

168

Dr Parnell saying that he thought Catullus rather too indelicate for a young girl to read. If this were so, for Belinda's scanty knowledge of Latin would not enable her to find out for herself, how much more indelicate must the great Roman poet be for a young curate! 'There is a pretty translation of one of his poems by Thomas Campion,' she said vaguely, 'but I suppose it's not like reading the original.'

'No, my friend Olivia Berridge always says that. You remember perhaps, she's Mrs Hoccleve's niece,' explained the curate.

'Oh, yes,' said Harriet, 'she knows Anglo-Saxon and things like that, doesn't she? And of course she made you those socks. I thought the toes were not very well grafted, in that grey pair you showed me. It's quite easy to do, really. You just say knit and slip off, purl and keep on—or it may be the other way round.'

The curate looked mystified. 'She's very clever,' he said. 'I expect she knows that.'

Harriet looked a little annoyed and the conversation flagged. Mr Donne got up to go.

'Perhaps you would like to borrow some books?' suggested Belinda, seeing that he was looking at the shelves. It was a little difficult to guide his choice, but eventually he went away with some thrillers and the selected poems of the Earl of Rochester, a volume of which Belinda was particularly fond. It had been given to her by Dr Parnell on her twenty-first birthday. Belinda felt that it would not be likely to harm Mr Donne's morals, as it professed to be *a collection of such pieces only, as may be received in a vertuous court, and may not unbecome the Cabinet of the Severest*

169

He had hardly gone out of the front door, when Harriet turned eagerly to Belinda and said, 'Now tell me *all* about it.'

Belinda looked up from her knitting rather startled. 'But, Harriet,' she protested, 'there's really nothing to tell. Henry read aloud to me and then we talked a bit and then he persuaded me to stay to supper, which I did. But I don't know whether I ought to have done that,' she added rather unhappily. 'I mean, I shouldn't like Agatha to think . . .'

'No, no, of course not,' said Harriet soothingly. 'Now wouldn't you like a nice cup of Ovaltine?' she said, fussing round Belinda like a motherly hen.

'Well, I don't know, I think I would,' said Belinda. Perhaps a nourishing milky drink was needed to bring her down to earth but it seemed an unromantic end to the evening.

Harriet had already gone into the kitchen and soon returned with the Ovaltine and a selection of biscuits and cakes.

'Now,' she said, as if speaking to an invalid, 'drink it up while it's hot and don't try to talk till you've finished. There'll be plenty of time for you to tell me all about it.'

'But what is there to tell?' protested Belinda, rousing herself. 'I've told you what we did.'

Harriet chose a chocolate biscuit. 'I do believe the Archdeacon has been asking you to elope with him!' she declared triumphantly.

'Oh, Harriet, how dreadful you are!' said Belinda, unable to help laughing at this monstrous suggestion. 'As if a clergyman, let alone an archdeacon, would do a thing like that.'

'Then he's been telling you that he's very fond of you, and hinting that he wishes he'd married you instead of Agatha,' went on Harriet, gallantly persevering.

'Well, hardly that,' ventured Belinda, growing a little more confidential, for the Ovaltine had loosened her tongue. 'I mean, it's a bit late for anything like that, isn't it? Henry is always loyal to Agatha and feels quite *differently* about her,' she added hastily, in case her sister should take her up wrongly.

Harriet agreed with this ambiguous statement. 'Yes, I'm sure he does,' she said, 'but there's no reason why he shouldn't be fond of you as well. Clergymen are always saying that we should love one another.'

'Oh, *Harriet*,' protested Belinda, rather shocked, 'you know quite well that isn't at all the same kind of thing. But of course Henry and I have always been friends and I hope we always will be.'

Harriet sighed. Poor Belinda was so unworldly, so sentimental.

'Of course he is fond of you,' she declared boldly. 'Anybody can tell that by the way he keeps smiling at you, when he thinks nobody's looking.'

Belinda had always thought that they were smiles of pity rather than of love. But hadn't one of our greater English poets said something about Pity being akin to Love? Or had she made it up herself? A vague recollection of Aristotle's *Poetics* came into her mind. But that was Pity and Fear, rather like her feeling for Miss Prior, not at all the same thing . . .

'I'm sure everyone knows,' persisted Harriet,

nothing daunted by her sister's unwillingness to confide in her and determined to make something interesting out of Belinda's evening at the vicarage.

'Knows what?' asked Belinda, rather startled.

'Why, that you love each other,' beamed Harriet, as if she were giving her blessing to a young couple, instead of making rather a scandalous suggestion about a married archdeacon and a respectable spinster.

Belinda was now rather agitated and could not think of anything to say.

'Don't deny that he's making the most of Agatha's absence,' Harriet went on, 'and anyway everybody knows that you knew him long before Agatha did.'

'I don't see what that has to do with it,' said Belinda. 'One can hardly claim people on that basis.'

'But didn't he say *anything?* Surely you weren't just reading poetry *all* the time?'

'No, not all the time.' Belinda smiled as she remembered their conversation. 'We talked about the dust on the mantelpiece.'

'Oh, Belinda, surely . . .' Harriet searched vainly in the tin for another chocolate biscuit.

'And I said that of course things did go wrong when there was no woman at the head of things,' Belinda went on. 'I mean, servants neglect their duty and that sort of thing. I think I said, "It's different when Agatha's away", or something like that.'

'Oh, Belinda, wasn't that rather obvious?'

Belinda looked startled. 'Oh, I meant things in the house, naturally. He surely couldn't have taken it any other way?'

'Well, what did he say to that?' went on Harriet relentlessly. 'Do you remember?'

'Oh, yes. I always remember everything Henry says.' She smiled. 'Thirty years of it. It's a pity I don't remember other things so well. He said, "Yes, it is different, but there it is. We can't alter things, can we?"'

Harriet let out a cry of joy. 'Go on,' she said. 'What happened next?'

'Oh, then Nicholas came in and we had supper.' Belinda paused. 'Well, dinner really, because there was soup, though I *think* it was tinned. Still, it was very nice, mushroom or something. It had little bits of things in it.'

'Oh, Belinda, I don't want to hear about the soup,' said Harriet. 'How sickening that Nicholas should have come in just at that moment. Just like him,' she grumbled. 'To think of it, the moment you've been waiting for for thirty years!' She paused dramatically.

'But you know I've never expected anything,' protested Belinda. 'I've no right to.'

'But don't you see what he meant when he said that about not being able to alter things?' said Harriet. 'He meant he'd rather have you than Agatha, only of course he couldn't put it quite as crudely as that.'

'We never mentioned ourselves,' said Belinda hopelessly. 'We were talking about his study not being dusted.'

'Now if only he were a *widower*,' mused Harriet.

'But he isn't,' said Belinda stoutly.

'No, and Agatha's very tough in spite of her rheumatism,' lamented Harriet. 'And soon he

173

won't even be a grass widower because she's coming back.'

'Yes, she's coming back,' said Belinda, even more stoutly. How odd if Henry were a widower, she thought suddenly. How embarrassing, really. It would be like going back thirty years. Or wouldn't it? Belinda soon saw that it wouldn't. For she was now a contented spinster and her love was like a warm, comfortable garment, bedsocks, perhaps, or even woollen combinations; certainly something without glamour or romance. All the same, it was rather nice to think that Henry *might* prefer her to Agatha, although she knew perfectly well that he didn't. It was one of the advantages of being the one he hadn't married that one could be in a position to imagine such things.

Belinda gave a contented sigh. It had been such a lovely evening. Just one evening like that every thirty years or so. It might not seem much to other people, but it was really all one needed to be happy. But Harriet was saying something, so she could not indulge in such thoughts for long.

'I don't like the way Mr Donne keeps mentioning that Olivia Berridge,' she said. 'Although he did say that he was definitely *not* engaged to her, one never knows.'

'He doesn't sound as if he were in love with her,' said Belinda doubtfully. 'But of course Miss Berridge may have made up her mind to marry him. She sounds a bit like Agatha,' she added.

'But Mr Donne is nothing like the Archdeacon,' said Harriet indignantly.

'No, I don't think anybody is quite like the Archdeacon,' said Belinda quietly.

174

CHAPTER FIFTEEN

During the next week or so the village began to look forward to the homecoming of the Archdeacon's right hand, as many of the church workers called Mrs Hoccleve. They were conventional enough to use this expression, which they had often heard, without troubling to ask themselves whether it could really be applied here. It was a known thing that the wives of clergy often were their right hands, and even if the Hoccleves were sometimes rather snappy with each other there was no doubt that she was the power behind him. The news that she was to be accompanied by the Bishop of Mbawawa had spread rapidly, and little groups of eager Sunday School teachers could be seen talking about it. Some had heard that he was black, a real African bishop, but Harriet soon put them right on this point and achieved a new importance through having known him as a curate. Belinda did not share in this glory, for after so many years she found it difficult to remember which of the many curates her sister had cherished was Theodore Grote.

'He was thin and dark, wasn't he?' she said anxiously. 'But somehow I can't see his face.' There was a blank above the clerical collar, as it were, for so many had been thin and dark.

'Oh, Belinda, you *must* remember him at that Whist Drive,' said Harriet smiling tenderly, for she had no difficulty in recalling him as one of the most sought-after curates in the history of the Church of England. In his heyday there had been quite a procession of doting women towards his lodgings, carrying cooked pheasants and chickens, iced cakes, even jellies in basins ... Harriet sighed over her reminiscences and then remarked in a regretful tone of voice that she did not think Belinda had really made the most of Agatha's absence.

Belinda could not but agree, for Harriet was perfectly right. And yet, how could one make the most of the absence of an archdeacon's wife. It was a thing no truly respectable spinster could or would do. She pointed this out to Harriet, who refused with characteristic obstinacy to understand and merely remarked that we none of us got any younger.

Ah yes, thought Belinda, as she turned to knitting the dull grey jumper that might have been a pullover for the Archdeacon, that was it. She thought about it so seldom but now she became melancholy at the realization that the fine madness of her youth had gone. She was no longer an original shining like a comet, indeed, it would have been unsuitable if she had been. *Change and decay in all around I see ... All, all are gone, the old familiar faces* ... Dear Nicholas was back in the Library, John Akenside was in heaven, while his earthly remains rested in an English cemetery in the Balkans, and if Harriet married Theodore Mbawawa, even she would be gone ... Who was there apart from the forbidden Archdeacon? One's women friends, of course, people like Edith Liversidge and Connie Aspinall, but they were a cold comfort. Belinda grew even more melancholy, and then she remembered Count Bianco. There was always Ricardo. Perhaps they could read

Dante together and find some consolation in the great Italian poet. She did not think she would be equal to reading Tacitus.

In the meantime Belinda had promised to go to the station with the Archdeacon to meet Agatha and the Bishop. On this day she was classed with Agatha's nearest and dearest in a way which seemed to her rather ironical. Who but a man could be so lacking in finer feelings as to think of such a thing? she wondered. But of course she said she would go.

'After all, you both love the Archdeacon,' Harriet had explained, and Belinda supposed that it was true, though one could hardly admit it even to oneself. Possibly, thought Belinda, I love him even more than Agatha does, but my feeling may be the stronger for not having married him.

As they waited on the station, Belinda decided that her sister had been wise to stay at home, for it was bitterly cold. Harriet liked her comfort and had decided that she would appear to better advantage in a less bleak setting.

'The Bishop will surely find our climate very different from that of the tropics,' remarked the curate, as they were stamping their feet on the platform to keep warm.

Belinda thought this remark to be so obvious as not to require an answer, so she turned to the Archdeacon and said that she thought his watch must be fast, as they seemed to have been waiting a long time.

'Oh, no, but the train is late,' he said, with a superior smile. So Milton's Adam must have smiled on Eve. He was not pleased at the prospect of having to entertain the Bishop for an indefinite length of time, but nevertheless he was looking forward to it with a kind of grim relish. He remembered certain minor discomforts about the spare room at the vicarage as he stood there on the cold platform. It was a gloomy room with a northerly aspect and a tall, dark monkey-puzzle growing close to the window, which looked out on to an old potting-shed, full of flower-pots and dried-up roots and bulbs. And in addition, although the Archdeacon had not personally made the bed, he knew that there were sides-to-middle sheets on it, for Florrie had come into his study that morning, very agitated because all the whole sheets were still at the laundry. The Archdeacon was delighted. He seemed to remember also that the mattress was a particularly lumpy one, worn into uncomfortable bumps and hollows by a variety of visiting clergy, and that the bedside lamp did not work. All the same he had taken pleasure in making a suitable selection of books for the bedside table—a volume of Tillotson's sermons, Klaeber's edition of *Beowulf*, the Poems of Mrs Hemans, an old Icelandic grammar, and, as a concession to the Bishop's connection with Africa, a particularly dull anthropological work, which had been included with some other books he had bought at a sale. The Bishop would naturally want thrillers—the clergy always did, he found—but he was keeping his own supply locked up in his study.

Belinda saw him smiling to himself and wondered whether it could be because Agatha was coming home. Naturally it must be, as she knew he was not pleased at the prospect of the Bishop. Prospect of bishops, she thought, liking the phrase, but at that moment the curate espied the train coming round the bend into the station.

'There they are!' he shouted, rushing towards a first-class carriage where Agatha's face had appeared at the window.

'I thought you would be travelling at the rear. I didn't look for you at the front,' said the Archdeacon rather reproachfully.

He kissed his wife, not very affectionately, Belinda thought, but she had kept herself rather in the background, waiting for this reunion of nearest and dearest to be over. There was a forced smile on her face to be used when needed. She looked about her and saw emerging from the railway carriage what she imagined must be the Bishop of Mbawawa. He too was looking as if he did not quite know what to do with himself.

Belinda moved towards him and introduced herself. 'I don't suppose you remember me,' she said, smiling rather awkwardly. Nor did she remember him, if it came to that, for she could have sworn that she had never seen him in all her life. Could a beautiful curate have grown into this tall, stringy-looking man, with a yellow, leathery complexion? His expression reminded Belinda of a sheep more than anything; his face was long, his forehead domed and his head bald. He was even rather toothy, a thing that Harriet abhorred. Could it be the same person? she wondered.

'But I certainly do remember you,' he was saying. 'You knitted me a beautiful scarf when I was a curate.'

Belinda was decidedly taken aback. She had always thought it rather wonderful that she had never done anything of the kind. He must have been thinking of Harriet or another of his many

179

admirers.

'Oh, did I?' she said vaguely, which helped neither of them, and caused the Bishop to be assailed with doubts.

'You did such splendid work with the Guild of St Agnes,' he went on, less certainly.

Belinda, who had never heard of any such guild, felt rather foolish. 'I daresay you remember my sister better,' she ventured, 'Harriet, you know.'

'Ah, *yes*.' His face cleared. 'I shall look forward to renewing my acquaintance with her,' he said politely. 'She was always interested in missions, if I remember rightly.'

'Oh, yes, she was,' said Belinda, thinking that she might as well agree for a change. 'She is looking forward to seeing you so much.'

The Bishop was just saying something about the pleasure of meeting old friends and looked as if he might almost be about to quote some Mbawawa proverb, when Agatha came over to them and Belinda found herself shaking hands cordially and telling her how well she looked.

'You're looking *splendid*,' said Belinda, and indeed Agatha was quite fat in the face and seemed in very good spirits. Belinda was shocked to find herself wondering whether a month's absence from her husband could have anything to do with it.

The curate was now bundling them all into a taxi, saying that he would walk as he had to call and see one of the church wardens. So Belinda found herself sitting by Agatha, while the Bishop and the Archdeacon squatted rather incongruously on the little folding seats.

'I don't think Henry is looking very well,' said

180

Agatha, with something of her old sharpness, so that Belinda felt that it was her fault.

'Oh, I think he's quite well really,' said Belinda quickly. 'A little tired, perhaps, but then he's had so much to do while you've been away.'

The Archdeacon was unable to resist joining in this interesting conversation, so he rather rudely interrupted the Bishop, who was telling him something about the organization of his diocese, to remark that he was really quite exhausted and did not know how he was going to get through the rest of the winter.

'Oh, I expect you'll manage all right,' said Agatha lightly. 'I'm sure Bishop Grote will be only too glad to help with some of the services.'

'Indeed I shall,' said the Bishop, 'and I daresay my own experience in organizing a large diocese will be of use to you. My African priests are dear, good fellows, but they sometimes need a helping hand.'

Belinda did not dare to look at the Archdeacon's face, but she could feel the blackness of his look and she wondered if her own indignation on his account could be seen in her face. To class an English archdeacon with African priests! Surely that was going too far? Not, she hastened to assure herself, because they were Africans: she was certain that, as the Bishop had said, they were dear, good fellows, but she was surprised that he should have so little sense of what was fitting to the occasion.

The remainder of the drive was taken in silence. Fortunately it was not far, but it was long enough for Belinda to realize that the Bishop and the Archdeacon had taken an instant dislike to each

181

other. This was in some ways rather unlucky, as it was essential to the success of Harriet's plans that the Bishop should stay some time, and if the Archdeacon were really rude to him, as he might very well be, there was no knowing what might happen. Of course Harriet might not feel so enthusiastic after she had seen the Bishop. Belinda hoped that this might be so, as she did not think she would like him as a brother-in-law and she certainly did not want her sister to leave her and go to Africa.

They reached the vicarage and Belinda hovered uncertainly by the front door.

'Belinda will stay to tea, of course,' said the Archdeacon quickly.

'Oh, yes, certainly,' said Agatha. 'We want to hear all the parish news.'

'I should like a little moral support,' said the Archdeacon in a low voice. 'I am not sure that tea will be enough.'

Belinda walked quickly into the hall after Agatha. The Bishop followed them, but the Archdeacon stayed behind to supervise the unloading of the luggage.

'I hope it isn't inconvenient,' said Belinda in her usual apologetic manner.

'Not at all,' said Agatha coolly. 'One extra for tea is no trouble at all—I never find that it is.'

'Oh, no, nor do I,' said Belinda, floundering deeper. She was quite grateful to the Bishop for turning the conversation to the Mbawawa hunting customs, by which it appeared that when an animal was killed unlimited hospitality was extended to all neighbouring tribes.

'What a nice custom,' said Belinda inadequately,

'but I imagine they would have to have more than one animal, wouldn't they?'

'Oh, it is a ritual eating,' the Bishop explained. 'The meat is not actually consumed.'

'Well, I hope our tea will be a little more satisfying,' said Agatha, smiling indulgently at the Bishop. 'Where is Harriet, by the way?' she asked Belinda, in a sharper tone. 'She couldn't come to the station,' said Belinda evasively. After all it was none of Agatha's business where Harriet was. She could hardly have told the assembled company that Harriet preferred to wait for some more elegant occasion before renewing her acquaintance with the Bishop. She had visions of herself advancing towards him graciously in her brown velvet or wine crêpe de Chine, and such clothes would hardly have been possible at the station on a cold winter afternoon.

'I hope she is quite well?' said Agatha politely.

'Yes, thank you,' said Belinda. 'She was doing something else, as a matter of fact.'

'With Ricardo, perhaps?' suggested the Archdeacon helpfully.

'Is she married then?' asked the Bishop. 'I did not know.'

'Oh, no,' said Belinda confusedly. 'Ricardo isn't her *husband*. He is an Italian count,' she added quickly, as if that did away with any possibility of a misunderstanding. 'One of our oldest friends here.'

'Of course everybody in the village knows him,' said Agatha. 'He is a charming man, most friendly. I ought not to gossip, I know, but I don't think anybody would be surprised if he were to marry Lady Clara Boulding, the widow of our former

Member of Parliament,' she explained for the Bishop's benefit.

'There is no reason why you shouldn't gossip, my dear,' said the Archdeacon, 'but I think a great many people would be surprised if things happened as you suggested. I had an idea that Ricardo's fancy lay in quite another direction.'

At this the Bishop directed a rather coy glance towards Belinda, who began talking quickly about missions and the very interesting preacher they had had one Sunday evening, from the diocese of Ndikpo, or some such name.

'Ah, yes, Ndikpo,' the Bishop shook his head. 'The labourers are indeed few in that field. They have no African priests there.'

'I suppose some parts are more backward than others,' Belinda ventured. 'I mean it takes some time before the natives are ready to be ordained.'

'Ah, yes, yes. Time and Money,' the Bishop nodded again and then asked whether the Archdeacon gave out collecting boxes for missions to his parishioners.

'No,' replied the Archdeacon shortly. 'We have a collection at Mattins every now and then.'

'But surely it would be more lucrative if people took collecting boxes?' suggested the Bishop. 'You would find that the spirit of friendly rivalry would increase the amount considerably. You might publish the results in the parish magazine when the boxes were opened. I have always found that the best way.'

'It wouldn't work here,' said the Archdeacon emphatically.

'I think it's an excellent idea,' said Agatha. 'Miss Smiley does it for the Zenana Mission, you know.'

'Does she?' said the Archdeacon. 'I really could not undertake to do anything about it myself, I am much too busy, as you will realize when you have been here a little longer, my dear Bishop.'

Belinda could only wonder how he was to be made to realize this, but, loyal as ever, she agreed that the Archdeacon was much too busy and, much to her own surprise and dismay, heard herself offering to take on the organization and distribution of the boxes.

'I knew it!' said the Bishop. 'As soon as I saw Miss Bede, I said to myself "here is one of *us*—that splendid work for the Guild of St Agnes"—do you know, Archdeacon, she even denied that she had been connected with it?'

Belinda was by now covered with confusion and began to wonder whether she had indeed worked splendidly for the Guild of St Agnes; after all, her memory was not always completely reliable. Perhaps she had also knitted the Bishop a beautiful scarf. She felt that it was time to be going.

'Oh, Belinda is a very excellent person altogether,' said the Archdeacon with casual charm. 'I don't know what we should do without her.'

Belinda reflected a little bitterly on these words as she walked home, but the sight of Ricardo and Edith Liversidge, deep in conversation, soon turned her thoughts to other matters. She could guess what they were talking about and was not surprised to hear Ricardo saying that he had hoped the tombstone would be of white marble rather than commonplace grey stone.

'Well, as long as he's dead I don't see that it

matters what his tombstone is like,' said Edith very sensibly, but with a lack of feeling regrettable in one who had lost her love so tragically. 'I'm sure John wouldn't mind,' she went on jovially. 'He was never all that particular about appearances.'

'A mind and spirit as great as his needed no outward decoration,' said Ricardo solemnly.

Belinda waited until he had gone before interrupting with an invitation to Edith to come in for a cup of tea.

'I've had mine at the vicarage,' she explained, 'but I expect Harriet will still be having hers.'

'Well, if it isn't a nuisance,' said Edith, with unusual consideration.

'Oh, one extra for tea is no trouble at all,' said Belinda gaily. 'I never find that it is.'

'It might quite easily be,' said Edith. 'If there were only a small piece of cake left, for instance.'

Belinda was confident that the tea table would be well stocked and was quite ready to forget that she had had her own tea at the vicarage. After the little strains and awkwardnesses there she felt that she deserved a second tea and was able to do full justice to the potato cakes and her favourite Belgian buns.

At tea they were all very gay, in the way that happy, unmarried ladies of middle age often are. Naturally they talked about the Bishop. Try as she would, Belinda could not give a flattering description. After several attempts to soften the blow, she burst out, 'Well, Harriet, there's no getting away from it, he reminds me of a *sheep!*'

'But surely a very handsome sheep?' Harriet protested. 'Of course I haven't seen him for many years, but people don't alter all that much, and he

186

was such an exceptionally good-looking curate.'

'Are you sure you're thinking of the same one?' suggested Belinda timidly. 'You've known so *many . . .*'

But Harriet indignantly denied the possibility of such a mistake. 'And anyway,' she went on stoutly, to justify herself in case of a possible disappointment, 'you can't judge a person by his face.'

'No, of course not,' Belinda agreed. 'I'm sure he's an excellent man,' she said doubtfully. 'Have you ever heard of the Guild of St Agnes, by the way?'

'Oh, I don't think so,' said Harriet. 'There's the Society of St Monica, but that's for widows, I believe.'

'You mean you have to be a widow?' said Belinda. 'I think it could hardly be that.'

'I know,' said Edith suddenly, 'it does work among Fallen Women—Connie's patroness was the President I believe. They used to have teas and sales of work in the house in Belgrave Square.'

'So that's it,' said Belinda, who hardly knew what advice she could give to a Fallen Woman, let alone what kind of splendid work she could have done. She explained the connection and they all laughed very heartily.

When they had finished tea Edith suddenly began doing a Balkan folk dance which encouraged Harriet to give a very ludicrous imitation of Mr Mold's proposal. But as Belinda laughed she found herself almost wishing that Harriet were even now Mrs Nathaniel Mold. Then at least there could be no danger of having the Bishop of Mbawawa for a brother-in-law.

CHAPTER SIXTEEN

It was the morning after the Bishop's arrival and there was a feeling of suppressed excitement in the air. At the Misses Bede's house the morning passed in the usual way until just before luncheon, when the front-door bell rang. Before Belinda and Harriet could begin to guess who it was, Emily had announced the Archdeacon.

It was at once evident that he was in a good temper, which Belinda thought rather surprising, although there was a certain relish in disliking somebody, she supposed, which might account for it.

'I hope the Bishop is well?' she ventured.

'Oh, tolerably well, I think,' said the Archdeacon, rubbing his hands in front of the fire. 'I believe he did not sleep very well, but our spare bed is notoriously uncomfortable.'

'We could easily have him here,' said Harriet, 'our spare bed has a new mattress and is really most comfortable. I have tried it myself.'

'That is kind of you,' said the Archdeacon, 'but the clergy are used to discomfort. They even enjoy it, you know.'

Belinda looked at him doubtfully, but he appeared to be quite serious.

'I hope you are writing to poor Nathaniel Mold,' he said, seeing that Harriet was seated at the writing-desk.

'Oh, no,' said Harriet, thinking it rather interfering of the Archdeacon. 'That is all finished. I was writing to Gorringes' for a new winter

188

dressing-gown.'

'Well, they say that a bird in the hand is worth two in the bush,' declared the Archdeacon.

'I'm not sure that I understand your meaning there,' said Harriet coyly. 'What do you mean by two in the bush?'

'Why, Ricardo and the Bishop,' said the Archdeacon slyly.

Belinda felt inclined to add that poor Ricardo was almost as good as in the hand, but she said nothing as she thought the conversation rather unbecoming. It would have been quite another matter if Edith or Connie had been there instead of the Archdeacon, but for somebody of Harriet's age to discuss her suitors with the vicar of the parish seemed to Belinda hardly the thing.

'But I haven't seen the Bishop for over thirty years,' protested Harriet, enjoying herself very much.

'Then you will see him tonight,' said the Archdeacon.

'*Tonight?*' echoed the sisters incredulously, as if it were the most unlikely thing in the world.

'Yes, I came to see you about it. The Bishop is giving a lantern lecture with slides, and I wanted to know if you would be good enough to work the lantern,' said the Archdeacon, turning to Harriet.

'Why, I should love to,' said Harriet, for she had an unexpected genius for working the lantern and had done it for many years now.

'It should be an unusual experience,' said the Archdeacon, 'to renew your acquaintance with the Bishop over a slide put in upside down.'

Harriet went off into a peal of delighted laughter.

189

'What's the lecture to be about?' asked Belinda, thinking that somebody ought to show an intelligent interest in it.

'Oh, his natives I believe,' said the Archdeacon rather scornfully. 'Songs and dances and that kind of thing!'

'It should be very interesting,' ventured Belinda.

'And amusing too,' said the Archdeacon. 'The Bishop was practising this morning.'

'The songs or the dances?' asked Harriet.

'Oh, the songs, as far as I could hear. I daresay it will not be possible to demonstrate the dances.'

'I hope *not*,' said Belinda rather indignantly, for from what one heard about these native dances it did not seem as if they were the sort of thing that could properly be performed in a parish hall.

Moved by a sudden impulse of friendliness, Harriet asked the Archdeacon if he would stay to luncheon. 'We're having pheasant,' she added temptingly.

'I'm so sorry,' he said, 'but I'm afraid Agatha will be expecting me. Otherwise nothing could have given me greater pleasure.'

'Yes, that's the worst of having a wife,' said Harriet jovially.

'It is really much wiser for a man to stay single,' said the Archdeacon, 'and then it doesn't matter if he's late for lunch.'

After he had gone Harriet remarked that if he had been single *now*, he might have discovered that there were even greater advantages, but she soon changed the subject, and began asking Belinda's opinion about her hair. Should she leave the back in a neat roll or comb it out into fluffy curls?

Belinda gave some sort of an answer, as she realized that Harriet was determined to have the fluffy curls, and wondered whether she herself should wear her blue marocain or an old wool dress. The parish hall was inclined to be draughty and she had no particular wish to impress the Bishop. On the other hand, the Archdeacon would certainly be there and she did not wish to appear dowdy before him. It was a difficult problem. Harriet had already decided that she would wear her brown velvet, and possibly her fur cape, though working the lantern she would probably be warm enough without it.

Emily was also going to the lecture with the vicarage Florrie, who had given her a most glowing account of the Bishop. He had apparently given her some very pretty African beads and a wooden comb, carved by one of his native converts.

'Putting silly ideas into her head,' Harriet had said to Belinda after hearing this. 'Theo ought to be careful,' she said ominously.

The lecture was to begin at eight o'clock, but Harriet insisted that they should be in good time as she had all sorts of things to do in connection with the lantern, which was inclined to be temperamental.

'And you will want to get a good seat,' she said.

'Oh, not particularly,' said Belinda. 'I don't suppose the hall will be very full and all the chairs are equally hard.'

The problem of where to sit was settled by their meeting Miss Liversidge and Miss Aspinall at the door of the hall.

'Let's go somewhere at the back, where we can have a good laugh,' said Edith.

191

Belinda agreed that she would also like to sit somewhere at the back, although she did not give any such crude reason for her preference. Poor Miss Aspinall would have liked to sit nearer the front, in case Lady Clara Boulding should be there, but she knew it was no use saying so, and sat meekly on Belinda's other side, glancing hopefully back at the door when anybody came in. Harriet was looking very important, perched up on a table, manipulating the lantern and trying out some specimen slides. Canterbury cathedral, a field with cows, and the head and shoulders of a bearded clergyman followed one another in quick succession: the lantern was obviously working well.

The hall began to fill up until there were very few vacant seats and the Bishop could be seen threading his way among the chairs towards Harriet, carrying a box of lantern slides. Belinda craned forward eagerly, yet as unconcernedly as she could, to witness their reunion after so many years. Edith Liversidge did the same and even went so far as to stand up for a better view.

'How many years did you say it was?' she inquired.

'I can't remember exactly, but I think it must be nearly thirty,' said Belinda in a more subdued tone of voice, for she did not want Miss Beard and Miss Smiley, who were sitting in front of them with a group of fellow teachers, to hear all their conversation. Things half heard were apt to be wickedly exaggerated and Miss Beard, in spite of being an excellent Sunday school teacher, was very much inclined to gossip.

'What a long time!' breathed Connie. 'There is something very wonderful in meeting a friend

192

again after many years.'

'That rather depends,' said Edith brusquely. 'I can think of some I'd much rather not meet.'

'I suppose in that case you would hardly call them friends,' said Belinda. 'Although one doesn't really know what a person is going to be like after thirty years.'

Harriet's position on the table made it necessary for the Bishop to gaze up at her. She bent graciously and extended her hand as if to take his, but received instead the box of lantern slides. Belinda was indignant. How rude and casual of him! she thought. How like a bishop! she went on and then stopped, realizing the injustice of this generalization. For she was certain that Willie Amery or Oliver Opobo and Calabar would not have behaved like this. Theodore Grote was cold, a cold fish as she remembered their dear mother calling him. *Legless, unloving, infamously chaste*, she thought detachedly, remembering Ricardo's goldfish, and was then ashamed of herself for thinking of it. There could be no excuse, for Leigh Hunt was not even one of our greater poets. Still, there *was* something fishlike about Bishop Grote. Fish and sheep. Was that possible?

'I do wish I knew what they were saying,' said Connie, 'though of course it's the most unpardonable curiosity. Meetings like this ought to be really *sacred*.'

'He's obviously just saying something about the slides,' said Edith. 'Connie is much too romantic. I suppose she thinks he ought to be quoting poetry.'

'Well, he might,' said Belinda, 'if he were that sort of a person, which I doubt. He didn't even shake hands, otherwise he might have quoted that nice line of Cleveland's, where he describes a lady's hand *tender as 'twere a jelly gloved* . . . I always like that, but somehow it doesn't apply to peoples' hands now.'

Edith looked down complacently at her own fingers, gnarled and stained. 'Not in the country,' she said, 'though Connie's always fussing about hers, rubbing them with lotion and all that sort of nonsense. I always tell her that nobody's likely to want to hold her hand now, so why bother.'

Belinda thought this rather unkind and sympathized with Connie. It wasn't exactly that one hoped to have one's hand held . . .

'Look, there's the Archdeacon and Father Plowman,' said Connie. 'I suppose it must be going to begin.'

'I imagine one can smoke here?' said Edith, producing a squashed paper packet of Woodbines and offering it to Belinda.

'No, thank you,' said Belinda. She felt that it would be unbecoming for her to smoke, though it seemed right that Edith should do so. Anything that she did seemed to be in character. Her appearance tonight in a homespun skirt with white blouse and Albanian embroidered waistcoat made Belinda feel dowdy and insignificant, one of the many thousand respectable middle-aged spinsters, the backbones or busybodies of countless parishes throughout the country.

The Archdeacon had mounted the platform and was introducing the Bishop in a short and almost gracious speech.

'I, for one, am eagerly looking forward to hearing more about this fascinating country and its people,' he said. 'Many of us will envy Bishop

194

Grote his unique opportunities. It may even be that I too shall feel the urge to labour in a foreign field,' he concluded, with what Belinda could only think was sarcasm, for nothing more unlikely could be imagined.

The audience settled down on the hard chairs. Belinda noticed that Agatha was wearing a becoming new dress, dark green, with little pleated ruffles at the shoulders and neck. From the best houses, she thought, with sad resignation.

'The climate of Mbawawa is temperate and the soil very fertile,' began the Bishop, waving his pointer vaguely in the air.

The first slide appeared. It showed a seascape with some kind of tropical palms in the foreground. Belinda had seen the same type of picture on the covers of dance tunes about the South Sea Islands.

'When I say temperate,' went on the Bishop, 'I dare say many of you might find it rather hot.' He paused and tapped his pointer vigorously on the floor.

There appeared in rapid succession several pictures of handsome natives, dressed in bunches of leaves and garlands of flowers. Some members of the audience were inclined to giggle at these, but the Bishop hastily explained that the pictures were of the natives as they *used* to be.

'We have since introduced a form of European dress which is far more in keeping with Christian ideas of morality,' he said. Another slide followed, showing the natives clad in this way. 'I should like to add here,' he went on, 'that we are often very much in need of garments for our people and should welcome gifts of clothing or material—light cotton materials, of course, nothing elaborate or costly.'

It would be typical of the perfidy of human nature, thought Belinda indignantly, if the church workers fell so much in love with the Bishop that they forgot about all the other more deserving charities such as the Clothe-Our-Children League and the Society for helping the Poor in Pimlico to which they were accustomed to contribute. She could already notice in the half darkness the beaming looks of approval on their faces, as they nodded and smiled to each other, planning working parties and schemes to raise money. Of course the Mbawawa *were* a deserving cause, she supposed, but were they not happier in their leaves and flowers? Naturally one wished them to have the benefits of Christianity; it was rather difficult to see where one should draw the line. They could hardly appear at a service in a dress of leaves, she reflected, when she herself felt that a short-sleeved dress was unsuitable. But need they wear those shapeless cotton garments? Perhaps the architecture of the church had something to do with it: one's style of dress ought to be somehow in keeping . . . her thoughts wandered on against a background of bleating Bishop's voice. He had somehow got on to the subject of music.

'The language is well suited to singing,' he declared. 'It is soft and pleasing, vowels and liquid sounds predominating. You may be interested to hear that the alphabet contains only eighteen letters,' he went on, 'and I think that if you saw it written you would hardly call it an alphabet at all. Such an odd collection of letters with long tails and squiggles! You see, the Mbawawa had never written their language down until a few years ago, when missionaries attempted it. Then some clever people in London, experts in African languages, made up this alphabet, and I think nobody was more surprised than the Mbawawa themselves!' The Bishop laughed heartily and wiped his brow. 'But I haven't come here tonight to tell you about the alphabet. I think we can safely leave that to the clever people in London,' he added, with what Belinda felt was insufferable patronage, considering the distinction of his audience, which contained at least four University graduates, five, if one counted Father Plowman's failed B.A.

'Their chief musical instrument is the Mhamha, M-H-A-M-H-A,' he spelled the word out and one of the Sunday school teachers could be seen fumbling in her handbag for pencil and paper. There now followed another slide of grinning natives holding musical instruments.

'I dare say some of you would like to hear what the language sounds like,' said the Bishop, 'so I am going to sing a few verses of a song which the Mbawawa adapt to many occasions, birth, marriage, death, all the great events in this mortal life have their own form of it.' He paused, as if wondering which was most suited to a gathering in a parish hall. 'Let me try and give you a gay marriage song,' he said. 'Imagine yourselves taking part in a Mbawawa wedding.'

'I do not feel myself equal to that,' whispered Edith to Belinda. 'Death would have been a better choice, or even birth.'

The voice of the Bishop rang out through the hall in song. Many handkerchiefs were taken out hastily, especially among the younger members of the audience, for the noise which filled the hall was quite unexpected. Even Belinda, who had heard the Bishop sing as a curate, was a little unprepared. And yet perhaps the Mbawawa *did* have voices like that and it was wrong to feel that one wanted to laugh. Belinda glanced at Harriet to see how she was reacting. As far as it was possible to see, she was displaying remarkable self-control, for she was very prone to giggle, and appeared to be gazing at the Bishop with rapt attention. Most of the audience were stirring uneasily. Even Agatha was smiling a little, but she managed to make it look as if she were not really amused, but pleased and approving, which was quite another matter.

At last the noise stopped, and some people relieved their feelings by clapping.

'The song has many more verses,' explained the Bishop. 'Indeed, if the singer is particularly gifted he can go on almost indefinitely; I have known the marriage song go on all night, but I fear I should find the hall empty if I attempted that.'

During the laughter which followed he tapped his pointer on the floor and another slide clicked into place.

'Now this is another characteristic musical instrument. It is called the Hmwoq, spelled H-M-W-O-Q.'

Everyone looked with interest at the curiously shaped object which had now appeared on the screen. It was certainly a very peculiar shape and there was more giggling from the back of the hall. It could hardly be what it seemed to be, thought Belinda doubtfully, though one knew that among primitive peoples one might find almost anything.

The anthropologist who went among them must go with an open mind . . .

The Bishop turned towards the screen and prodded it uncertainly. Then he advanced towards the edge of the platform and said in a loud clear voice, 'I think that slide is upside down.'

Everyone turned to look at Harriet, who was not in the least embarrassed at having such attention drawn to her. Indeed, Belinda could not be absolutely sure that her sister had not purposely put the slide in upside down.

'I am *so* sorry, My Lord Bishop,' Harriet's voice rang clearly through the hall. 'How *stupid* of me,' she said, smiling most charmingly into the darkness.

The Bishop responded graciously enough by saying that he feared *he* was too stupid to explain the picture unless it were the right way up, and his explanation was very confused even when the slide was correctly shown. Leaving it rather hurriedly, he produced a large sea shell from an inner pocket and applied it to his lips.

By this time his hearers knew more or less what to expect, so that they were able to bear the strange sounds which came out of the shell with more composure. The noise seemed to be a hollower and more resonant version of the Bishop's own singing voice.

'Wonderful how he does it, isn't it?' whispered Father Plowman to Agatha Hoccleve, who could not but agree that it was indeed most wonderful.

'This instrument is used particularly in agricultural rites,' explained the Bishop, 'where the ceremony of propitiating the earth goddess is carried out.'

'Phallic,' murmured Edith, nodding her head. 'Quite the usual thing.'

Fortunately the Sunday school teachers did not know the word, thought Belinda, or they would most certainly have turned round. It was rather like Edith to show off her smattering of anthropological knowledge, she felt, particularly if it were something rather embarrassing.

After the music came more slides of wedding and funeral scenes, and finally one of the Bishop himself in gaiters and leafy garlands, at which everyone clapped vigorously. It was a relief to be able to let off steam, for much laughter had been bottled up. But the climax came when he turned his back on the audience, fumbled in a suitcase and reappeared facing them in a huge painted wooden mask, with hinged beak, large round eyes and hanging raffia mane, which completely covered his head and shoulders. This brought the house down and there was laughter and clapping from the front seats, stamping and whistling from the back benches.

All that followed was inevitably an anticlimax. The Bishop went on to give a list of rather stray facts which he might have got out of the *Encyclopaedia Britannica*. He mentioned that they tattooed little, that the native chiefs sometimes weighed as much as one hundred and eighty pounds, and that although infanticide was prevalent, cannibalism was almost unknown. They lived chiefly on yams and millet, but rats and mice were also eaten. Beer was brewed from guinea corn; fire was made from a paste of salt, pepper and lizard dung.

'And in conclusion,' he added, 'for the benefit of

any anthropologists who may be listening to me, I may as well state that the basic social unit is an exogamous patrilineal kindred or extended family or even clan. I don't think we need worry overmuch about that.'

Hearty laughter greeted these remarks. There was no anthropologist in the audience.

Father Plowman mounted the platform and began to propose a vote of thanks.

'I for one shall never forget this fascinating lecture,' he said. 'I am sure that after tonight there will be many who will be eager to visit this beautiful country and see all these wonders for themselves.'

'Putting ideas into their heads,' muttered Edith, and she was not far wrong, for one of the Sunday school teachers was even at that moment toying with the idea of asking the Bishop whether he could find a place for her in his Mission, and even Miss Aspinall was wondering whether it might not be possible to go out there to teach the gentler arts.

'Truly the wonders of this world are without number. Let us thank God for His goodness to us,' concluded Father Plowman, and everyone agreed that it was a most fitting end to the evening.

It was a little spoilt by the Archdeacon rising to his feet and saying that he was sure everyone would wish him to thank Miss Harriet Bede for her admirable working of the lantern, without which the lecture would not have been half so enjoyable. Of course it was right that she should be thanked, but several people felt that Father Plowman's words should have been the last. Only Belinda was pleased, both because of his acknowledgment of her sister and because no evening was complete for her which did not include a few words from the Archdeacon.

'So like him, that kind thought,' she said to Edith, 'remembering Harriet when the Bishop never said a word, nor Father Plowman for that matter. I knew the Archdeacon wouldn't forget.'

'Oh, I expect he just wanted to be different,' said Edith, struggling into her mannish navy blue overcoat. 'What happens now?'

'I think we go home,' said Belinda, 'but I dare say Harriet will go and have refreshments at the vicarage with the Bishop. They'll probably have coffee and sandwiches or something light.'

'Oh, I hate standing about balancing a cup and plate and making conversation,' said Edith. 'Come along, Connie,' she called, turning round, 'we're going home.'

But Connie, with a hasty gathering up of bits and pieces and a fluttering of grey draperies, had hurried towards the front of the hall, where she could be seen among the little cluster of people waiting to shake hands with the Bishop.

'Don't make her come away,' pleaded Belinda. 'She would probably like to go to the vicarage with the others.'

'Well, come and take pot luck with me,' said Edith roughly. 'Just coffee and baked beans—you know our kind of supper.'

'That will be lovely,' murmured Belinda.

At the door of Edith's cottage a big, shaggy dog came bounding towards them, his muddy paws scrabbling against their coats and stockings, and inside the living-room, for it could hardly be called a drawing-room, everything was so primitive and

202

comfortless that Belinda felt really sympathetic towards poor Connie. After Belgrave Square too ... Her harp, shrouded in a holland cover, seemed out of place in the untidy room with its smell of dog and cigarette smoke.

Belinda stood uncertainly on the threshold of the little kitchen, watching Edith cutting bread and scooping the beans out of their tin into a saucepan.

'Hand me that ash tray, will you?' said Edith, but not before Belinda had seen a grey wedge of ash drop into the beans. 'Drat it,' she said. 'Too late. Hope you don't mind?'

'Of course not,' said Belinda nobly, remembering Miss Prior and the caterpillar. Perhaps there was something after all in being a gentlewoman.

CHAPTER SEVENTEEN

When Belinda awoke next morning, she decided that she did not feel very well. She was not sure whether this was because of the ash in the baked beans, the half-empty bottle of Empire port that Edith had found in the back of a cupboard or the damp walk home, in rather thin shoes. She was inclined to think it must be the last, for what else could have given her such an unromantic, snivelling cold?

'Oh, dear,' said Harriet, sitting down heavily on Belinda's bed, 'the Bishop was coming to tea and I suppose I shall have to put him off if you're going to be ill.'

'Why?' asked Belinda stupidly.

'Well, really, what would people think?'

'They needn't know I'm in bed, and after all, it's only a matter of time,' said Belinda, who was in no mood to humour her sister's coy scruples.

'Yes, perhaps it is,' agreed Harriet, but rather doubtfully. 'He asked particularly if you would be here, though.'

'Did he? Well, we certainly can't have tea in my bedroom,' said Belinda plaintively.

'No, of course not,' Harriet agreed. 'Now are you sure you couldn't fancy a little sausage?' she said brightly. 'Emily will have cooked enough for both of us.'

Belinda did not think she fancied anything at all, but was persuaded to try some weak tea and a piece of toast. And would Harriet be very kind and bring her the *Oxford Book of Victorian Verse*? She might feel like reading later on.

Harriet went downstairs and came back with a tray and the book.

'Isn't it rather heavy to read in bed?' she ventured. 'I've brought you something smaller as well. Here's the Fourth Book of Virgil. I know you like the part about Dido and Aeneas. It's such a nice thin little book.'

'Oh, Harriet, how kind. But it's all in Latin, and you know I can't read it.'

'Never mind, dear,' said Harriet soothingly. 'I shouldn't read at all, if I were you. Just try and rest.'

'I can't think how I caught this cold,' said Belinda.

'I'll go and get you some whisky from the Crownwheel and Pinion,' declared Harriet. 'I shall go as soon as it's open.'

'Oh, Harriet, don't go *there*,' said Belinda, rather

concerned. 'I'm sure you could get some at Abbot's, and anyway I don't think I really need it. If I stay in bed and keep warm I'm sure to be better in a day or two. Hot lemon is really a much nicer drink.'

'You never know when you may need whisky,' said Harriet mysteriously. 'It's just as well to have it in the house.'

'I seem to remember a recipe in *Tried Favourites*—a sort of substitute for whisky,' said Belinda. 'I dare say it would be quite easy to make.'

'I think our guests would hardly thank us if we offered them that,' said Harriet.

'Our guests?' Belinda sank back weakly on to her pillows, unable to face the idea of guests who needed to be entertained with whisky. 'I think I'll just rest until lunch-time,' she said. 'I dare say I shan't read after all.'

So Harriet left her and went out to do the shopping. She met several people and told each one about her sister's indisposition, making little or much of it according to the status of her hearer. To the Archdeacon she gave the most exact details, thinking that somehow he ought to be possessed of all the facts.

'She had weak tea and dry toast for breakfast,' said Harriet confidentially, 'and then she asked for the *Oxford Book of Victorian Verse*.'

'She called for madder music and for stronger wine,' said the Archdeacon, but Harriet was not familiar with our great Victorian poets and so the quotation passed over her head.

She pointed out rather sharply that strong wine was the last thing that should be given to an invalid, although a little brandy might be helpful in cases of biliousness.

'But of course Belinda isn't bilious,' she said hastily. 'Nothing like that.'

'Poor Belinda, I am really extremely sorry. Do tell her how very sorry I am. I only wish I could go and see her.'

'Oh, she's not at all seriously ill,' said Harriet. 'Just a little chill. I'm sure it would alarm people if you were seen going to the house. People always think the worst when they see a clergyman.'

'Dear me, I hardly know how to take that,' said the Archdeacon. 'I should have liked to think that we brought comfort to the sick.'

'Oh, well, I suppose you do, in a way,' said Harriet, who was finding it difficult to convey that it all depended on the clergyman.

'I must look out some books for her to read,' said the Archdeacon.

'Thank you very much, but she really has plenty to read.'

'All the same, there might be something she'd like,' persisted the Archdeacon. 'I sometimes wish that I could afford to be ill so that I could read some of the things I normally never have time for.'

Harriet looked contemptuous but said nothing. 'I must be going now,' she said at last. 'I still have quite a lot of shopping to do.'

On her return she found that Belinda had been to sleep and felt a little better.

'I saw the Archdeacon,' said Harriet triumphantly. 'He seemed quite concerned to hear that you were ill and almost suggested coming to see you, but I soon nipped that in the bud.'

Belinda gathered her faded pink bed-jacket

more closely round her shoulders. 'Oh, no, I couldn't have him coming to see me,' she said. 'Not without warning, anyway.'

'Well, of course,' said Harriet pompously, 'it is, or should be, customary for a clergyman to visit the sick in his parish. But perhaps that's only for the poor people really, to see if they have all they want and so on.'

'Yes, I suppose I have everything I want,' said Belinda rather sadly.

'Naturally if you were seriously ill or dying it would be another matter,' went on Harriet reassuringly.

'But I'm not,' said Belinda regretfully, thinking of Henry reading *Samson Agonistes* to her on her death-bed.

After lunch she settled down to her own thoughts. Harriet had brought up a light novel from the circulating library and this lay with the *Oxford Book of Victorian Verse* on the eiderdown. But Belinda did not feel like reading. She was quite enjoying her illness now that she felt a little better and could allow her thoughts to wander at random in the past and future without the consciousness that she ought to be more profitably employed. She had no doubt that there would soon be another proposal of marriage in the drawing-room, perhaps even this afternoon, although she judged the Bishop to be a more prudent man than Mr Mold. He had certainly not behaved very cordially to Harriet at the lecture, but Belinda was sure that he would not be able to hold out long against her charms. Nor had Harriet seemed as enthusiastic as might have been expected. Could it be that she had found him less attractive than she anticipated, or was it the very depth of her feeling that kept her from speaking of it? Belinda puzzled over this for some time and then fell to thinking of her own life.

There was very little new to be said or thought about it, she decided. She had loved dear Henry for so many years now that she no longer thought of her love as a hopeless passion. Indeed, Belinda felt that no spinster of her age and respectability could possibly have such a thing for an archdeacon. The fierce flame had died down, but the fire was still glowing brightly.

> *My very ashes in their urn,*
> *Shall like a hallowed lamp for ever burn . . .*

How much more one appreciated our great literature if one loved, thought Belinda, especially if the love were unrequited! She touched the books affectionately but made no effort to read either of them. As Harriet had said, the *Oxford Book of Victorian Verse* was rather heavy to hold, and many of the poems in it were uncomfortably sentimental for afternoon reading.

Suddenly there was a noise in the hall. Belinda sat up in bed and listened. At first she thought it must be the Bishop arriving rather too early for tea, but then she realized that it was a woman's voice. It sounded almost like Agatha's. She crouched under the bedclothes and began to wonder whether she had a temperature after all and ought not to see people. It was surely not normal to have a sudden longing to hide under the bedclothes when one heard the vicar's wife in the hall, even if one did love her husband better than she did?

Belinda sat up bravely and took out her hand-mirror. She knew that she looked most unattractive and thought what a good thing it was that she was not seriously ill or dying. Her hair was out of curl, her cheeks were pale and her nose needed powdering. She would not have liked Henry to see her like this, even on her death-bed.

Agatha was all too soon in the room, saying, 'Poor Belinda, I was so sorry when Henry told me you were ill. I thought I'd come and see how you were.'

Belinda, who was trying to smuggle the hand-mirror out of sight, murmured that it was very kind of Agatha and that she was feeling much better.

'And now,' said Agatha, rather too briskly, 'what has been the matter with you?'

'Oh, I think I must have caught a slight chill,' said Belinda vaguely. 'Perhaps I was sitting in a draught at the Bishop's lecture,' she ventured, feeling ashamed of not knowing exactly what was the matter with her and why. 'The lecture was most interesting, wasn't it?'

'Oh, yes, fascinating,' said Agatha. 'The Bishop is such a dear man, so kind and amusing.'

He must be especially pleasant to Agatha, thought Belinda, who had not formed at all that impression of him. Indeed Agatha was quite animated when she spoke of him and even looked a little flushed.

'He asked where you were last night after the lecture,' she went on. 'We had quite a little gathering at the vicarage, you know.'

'I thought you would probably have enough people there without me,' said Belinda weakly, feeling as she so often did with Agatha that she had somehow done the wrong thing. 'I went to supper with Edith Liversidge. I'm surprised that he should have remembered me at all.'

'Well, of course it is a bishop's duty to remember people,' said Agatha. 'My father had a wonderful memory for names and faces.'

'Yes, I suppose they meet so many people,' said Belinda, feeling rather damped. Not that she wanted the Bishop to remember her particularly, but it was like Agatha to take away any illusions she might have cherished.

'It's some years since you last met, isn't it?' said Agatha conversationally.

'Oh, yes, about thirty years, I think. We none of us grow any younger, do we? *Timor mortis conturbat me*,' murmured Belinda, staring straight in front of her.

Agatha looked at her sharply. Sometimes she wondered whether Belinda was quite all there. She said such odd things.

There was a short pause, but before it had time to become awkward a hearty voice was heard outside the door and Edith Liversidge strode into the room, followed by Connie Aspinall. Their arms were full of books and parcels.

'I must be going now,' said Agatha, who disliked Edith. 'Too many visitors at once will tire you.'

Belinda thanked her for her kindness, but was quite relieved to be left alone with Edith and Connie.

'We've brought you some books,' said Edith. 'And Connie's made you a sponge cake. You know I'm no hand at that kind of thing.'

'Oh, how kind . . .'

'I thought you might like to see some copies of *The Gentlewoman*,' said Connie. 'There's a picture of Lady Grudge's daughter in one of them.'

'How interesting, I shall look forward to reading them,' said Belinda. 'You must point her out to me.'

At this moment the front-door bell rang. 'That must be the Bishop arriving,' said Belinda.

'The Bishop?' asked Edith, rather surprised.

'Yes, he is coming to tea today.'

'Does he know you're ill or is he expecting to see both of you?'

'Oh, I'm supposed to be there too, but I suddenly woke up ill,' said Belinda pathetically. 'So Harriet will have to entertain him alone.'

'Alone?' said Edith. 'I don't think he'll like that.'

'Why ever not?' asked Belinda, rather worried. Life was quite difficult enough without Edith making disturbing suggestions. Harriet was going to marry the Bishop and Belinda would be left in her old age to die a lonely death, or with nobody but a paid companion to cheer her last hours. Surely that was enough? She had been trying to prepare herself for the worst and did not wish to be unsettled.

Meanwhile Edith expounded her ideas of what a bishop would think quite proper. 'I don't think Harriet will get him,' she said bluntly.

Belinda had been thinking the same thing not so long ago, but now she was inclined to disagree. After all, dear Edith had had little or no experience of bishops, although poor John had been a very good man in his way.

'I think he has successfully avoided so many women in his life that not even Harriet will be able

211

to catch him,' she went on. 'I know his sort.'

Belinda thought this rather a vulgar way of putting it, though it could hardly be denied that it was what Harriet intended to do.

'I believe women can do almost anything if they are really desperate,' she ventured. 'In one of Lyly's plays, *Endimion*, I think . . .'

'But I don't think Harriet is really desperate,' Edith interrupted. 'Do you?'

'I really couldn't say,' said Belinda plaintively. 'I think I should like a drink of barley water. It's on the little table.'

'Oh, let me get it for you,' said Connie, coming forward with a glass and a copy of *The Gentlewoman* in her hand. 'This is Lady Joan Grudge,' she said eagerly, indicating a group of people enjoying a joke at a race meeting.

'Yes, she's very pretty, isn't she,' murmured Belinda, and was then informed that she had been looking at the wrong girl, for nobody could call Lady Joan pretty. 'Such a nice expression,' she emended. 'She looks very jolly.'

'Yes, she is a *very* sweet girl . . .'

Downstairs Harriet had just made the discovery that Bishop Grote never ate anything for his tea.

Now this was exceedingly awkward, for how can any real contact be established between two persons when one is eating and the other merely watching? For some minutes Harriet did not know what to do. Her recollections of the Bishop as a curate had included cream buns and hot buttered toast, with licking of fingers. Eventually she had to resort to the kind of arch scolding, which was really more suitable for very young curates than for bishops.

'Now, that's *naughty* of you,' she said. 'I expected you to have a really good appetite. I shall be *much* too embarrassed to eat alone,' she added, liberally spreading a piece of buttered toast with strawberry jam.

'I am really very sorry,' said the Bishop complacently, but with no intention of changing his habits even to be polite to his hostess. 'But your sister will be eating something, won't she?' he inquired, looking anxiously towards the door for a sign of the elder Miss Bede.

'Oh, I forgot to tell you,' said Harriet airily, 'poor Belinda is in bed today. She isn't well.'

The Bishop started and half rose from his chair. 'Nothing infectious or contagious, I hope?' he asked, rather too eagerly.

'No, no,' Harriet smiled reassuringly, but at the same time a little dangerously, so that the Bishop knew that there was as yet no possibility of escape. 'Just a slight chill,' she explained, 'but one can't be too careful.'

The Bishop murmured some words of regret but he found it difficult to keep a note of displeasure out of his voice. So might he have rebuked a rebellious African who appeared at Divine Service in his flowery but inadequate native costume. To begin with, he was not sure that he believed this story about Belinda's illness. People didn't suddenly become ill like this, he told himself angrily, and Belinda had seemed quite well at the lecture last night. If she were really indisposed why hadn't Harriet written or sent a message, changing the invitation to another day? She could so easily have done this. That nice maid who had answered the door would have been only too willing to take a message to the vicarage. It was only a few minutes away. Besides, he wanted to see Belinda. He thought her much nicer than Harriet and she had knitted him such a beautiful scarf when he was a curate, however much she might deny it. Harriet must indeed be heartless to leave her sister lying alone and ill upstairs while she entertained guests—the Bishop's indignation had got the better of his accuracy—in the drawing-room.

Harriet interrupted his thoughts by asking if his tea were too strong.

'Oh, no, it is very nice, thank you,' he said quite civilly.

'Perhaps you would like some more sugar in it?' she persisted.

'No, thank you. I never take more than one lump.'

There was a pause while Harriet, who was finding dear Theo not at all as she had imagined, racked her brains for something to say. Surely he had lost some of his charm of manner? she asked herself anxiously. It went without saying that he had once had charm of manner, but what had happened to it now? He did not appear to be enjoying himself at all and was behaving almost as if this visit were a duty rather than a pleasure. She stretched forward and helped herself to another piece of buttered toast. And how extremely irritating this not eating was. It was impolite, too, most impolite.

'I suppose it was in Africa that you got into the habit of not eating any tea?' she asked brightly.

'Oh, no, it was when I was a minor canon,' he replied seriously. 'I found that it interfered with

Evensong.'

Harriet burst into a peal of laughter. She thought this very funny and stored it up to tell Belinda. But the Bishop's sheep's face hardly altered its expression.

'A minor canon,' she giggled. 'Now when you were a deacon I seem to remember you eating crumpets for tea,' she said, trying to bring back to him the remembrance that he had once been a typically charming curate with endearing human weaknesses. '*Sic transit gloria mundi*,' she added.

'I beg your pardon?' The Bishop's voice held a note of surprise. He thought Harriet an extremely silly woman and was wondering how soon he could decently get away. It was in vain that Harriet asked him intelligent questions about the flora and fauna of the Mbawawa country and tried to draw him out on the missionaries' attitude towards polygamy. He seemed disinclined for conversation and at five o'clock got up to go.

As they went out into the hall, Miss Liversidge and Miss Aspinall came down the stairs from Belinda's room.

'Poor Belinda,' said Connie, 'I think she seems rather low. I must say I thought her looking *not at all well*.'

'Rubbish,' said Edith. 'It's only a chill. She'll be up and about in a day or two.'

'I am indeed sorry to hear this,' said the Bishop. 'Will you give her my very kindest regards and good wishes for a speedy recovery? In my diocese we have a special song for such an occasion. It is almost entirely on one note.'

The three ladies looked up expectantly.

'Perhaps I had better not sing it now,' said the

215

Bishop. 'It might disturb Miss Belinda. The African temperament is not quite like ours.'

'Oh, Belinda, he's so stupid and *dull!*' Harriet burst out, when the visitors had gone. 'He sent you his kindest regards. I don't think he really believed you were ill until he saw Edith and Connie.'

'I'm sorry he was such a disappointment,' said Belinda, 'but perhaps he will improve on further acquaintance. He is really quite the opposite to Mr Mold, isn't he? I mean, perhaps he doesn't have all his goods in the shop window.'

Harriet laughed scornfully and became absorbed in looking at *The Gentlewoman*.

'It was kind of Connie to bring these,' said Belinda. 'It makes one feel so secure to look at a paper like this.' She pointed out Lady Joan Grudge, enjoying a joke with friends at a race meeting, a group at a dance held in Eaton Square for somebody's debutante daughter, a party of titled people at a night club and other comforting unrealities. Lulled in security and contentment, they passed the next half-hour very pleasantly until there was a ring at the front door and the sisters started up in agitation.

'Oh, dear, I wonder who that is?' said Harriet, hastily squeezing her feet into the elegant shoes which she had kicked off after the Bishop had gone.

'I really don't think I can do with any more visitors tonight,' said Belinda feebly. 'What is it, Emily?' she asked, as the maid appeared in the doorway.

For answer Emily thrust forward a large bundle, shrouded in many sheets of blue tissue paper. 'Flowers for the invalid, Miss Belinda,' she said brightly, in a nurse's tone.

Harriet rushed forward. Nobody ever sent *Belinda* flowers, but the florist's label was clearly addressed to Miss Belinda Bede. Harriet unwrapped the tissue paper to reveal a dozen beautiful chrysanthemums, bronze and white.

Belinda's heart leapt. They were from Henry. Harriet had seen him that morning, so he knew she was ill, but in any case Agatha would probably have told him.

'There doesn't seem to be a card with them,' said Harriet, fumbling with maddening deliberation. 'Oh, yes, here we are.' She tossed the little envelope over to Belinda, who tore it open eagerly.

When one has reached Belinda's age, and even before, one takes these small disappointments calmly. Of course the flowers were not from the Archdeacon, how could they have been? It would have been most unsuitable, unless, of course, Agatha had joined in the gift, Belinda told herself, as she struggled to decipher the unfamiliar handwriting.

'*With best wishes for a speedy recovery—Theodore Mbawawa.*' she read. 'Oh, Harriet, from the Bishop!' she sank back weakly on to her pillows. 'I really don't think I can bear any more today. Theodore Mbawawa . . . doesn't that sound odd . . . I suppose it's what he calls himself . . .'

CHAPTER EIGHTEEN

Belinda did not keep to her bed for very long, and was soon about again. The Bishop stayed on at the vicarage, though it was evident that he and the Archdeacon disliked each other. Agatha, however, seemed to prefer his company to that of her husband, and Belinda could not help noticing the way she beamed at him when beaming was certainly not one of her normal expressions. Perhaps she felt naturally more at ease with bishops, as her father had been one, and it may have been a disappointment to her that her husband was only an archdeacon. Certainly she and Bishop Grote made a very suitable couple, if only because there was something slightly unpleasant about each of them. Belinda began to weave a little fantasy in which they somehow 'came together' and the Archdeacon was left alone and in need of comfort. How this was to come about she did not know, as divorce was against her principles and the Archdeacon's too, she imagined, and she would hardly have wished the Archdeacon to be removed by death and so put beyond the reach of her comfort. It was somehow out of the question, even in a fantasy, that Agatha should die. People like Agatha didn't die. It might of course be discovered that the marriage of Henry and Agatha had not been legal, but that happened only in the novels of Mrs Henry Wood. And supposing Henry were to be left alone and apparently in need of comfort, and did not turn to Belinda? How was that to be borne? It might well be that he would find Agatha's absence comfort enough. When she got to this point, Belinda was firm with herself and set to work helping Emily with the mincemeat and Christmas puddings, for it was already December and it was even rumoured that the Bishop was to spend Christmas at the vicarage.

Soon Christmas cards began to arrive and every post brought something.

'*A Happy, Holy Christmass,*' said Harriet, reading from Father Plowman's card. 'Very nice wording, and such a pretty picture of the Nativity. I think Christ*mass* is rather nice, Belinda. The Archdeacon's card is *very* ordinary, just *A Happy Christmas and a Bright New Year, from Agatha and Henry Hoccleve*, and no picture at all.'

'I expect Agatha had them done,' said Belinda. 'I imagine Henry would have wanted some quotation, but it was probably cheaper without. Of course Christ*mass* is rather High, isn't it, I mean, the use of the word *mass*. It always looks like a mis-spelling to me.'

'I wonder what Mr Donne's will be like,' said Harriet anxiously. 'I hope he will remember us.'

'Oh, surely,' said Belinda, indignant not so much for herself as for her sister and the many delicacies she had prepared for him. 'He has been here so much.'

'He might even send a calendar,' mused Harriet. 'That's one degree better than a card.'

'Yes, one of those with a quotation from Shakespeare or a Great Thought for every day. I always think it's nice to have one in some convenient place so that you can read it at the beginning of the day. And yet the thoughts they

219

choose are often so depressing, aren't they, as if Great Thinkers were never cheerful.'

'Well, Mr Donne's calendar certainly won't go *there*,' said Harriet, bristling. 'It shall go in the dining-room, where we can read it at breakfast.'

'Yes, dear, that's what I mean.'

But Mr Donne upset their plans by calling round in person with his present, or rather presents, an expensive looking box of chocolates with a coloured picture of Hampton Court on the lid which the sisters felt he could ill afford, and a photograph of himself which he gave to them rather shyly, obviously embarrassed by Harriet's cries of joy.

'Oh, how *lovely!* And how good of you! Belinda, isn't it *good* of Mr Donne?' She thrust the photograph at Belinda; who was rather at a loss, as it looked so exactly like any of the other photographs of curates in Harriet's collection upstairs that she could hardly think what to say.

'The lighting is very good,' she ventured, noticing it on his nose and clerical collar. 'So often a photograph is spoiled by bad lighting. You look very serious,' she added, with what was for her a forced note of playfulness. 'Almost as if you were thinking out a sermon.'

'Oh, we shall have you for tomorrow morning, shan't we,' said Harriet, for the Archdeacon, contrary to his normal practice, had been trying out a course of sermons on the evening congregation, sermons written in so-called 'simple language' and full of sentiments to which every bosom might be expected to return an echo, though he had not, of course, mentioned Harriet's Apes of Brazil. Some of his hearers had found the sermons almost too simple and were even beginning to wonder whether the Archdeacon himself were not returning to his second childhood.

'Oh, no, Bishop Grote is to preach on Sunday morning,' said the curate.

'Well, I suppose he must keep his hand in,' said Belinda. 'I expect it will be about Christmas as it's so near.'

'Yes, on Tuesday,' said the curate. 'I can hardly believe it myself, the weather's so mild.'

'They say a green Christmas means a full churchyard,' declared Harriet with satisfaction. 'I dare say some old people will be taken.'

'Taken?' The curate looked puzzled. 'Ah, yes, I see. I suppose we must expect that.'

They were silent for a moment, until Belinda, not liking to see his young face clouded over, said, 'I really can't think of any old people who are likely to die at the moment. Besides, it's the weather *after* Christmas that we have to fear, isn't it?'

'Oh, yes, if it's mild at Christmas it will be cold afterwards,' agreed Harriet. 'It makes one feel very anxious.'

Belinda, looking at Harriet's sturdy figure, could hardly help smiling.

When Sunday came it occurred to Belinda that perhaps the Bishop had his uses after all. For when the Archdeacon came to give out the notices of the Christmas Services it appeared that Bishop Grote and Mr Donne were to take the seven and eight o'clock Celebrations of Holy Communion, while the Archdeacon himself was to preach at Mattins and conduct the Celebration afterwards at twelve, for the benefit of the elderly and lazy. He took the opportunity to say a few words of warning to those who intended to go to Midnight Mass at Father Plowman's church, dwelling darkly on the dangers they might meet there and pronouncing the word *Rome* with such horrifying emphasis that many of his hearers were quite alarmed, and those who had thought of doing such a thing began to tell themselves that perhaps the parish church was more convenient after all.

The Bishop's sermon, when it came, was not particularly suited to the season, being very much like his lecture suitably adapted for the pulpit. He had chosen for his text a verse from the psalms, *In them hath he set a tabernacle for the sun, which cometh forth as a bridegroom out of his chamber, and rejoiceth as a giant to run his course.*

Belinda hoped that Harriet would not be upset by the reference to bridegrooms, but she appeared to be quite unmoved and it was evident that she had very sensibly put away any hopes she might once have had. She even whispered to Belinda that he certainly wasn't the preacher he used to be, though he still had that same way of gripping the edge of the pulpit when he wished to emphasize a point.

The text seemed to have little reference to the sermon, although the more intelligent of the congregation saw it as referring to the Bishop himself. He was the giant and his course was the Mission Field. Belinda noticed, however, that when he prayed for his flock he gave the impression that they were so entirely heathen that she began to wonder whether dear Theo had done such wonderful work among them after all. What if

222

the whole of his life had been so taken up with avoiding designing spinsters and widows that no other work had been possible? It was an interesting idea and one which she was able to follow up that evening, when she and Harriet were invited to supper at the vicarage.

Belinda was not sure why they had been asked, but it seemed as if Agatha had decided to dispose of several people to whom she owed invitations, for the company included, besides themselves, the Bishop, Father Plowman, Mr Donne and Miss Aspinall, who had been asked at the last minute instead of Lady Clara Boulding, who had suddenly decided to spend Christmas in Switzerland with her married daughter. Miss Aspinall was radiant, or as near it as she could be, glittering with beads and chains and agreeing rapturously with everything that everybody said. This was rather difficult with four clergymen present, as, with the exception of the curate who hardly ventured an opinion on anything, they tended to disagree with each other wherever they could.

It was such a pity, Belinda reflected, that clergymen were so apt to bring out the worst in each other, especially with the season of Peace and Goodwill so near. As a species they did not *get on* and being in a small country village made things even more difficult. These embarrassments would not arise in London where the clergy kept themselves to themselves in their own little sets, High, Broad and Low, as it were. It was so odd to hear Father Plowman calling the curate Father Donne, though the curate himself did not appear to think it so. On the contrary, he had that evening preached a most successful sermon in Father

223

Plowman's church on the text *We heard of the same at Ephrata and found it in the wood*, and had been very much impressed by the elaborate service. He would discuss it with Olivia Berridge some time; she was always so sensible and would be sure to give him good advice. He would be seeing her in the New Year as he had been invited to stay for a few days with the chaplain of his old college, in whose rowing he still took a very keen interest. When there was a suitable pause in the conversation, he ventured to mention this visit.

'Oh, if you should see Mr Mold, do give him my very kindest regards,' said Harriet, fingering her long rope of cultured pearls.

'Do you think that is wise?' said the Archdeacon. 'Even kindest regards are a poor substitute for the deeper feelings. I hear that the poor fellow is in quite a bad way as it is.'

The Bishop looked a little alarmed and Agatha, frowning at her husband, hastened to turn the conversation to Olivia, and how glad she would be to see Mr Donne. 'She is generally up during the vacation, you know,' she explained. 'She does a good deal of reading then.'

Mr Donne looked rather embarrassed. 'Oh, yes, it will be jolly to see Olivia again,' he said heartily. 'I expect we shall go for some walks together. She's very keen on walking.'

'Has she made you any more socks?' asked Belinda innocently.

'Yes, indeed, and a pullover too,' said Mr Donne. 'She's really awfully good.'

'Well, I hope she knows how to graft a toe by now,' said Harriet bluntly. 'Belinda could show her.'

224

'Olivia is a very clever girl,' said Agatha. 'I'm sure she is quite equal to it.'

'I should hardly call her a girl,' said the Archdeacon spitefully. 'But I suppose women like to think of themselves as girls long after they are thirty.'

'Oh, Olivia is only thirty-one or two,' said Agatha impatiently, 'and her work on *The Owl and the Nightingale* has really been a most substantial contribution to Middle English studies.'

'All the same, it is important to know how to graft a toe,' persisted Harriet. 'What is it, Belinda, knit and slip off, then purl and keep on? I never can remember.'

Just as Belinda was thinking of a tactful answer, the Bishop broke in, saying with a reminiscent sigh, 'Ah, the socks I had knitted for me when I was a curate!'

'I know,' agreed Father Plowman, 'some small, some large, some short, some long, but all acceptable because of the goodwill that inspired the knitters.'

'I should have thought a sock was very little use unless it was the right size,' said the Archdeacon sourly.

When she heard this, Belinda was thankful that she had decided against knitting him a pullover and went cold with horror at the thought of what she had escaped. For there would surely have been something wrong with it. She attended to her soup, straight out of a tin with no subtle additions, she decided. Perhaps only one tin among so many, watered down or with potato water added. It certainly had very little taste.

'What delicious soup, Mrs Hoccleve,' said Miss

Aspinall timidly. 'Such a delicate flavour.'

'It reminds me of our native fermented porridge,' said the Bishop. 'The flavour is somewhat similar.'

'Oh, how *interesting*,' said Connie. 'How is it made?'

'My dear Bishop, I hope you will remember that we are at the dinner table and spare us a detailed description,' broke in the Archdeacon.

'Yes, I suppose these natives are very disgusting,' said Harriet complacently. 'It is better not to know too much about them.'

'Many of them will be celebrating the festival of Christmas on Tuesday, just as we shall be doing,' said the Bishop on a faint note of reproach. 'Perhaps it will not be exactly the same in detail, but their feelings will be as ours.'

'I suppose it is because of your work there that they will be able to,' said the curate.

The Bishop smiled and was about to answer when the Archdeacon gave a short bark of laughter and exclaimed, 'Ah, no, that's where you're wrong. The Romans were there first. Father Vigilio of the Padua Fathers, I believe.'

'Yes, certainly, but I had the honour of starting the first Church of England Mission among the Mbawawa,' said the Bishop, 'though the Roman Catholics *were* there before me.'

'What a shame,' said Harriet indignantly, but Belinda felt that her wrath was directed not so much towards the Church of Rome as the rather dry-looking rissoles, cabbage and boiled potatoes which were now set before them. *Rissoles!* Belinda could imagine her sister's disgusted comments later. At least one would have expected a bird of some kind, especially when there was a bishop present, when indeed all the gentlemen were in Holy Orders.

'I suppose the African's leaning towards ritual would make him a ready convert to Roman Catholicism,' Belinda ventured. 'I mean, one knows their love of bright, gaudy things,' she added rather unfortunately. 'The Church of England might seem rather plain to them.'

'Bright and gaudy?' said Father Plowman, on a pained note. 'Oh, Miss Bede, surely you cannot mean that?'

'I'm sorry,' said Belinda, in confusion, 'naturally I didn't mean to imply . . .'

'Well, Plowman is still with us, you know,' said the Archdeacon almost jovially. 'I don't think he need take your remarks so personally.'

Belinda chewed her stringy cabbage and listened gratefully to dear Henry talking about Frazer and *The Golden Bough*, which he thought remarkably fine.

'At one time I had the idea of giving a course of sermons based on it,' he said, 'but I came to the conclusion, regretfully I must admit, that with a congregation of limited intelligence it would be *too dangerous*.'

Belinda liked the sound of this and could almost have imagined them all back in Victorian days, when a father might forbid a book 'inimical to the faith of the day' to be read in his house.

'How debased anthropology has become since Frazer's day,' sighed the Bishop, 'a mere matter of genealogies, meaningless definitions and jargon, *words, words, words*, as Hamlet has it; lineage, sib, kindred, extended family, ramage—one doesn't know where one is. Even the good old term *clan* is suspect.'

'What is a sib?' asked Harriet. 'It sounds a nice, friendly kind of thing, or it might be something to eat, a biscuit, perhaps.'

The Bishop shook his head and said nothing, either because he did not deign to be associated with present-day anthropological terminology or because he did not really know what a sib was.

The Archdeacon recalled the Anglo-Saxon meaning of the word, and talked for some minutes about the double meaning of peace and relationship, but Harriet had lost interest and soon they were all in the drawing-room, drinking coffee made with coffee essence. When the gentlemen joined them it was suggested that Harriet should play the piano and she gave a showy performance of Manuel de Falla's *Pantomime*. Then the Bishop sang an unaccompanied Mbawawa Christmas carol, which everyone agreed was very moving. When he had finished, Father Plowman suggested with admirable good manners that the Archdeacon should read aloud to them.

The Archdeacon was so surprised at this that for some minutes he could not even think of anything to read.

'Let it be something that all can understand,' suggested Father Plowman, thinking of an occasion when the Archdeacon had insisted on reading Chaucer's *Canterbury Tales* with an attempt at the original pronunciation.

There was a pause, nobody liking or perhaps wishing to make any suggestion, until Miss Aspinall timidly ventured the observation that Keats had written some very lovely poems. She was, of course, remembering Lady Grudge's 'evenings' in Belgrave Square, when Canon Kendrick used to read aloud to them.

'Ah, yes, we will have *Hyperion*,' said the Archdeacon. '*Remarkably* fine.'

There was a murmur of assent, during which Harriet could be heard asking the curate if *Hyperion* were a very *long* poem; she had quite forgotten.

Belinda turned to the Bishop and made a chatty remark about always having liked the lines about *Sorrow more beautiful than Beauty's self*.

The Bishop nodded and gave her what Belinda thought was rather an intimate smile. 'I am sure that any poem you admire must be very fine,' he said in a low voice.

Belinda was so startled that she wondered whether she could have heard correctly. 'I'm afraid I like what I remember from my student days,' she said. 'I hardly ever read anything new.' *Hyperion* had no memories for her, as the Archdeacon had never read it to her then, so that she was able to listen to it quite dispassionately and join with the polite murmurs that followed his performance.

'And yet I think I prefer the earlier Keats,' she said rather boldly, 'I was always very fond of *Isabella* when I was a young girl.'

The Archdeacon smiled indulgently and Agatha said quite kindly, 'Well, of course, *Isabella* is rather a young girl's poem, isn't it?'

'Oh, yes, completely,' agreed Belinda. 'It is many years since I read it.' It would indeed be an ominous sign if she felt drawn to it at her time of life, she felt.

'What a fine poem Young's *Night Thoughts* is,'

said the Bishop. 'I have been reading it every night myself. I have a most interesting collection of books in my room,' he went on. 'There is an Icelandic grammar among them and I have been comparing that language with the Mbawawa.'

'But do you find any similarity?' asked Agatha doubtfully.

'Oh, none whatever,' said the Bishop almost gaily, 'but it is a fascinating study, *fascinating* . . .' his voice trailed off on a bleating note.

'I am surprised and gratified that you find the books interesting,' said the Archdeacon. 'I made the selection myself, but I had no idea of your tastes.'

The evening ended with a song from the curate. Harriet, who accompanied him, was anxious that he should try an Elizabethan love song, and after a rather faltering beginning he sang quite charmingly, Belinda thought, but without much conviction.

> *Love is a fancie,*
> *Love is a frenzie,*
> *Let not a toy then breed thee such annoy . . .*

Perhaps there was no frenzy in his feeling for Miss Berridge, and love was hardly a *toy*. Surely Count Bianco's affection for Harriet could not be so described, or Belinda's for the Archdeacon? And yet tonight she had the feeling that there might be some truth in what the poet said. It was excellent advice to those of riper years, especially when the imagination became too active. That intimate note in the Bishop's voice, for example, and the way he had seemed to look at her during

230

the reading of the poem. It might just as easily have been Connie Aspinall he was looking at. Belinda had been forced to mention the fact that the chrysanthemums he had sent her were still lasting very well. She almost wished that they might die, and noticed with relief when she got home that some of the foliage was tinged with brown. Suddenly she took them out of their vase and, although it was dark, went out with them to the dustbin. They *were* dead really and one did not like to feel that flowers from the wrong person might be everlasting.

CHAPTER NINETEEN

'I must go and see Ricardo,' declared Belinda, one morning early in the New Year. 'Edith tells me that he has a slight attack of gout which keeps him in the house. It's rather difficult to know what to take him, though.'

'Yes, you have to be very careful with gout,' said Harriet. 'No beef or strawberries or port wine. Do you think I ought to go as well?'

'That would certainly do him more good than anything, but you mustn't come with me. I'm sure he'd prefer to see you *alone*.'

'Yes, I really will go,' said Harriet. 'You may tell him to expect me,' she added graciously.

Now that Harriet's plans about the Bishop were clearly not likely to come to anything, Belinda was determined to bring Count Bianco and her sister together as much as possible. She felt this to be her duty, and although she was not particularly

231

anxious that Harriet should marry and leave her alone, she thought that if a marriage had been arranged in heaven she would prefer Ricardo to be the happy man. He was devoted to Harriet and they had many tastes in common: he came of an ancient Italian family and was very comfortable financially. The only thing that might possibly be against him was that he was not in the Church, but even this was not as great a drawback as might at first appear, for would there not always be tender curates in need of sympathetic attention and perfectly baked cakes?

So Belinda reasoned within herself as she walked up the drive to Ricardo's house. She walked slowly, for she was thinking rather sentimentally of how Ricardo had loved her sister well and faithfully for many years. Surely he deserved some reward for his constancy? She herself had loved the Archdeacon even longer, but naturally there was no hope of any reward for her now, at least not in *this* world, she reflected piously, and we are given to understand that we shall be purged of all earthly passions in that *other* life.

The Count was in and would be delighted to see her. Belinda had been careful to announce herself as Miss *Belinda* Bede, with special emphasis on the Christian name, for she did not want Ricardo to expect Harriet and then be disappointed.

He was in the library, reading a little here and there in his many books. His gouty foot was bound up and rested on a low stool. Beside him on a little table was a pile of letters, which Belinda guessed to be those of his friend, the late John Akenside. There was also a Serbo-Croatian dictionary and the works of Alfred, Lord Tennyson.

The Count greeted Belinda with a sad smile. 'It is indeed kind of you to call,' he said, attempting to get up, but Belinda put her hand on his arm and said how sorry she had been to hear about his gout.

'It is an inconvenience,' he said, 'but I am accustomed to it.'

Touched by his patience and resignation, Belinda wondered how she could show her sympathy. She found it a little difficult to make conversation with Ricardo at the best of times, and could do no more than touch on various matters of general interest. It was inevitable that they should find themselves talking about the Bishop, who showed no signs of moving from the vicarage, where he had now been for nearly two months.

'I hear that he is to be married soon,' said Ricardo, in a calm, patient tone.

'Oh, surely not!' exclaimed Belinda, wondering how it was possible that Ricardo should come out with a piece of news that she and Harriet knew nothing of. 'We haven't heard anything, and I can't really imagine that anybody would want to marry him.'

'I heard that your sister was to marry him,' said Ricardo pathetically.

Belinda now laughed aloud for joy, all the more because it might so nearly have happened. In fact, she told herself soberly, there was still time; but she could at least reassure Ricardo.

'It certainly isn't true at the moment,' she said, 'and I think it most unlikely that it ever will be. Wherever did you hear such a thing?'

Ricardo could not remember exactly; perhaps his manservant had heard it somewhere, or it may

233

have been the Archdeacon who had told him when he called a few days ago. Yes, he was sure now that it must have been the Archdeacon. He had seemed quite certain that he was not misinformed.

The wicked *liar*, thought Belinda angrily. An archdeacon making mischief and spreading false rumours, that was what it amounted to. Although, she told herself hastily, it was possible that Ricardo had misunderstood him, had read too much into a hint or taken a joke too seriously.

'There is no truth in it whatever,' she declared positively, hoping as she did so that the Bishop was not at this moment in their drawing-room asking Harriet to be his wife. 'Harriet does not really care for him at all,' she went on boldly.

Ricardo smiled and looked almost happy, but then his face clouded as he asked if the Bishop were still at the vicarage?

'Yes, he is still there,' said Belinda, 'but I do not think he will stay much longer. He will have to be getting back to his diocese.'

'Then there is still time,' said Ricardo despondently. 'Even now he may be asking her.'

Belinda shifted uneasily in her chair. Of course one never knew for certain what Harriet might be up to, or the Bishop, for that matter. She was grateful when Ricardo's manservant appeared with sherry and biscuits on a silver tray.

'Have you been working on the letters this morning?' she asked, indicating the pile on the table.

'Yes, I have been reading them before you came. How wise he was! He knew what would happen there; no man understood the Balkan mind as he did.'

'No, I'm sure they didn't,' said Belinda inadequately, for she was never quite clear as to what *had* happened there except that poor John had been killed in a riot.

There was a silence, during which Belinda racked her brains for something intelligent to say. But she was too late to stop Ricardo from getting back on to the subject of Harriet.

'It is many days since I have seen your sister,' he said. 'It may be that there is something she does not wish to tell me.'

The warmth of the room and the unaccustomed effect of sherry in the morning were beginning to make Belinda feel a little vague and carefree, in the mood to make rash promises.

'Harriet is coming to see you very soon,' she said. 'I can promise you that.'

'She will never marry me, she does not love me,' said Ricardo as if speaking his thoughts aloud.

'Now, Ricardo, you mustn't lose hope,' said Belinda comfortably. 'I know she is fond of you and even if she will not love you, always remember'—her eyes lighted on the works of Alfred, Lord Tennyson—'that it is better to have loved and lost than never to have loved at all. I always think those lines are such a great comfort; so many of us have loved and lost.' She frowned: nobody wanted to be one of many, and she did not like this picture of herself, only one of a great crowd of dreary women. Perhaps Tennyson was rather hackneyed after all.

But Ricardo did not appear to think so. 'You are so kind and understanding,' he said. 'I feel that there is a great bond between us.'

Belinda did not quite know what to say, so she

235

merely smiled and said that she was sure that some day everything would be just as Ricardo wished.

'Then I shall ask her again,' he declared, fired with fresh courage and looking as if he were about to quote Dante or Tacitus at any moment; probably the former, Belinda thought, for it seemed unlikely that there would be anything suitable in Tacitus.

'Yes, Ricardo, do,' she said, 'but not yet. Wait until the spring, when the daffodils are out in your meadow.'

'If I am spared till then,' said Ricardo sadly, looking down at his bandaged foot. He then went on to talk of the fine new bulbs that he had planted in the meadow and to calculate when they would be at their best.

Belinda left the house feeling that she had done good, and with a picture of daffodils and scyllas in her mind. She saw Harriet, the radiant Countess, picking grapes in the conservatory, adorning the head of Ricardo's dinner table, opening a garden fete or bazaar. But all this was in the distant future. For the present Belinda was glad that she had been able to cheer Ricardo and to give him a little hope. What a good thing it was that hope sprang eternal in the human breast! What would she herself have done without hope? Even if nothing came of it, she thought obscurely, for she could not have said exactly what it was that she hoped for *now*. It would be enough if things could return to normal and be as they were before Mr Mold and the Bishop had appeared in the village. They could get on very well without them.

Belinda took out her shopping list and stopped for a moment, deep in contemplation of it. Coffee, rice, steel wool, kitchen soap, written in her own hand and then, in Harriet's, tinned peaches, sponge cakes, sherry (*not* cooking), set of no. 14 knitting needles (*steel*) . . . Belinda frowned. They had plenty of knitting needles of all sizes and did they really *need* sherry or peaches or sponge cakes? Perhaps Mr Donne was coming to supper again.

'Good morning!' said a bright, cheerful voice, which Belinda did not at first recognize as Agatha's, calling to her from the other side of the narrow street.

'Good morning,' Belinda called back, and was just moving on when she saw that Agatha was hurrying across to speak to her.

'Isn't it a lovely morning?' she said, beaming with such unusual good humour that Belinda stared at her quite curiously, wondering what could have happened to bring about this change.

'Yes, isn't it. Really quite mild,' murmured Belinda expectantly.

'I have some great news for you,' said Agatha, smiling.

'News? For me?' All kinds of wild ideas rushed through Belinda's head, most of which she rejected hastily. Henry had been made a dean or a bishop, that was it. It seemed unlikely, in a way, and yet what else could it be?

'I had a letter from my niece Olivia this morning,' went on Agatha. 'She and Edgar are to be married—quite soon.' She paused and peered so intently and beamingly at Belinda that the latter drew back, a little embarrassed.

'Edgar?' said Belinda stupidly. 'Do I know him?'

'Why, of course you do! Our curate, Mr Donne,'

said Agatha with some of her usual impatience which made Belinda feel more at home. 'Such a suitable thing altogether, I've been hoping all along that it would happen like this.'

'But isn't she a lot older than he is,' said Belinda tactlessly.

'Oh, well, a year or two, but Mr Donne needs an older woman. Besides, he's rather shy and an older woman can often help things along, you know.'

'How do you mean?' asked Belinda. 'I suppose if young people want to marry, they will. I mean if they both do.'

'Ah, yes,' said Agatha, 'but there is often a natural hesitation on the part of the man, especially if he feels, as I know Edgar does, that a woman is far superior to him intellectually.'

And older too, thought Belinda perversely. 'Yes, I suppose a young man might well hesitate in those circumstances,' she said aloud.

'He who hesitates is lost,' said Agatha briskly. 'I told Edgar that and I dropped a hint to Olivia.'

'Oh, did *she* propose to *him?*' asked Belinda in a loud, interested tone. 'I've often wondered if it was done very much. I suppose it must be done a good deal more than one realizes.'

'Oh, yes,' said Agatha casually, 'it is not at all unusual. Men are understandably shy about offering what seems to them very little and when a woman realizes this she is perfectly justified in helping him on a bit, as it were.'

At this moment an idea came into Belinda's head. At first it seemed fantastic, then quite likely, and finally almost a certainty. Agatha had proposed to Henry. Why had this never occurred to her before? And now that it had, what was the use of it? Belinda could not answer this, but she knew that she could put it away in her mind and take it out again when she was feeling in need of comfort.

'Yes, I suppose it can happen like that,' she agreed calmly. 'There is no reason why it shouldn't. And yet,' she ventured, 'I don't think I should ever feel certain enough to take on that responsibility myself. I know men have to take it, but supposing one met somebody else afterwards . . .' she stopped in confusion.

'Ah, yes,' Agatha's face seemed to soften for a moment, 'That can happen too. One wonders how often it *does* happen when one knows that it *can*.'

Belinda hurried home in a great turmoil. So many exciting things to tell Harriet and somehow the curate's engagement seemed to be the least exciting of them all. Nevertheless, she could not help wondering how her sister would take the news. Not that one could say it had really been a 'disappointment' to Harriet in the usual sense, but what would she do without a curate to dote upon? It was unlikely that Miss Berridge—perhaps they would soon be calling her Olivia—would approve of anybody else doting on her husband, for Harriet would not like it to be suggested that she was too old and unattractive for there to be any danger, which led Belinda to speculate upon the age at which a single woman could safely have a curate to live with her without fear of scandal. She feared that whatever the age might be, seventy-five or even eighty, it would be many years before Harriet would attain it. What a solution it would be! Belinda sighed as she walked through the gate, fearful of what might happen.

But Harriet had already heard the news and although it was obvious that she was rather upset, her attitude was rather one of indignation and pity for Mr Donne.

'*Poor* young man,' she said, 'I could hardly believe it when I heard the news. Of course it's obvious that she's been after him for a long time. I expect *she* proposed to *him*.'

'Why, yes,' said Belinda eagerly, 'Agatha as good as told me so. And I think *she* proposed to Henry, and now she finds that she prefers the Bishop. At least,' she added, feeling that she had gone rather too far, 'she might not necessarily have meant that, but she did hint at it.'

'I can quite imagine it,' said Harriet. 'If only *you* could have thought of proposing, Belinda.'

'It wouldn't have occurred to me, I'm afraid. And think how dreadful it would be to be refused. I sometimes wonder how men can bear it, though they usually go off and ask somebody else, don't they, all except Ricardo, that is. But I think it's much better not to have asked, not to know definitely that one wasn't wanted,' said Belinda hastily. 'I always feel that a man should do his own proposing.'

'Yes, and then he can be blamed for the results,' said Harriet stoutly.

'Perhaps clergymen feel that they ought not to ask people to marry them,' said Belinda. 'The celibacy of the clergy, you know,' she added vaguely.

'It's much better for a curate not to marry. Just imagine, a *married* curate,' said Harriet in disgust.

'Ricardo has given me the recipe for ravioli,' said Belinda. 'He seemed rather low, I thought, and I

240

promised that you would go up and see him.'

'Oh, yes, I really ought to go,' said Harriet, 'perhaps this afternoon,' she added, brightening up a little, as if the thought of the Count's admiration would do something to make up for the prospect of a married curate. 'No, this afternoon won't do. I shall go tomorrow after I've had my hair done.'

'All right, but let it be soon,' said Belinda. 'It would cheer him up so much. I think I shall make some ravioli for supper; it seems quite easy.'

'Yes, that would be nice. We have some cold meat, haven't we, for the filling?' Harriet suddenly chuckled. 'I wonder if Agatha *does* prefer the Bishop to Henry,' she said. 'How ironical life is; he sent you those flowers and you weren't at all pleased.'

Belinda looked startled, almost as if she expected to see the chrysanthemums still there. But the place where they had stood was reassuringly filled with dried Cape gooseberries and honesty.

CHAPTER TWENTY

Belinda always liked working in the kitchen when Emily was not there and was glad that she had decided to make the ravioli on her afternoon out. Emily always seemed so critical, though generally in a silent way which was far more unnerving than if she had put it into words. Belinda could feel her scornful, pitying glances as she creamed butter and sugar or rubbed fat into flour. For this reason she usually chose some foreign dish of which Emily would be unlikely to have knowledge.

This afternoon she felt a great sense of freedom and spread the things around her in a most wanton manner, though the recipe did not need complicated ingredients. The secret seemed to lie in the kneading or rolling, which was to be carried out for a full half-hour or until the paste was quite smooth and 'of the consistency of the finest chamois leather', as the Count's translation of the Italian read.

When Belinda had been kneading and rolling for about ten minutes she felt she must rest. It was exhausting work, and the paste was nowhere near the desired consistency yet. It was sticky, full of little lumps and greyish looking—not at all like any kind of chamois leather.

Harriet was bustling in and out of the kitchen as she was expecting a visit from Mrs Ramage, the wardrobe woman. She had spread practically the whole of Belinda's wardrobe out on the floor, and was quite ruthless in brushing aside Belinda's feeble protest on seeing a nearly new green crêpe afternoon frock among the things to be sold.

'Oh, but Harriet, I rather like that dress,' said Belinda, 'and there's still a lot of wear in it. I'm sure Miss Prior could bring it up to date in some way, if it needs it. Perhaps a little lace collar or a contrasting jabot,' she suggested uncertainly.

'Neither lace collars nor jabots are being worn at the moment,' said Harriet firmly, 'and I've always thought it rather a trying shade of green. It makes you look yellow.'

Belinda paused in her kneading, remembering the many times she had worn the dress. Had she always looked yellow in it? It was a disturbing thought. 'I suppose that old tweed coat is past wearing,' she went on sadly, 'but I've always liked it so much.'

'It's no use being sentimental about things,' said Harriet. 'You shouldn't keep a clutter of clothes you never wear just because you once liked them.'

Belinda made no comment on this, for she was thinking that Harriet's words might be applied to more serious things than clothes. If only one could clear out one's mind and heart as ruthlessly as one did one's wardrobe . . .

'I shall see Mrs Ramage in the dining-room,' declared Harriet. 'I shall not take more than two or three things in at once. I shall start by asking £5 for your green dress.'

'But I believe it hardly cost that when it was new,' protested Belinda. 'What a good thing *you* are seeing her,' she added, thinking also that it was just as well that Harriet had something to take her mind off Mr Donne's engagement. 'I'm afraid I never have the courage to ask a big price but just agree to what she offers.'

Harriet snorted. 'She'd probably offer a pound for the lot if you asked her.' The front-door bell rang. 'There, that must be her now.' Harriet strode out with a purposeful step, carrying Belinda's old tweed coat and an old jumper suit of her own over her arm. She would lead up to the green crêpe dress artistically and not bring it out until the last moment.

Belinda returned to her kneading and rolling. The paste still did not seem quite right. Perhaps it was too sticky. She sprinkled more flour on the board and on her hands and went on rather grimly. Her back was aching a little now and she was startled when the front-door bell rang again, and stood for a moment undecided what to do. It was no use expecting Harriet to answer it and she herself with her floury hands and generally dishevelled appearance was really in no fit state to go. But of course it probably wouldn't be anybody who mattered. It certainly wouldn't be the Archdeacon at ten to three in the afternoon.

The bell rang again, a long ring, as if it had been firmly pressed. Belinda wiped her floury hands on her apron and hurried into the hall.

A man's figure showed through the frosted glass panel of the front door. A tall figure, but definitely not the Archdeacon's. It was probably a man selling something. A suitcase would be opened on the doorstep, full of combs, cards of safety pins and darning wool, packets of needles . . . Still, such things were useful, one could always do with them, thought Belinda opening the door, for she felt much too sorry for the men not to buy something.

'Ah, Miss Bede, good afternoon.' It was an unctuous voice, a clergyman's voice, a Bishop's voice. Why was it that they were so unmistakable? Only the Archdeacon's was different.

'Oh, dear, Bishop Grote.' Theodore Mbawawa. Belinda rubbed her hands vigorously on her grey tweed skirt—for her apron was already too floury to be of much use—and backed into the hall. 'I'm afraid I'm hardly in a fit state to receive visitors, but do come in.' She edged towards the drawing-room door and put out a still floury hand to open it.

But the Bishop was almost too quick for her. His hand reached the knob simultaneously with hers. For one panic-stricken moment she even imagined that it lingered for a fraction of a second, but then dismissed the unworthy thought almost before it had time to register in her mind. She was in an agitated state, and she had read somewhere that in any case middle-aged spinsters were apt to imagine things of this kind . . .

Inside the drawing-room Belinda stood uncertainly, while the Bishop advanced towards the fireplace, where a fire was laid but not yet lit. He made a remark about the weather, observing that it was a raw and chilly afternoon. In his diocese, he added, they would be enjoying some of the hottest weather now.

'It must be a lovely climate,' said Belinda, fumbling in the Toby jug on the mantelpiece for a box of matches. 'I'm so sorry about there being no fire. We usually light it just before tea.' She wondered if she could perhaps offer him a cup now. It was certainly a little early, but it would at least fill in the time until Harriet had finished with Mrs Ramage and would also give Belinda an opportunity to slip away and make herself more presentable. 'I will go and tell my sister that you are here,' she said crouching over the fire and setting a match to a corner of the *Church Times*. 'She will be so pleased to see you.'

The Bishop held up his hand. 'No, please, Miss Bede. It is *you* I have come to see.'

Belinda stood up. 'Oh?' Whatever could he want? *'Me?* Please sit down, won't you? I must apologize again for my untidiness, but I was doing something in the kitchen.'

The Bishop smiled. 'And doing it admirably, I'm sure.'

Belinda smiled uneasily. She began to wonder

245

whether she had thanked him enough for the flowers, though that was some weeks ago now, and was just going to make a remark about them when he began to speak in a hurrying way, as if he were not quite sure of himself.

'Miss Bede, I am sure you must have realized— have noticed, that is—my preference for you above all the other ladies of the village,' he said, and peered at her so intently that Belinda—they were sitting together on the sofa—drew back, considerably alarmed.

'No, I don't think I have,' she said anxiously. 'In any case you can hardly know me very well or you would realize that there is nothing very special about me.'

'Ah, well, one hardly looks for beauty at our time of life,' he said, with a return of some of his usual complacency. '*She is not fair to outward view* . . . how does Wordsworth put it?'

'Not *Wordsworth*,' said Belinda automatically. 'Coleridge, Hartley Coleridge, I think.' She felt rather annoyed. Not even a middle-aged spinster likes to be told in so many words that she is not fair to outward view. Besides, she felt that the Bishop had taken an unfair advantage of her, calling on Emily's afternoon off, when she had had no opportunity to tidy herself. 'Although I am not beautiful myself and never have been,' she went on, 'I must confess that I like to see beauty in other people.'

'You mean beauty of character, ah, yes. That is something we all like to see.'

'No, I mean beauty of person,' said Belinda obstinately.

The Bishop smiled. 'Then perhaps you will not

be so ready to accept what I have to offer,' he said, though it was obvious that he really thought quite otherwise.

'Offer?' said Belinda in a startled tone. 'I don't think I understand.' The man on the doorstep opening his suitcase was simpler and less alarming than this. She hardly dared to let herself guess what the Bishop meant; it was too fantastic and terrible to be thought of.

'Perhaps you are not accustomed to receiving such offers?' he went on. 'Or perhaps it is some time since you last had one? After all, this is a quiet country village; it is unlikely that you would meet many strangers.'

'That may be,' said Belinda feeling very angry, 'but I think I can say that I have had my share, in the past, that is. Naturally not lately,' she fumbled, her natural honesty getting the better of her.

'I think I had better speak more plainly,' the Bishop went on. 'I am asking you to marry me.'

There was a short but awkward silence, and then Belinda heard herself stammering out the first words that came into her head, 'Oh, but I *couldn't* . . .'

'My dear, you are equal to being the wife of a bishop,' he said kindly, making a movement towards her. 'You need have no fears on that account. When I was a younger man I held views about the celibacy of the clergy, young curates often do, you know,' he smiled indulgently, 'it is a kind of protection, if you see what I mean. But a man does need a helpmeet, you remember in *Paradise Lost* . . .'

Belinda interrupted him with a startled exclamation. *'Paradise Lost!'* she echoed in horror.

247

'*Milton* . . .'

'I think when one has reached er—riper years,' the Bishop continued, 'things are different, aren't they?'

A man needs a woman to help him into his grave, thought Belinda, remembering a remark Dr Parnell had made. Well, there would be plenty who would be willing to do that.

'I'm afraid I can't marry you,' she said, looking down at her floury hands. 'I don't love you.'

'But you respect and like me,' said the Bishop, as if that went without saying. 'We need not speak of love—one would hardly expect that now.'

'No,' said Belinda miserably, 'I suppose one would not *expect* it. But you see,' she went on, 'I did love somebody once and perhaps I still do.'

'Ah . . .' the Bishop shook his head, 'he died, perhaps? A very sad thing.'

They were both silent. He died, yes, it was better that the Bishop should think that, it sounded more suitable; there was even something a little noble about it. *She never married* . . . Belinda began to see herself as a romantically tragic figure.

'Of course, as Lord Byron says,' began the Bishop, and then paused.

Could Lord Byron have said anything at all suitable? Belinda wondered. *When we two parted in silence and tears?* Possibly, though the poem was not really applicable. 'Do tell me,' she said, her literary curiosity driving other thoughts from her mind. 'What *did* Lord Byron say?'

But the Bishop was standing up now and saying that he did not think he would be able to stay for tea, although Belinda was not conscious of having offered it. 'I think it is perhaps a little early for tea,

248

Miss Bede, and I have still another call to make.'

'Oh, I expect you will get tea there,' said Belinda in a full, relieved tone. 'Now that I come to think of it, we have only very little cake, just a small piece of gingerbread, I believe. When one has guests one likes to have rather more than that to offer them.' She frowned, wishing she had not used the word 'offer', but the Bishop did not seem to be at all upset, or even, indeed, to have noticed. 'I'm so sorry,' said Belinda ambiguously. 'I am really most honoured that you should have felt . . . but I'm sure you will understand how it is.'

'Do not give it another thought, Miss Bede,' he said briskly, 'I assure you that I shall not. After all, we must remember that *God moves in a mysterious way, His wonders to perform.*'

'Yes, certainly,' agreed Belinda, feeling a little annoyed that he should quote her favourite hymn. But perhaps it was presumptuous to suppose that God would be more likely to reveal His ways to her than to the Bishop. She did not quite see how the lines applied here, no doubt he had something else in mind. Perhaps he would come another day and ask Harriet? At all events he was not going to give her refusal another thought, so he could not care very much. It was not very flattering to her, though she supposed that as she was not fair to outward view she could hardly expect anything else.

It was not until they were in the hall that she realized that she had been offered and refused something that Agatha wanted, or that she may have wanted, for the hint she had given had been very slight. She wondered if the Bishop had any idea of it.

'It is nice that you have been able to stay so long here,' she said, with unaccustomed guile. 'I expect the Archdeacon and Mrs Hoccleve will miss you when you go back.'

'Yes, I think I can say that they will.' The Bishop smiled to himself. 'I have been able to give the Archdeacon a few tips, although a small country parish hardly presents the same problems as a large African diocese.'

'No, of course not,' said Belinda. 'Nobody would imagine that it did.'

'Mrs Hoccleve has been most kind in helping me to buy various things that I need to take back to Africa with me. She has also knitted me some socks.'

'Oh, how kind!' exclaimed Belinda. 'There is nothing like hand-knitted socks.'

'No, indeed, there isn't. Particularly when they are not quite long enough in the foot.' The Bishop laughed with a silly, bleating noise. 'Quite between ourselves, of course,' he added.

'Of course,' repeated Belinda, closing the front door behind him. She felt that she could almost love Agatha as a sister now. The pullover that she might have made for the Archdeacon would surely have been wrong somewhere, but as it had never even been started, it lacked the pathos of the socks not quite long enough in the foot. To think of Agatha as pathetic was something so new that Belinda had to sit down on a chair in the hall, quite overcome by the sensation. She began to find ways of making things better and more bearable. Agatha couldn't really have meant that she cared for the Bishop; nobody could love a man like that. She almost longed to see Agatha and to be

250

crushed by one of her sharp retorts, to know that she was still the same.

At last she remembered the ravioli, and was almost glad of an excuse to stop thinking about these disturbing matters. She paused for a moment by the looking-glass and studied her wispy hair, flushed face smeared with flour and faded blue overall. Looking like that one could not feel even a romantic figure whose lover had died.

The sound of raised, almost angry, voices came from behind the closed door of the dining-room. It was a clash of wills between Harriet and Mrs Ramage, but Harriet would win in the end. It was known that the Misses Bede had 'good' things— though hardly of the same standard as Mrs Hoccleve—and Mrs Ramage would be unwilling to leave without buying them.

Belinda went quietly back to the kitchen and sat down. She wished Harriet would come, so that she could tell her all about it. After all, she supposed, it was something to have been considered worthy to be the wife of a bishop, even if only a colonial one. There was something rather sad about the kitchen now. It was beginning to get dark, and the greyish mass of dough on the table reminded Belinda of the unfinished ravioli. Twenty minutes more kneading, and perhaps it would be of the consistency of the finest chamois leather.

The trivial round, the common task—did it furnish *quite* all we needed to ask? Had Keble *really* understood? Sometimes one almost doubted it. Belinda imagined him writing the lines in a Gothic study, panelled in pitch-pine and well dusted that morning by an efficient servant. Not at all the same thing as standing at the sink with aching back and hands plunged into the washing-up water.

'Three pounds, fifteen and six!' Harriet came triumphant into the kitchen, waving the notes in her hand. 'She was pleased with your green dress, but she wondered how you could ever have worn it. "Not at all Miss Bede's colour", she said.'

'No, I begin to wonder now myself how I could ever have worn it,' said Belinda. 'Perhaps it is hardly surprising that Bishop Grote does not think me fair to outward view, though I think I was wearing my blue marocain that evening at the vicarage, and I always think I look quite nice in that.'

'Oh, was it Theo who called just now?' asked Harriet. 'What did he want?'

'He wanted me to be his wife,' said Belinda, enjoying the dramatic simplicity of her announcement.

'*No!*' Harriet's surprise was a little uncomplimentary, but her joy and relief at having her sister spared to her more than made up for it. 'What a pity you and Agatha can't change, though,' she lamented. 'But of course he can't really care for her very much or he wouldn't have asked you, would he?'

'I don't know,' said Belinda, who was beginning to think that she did not understand anything any more. 'Anyway I don't suppose Agatha really cares for him. I ought not to have told you what she said.' She felt that she could not tell even Harriet about the socks and was glad when she left the subject and came out with a piece of news of her own. Mrs Ramage, in the intervals of bargaining, had told her that she had heard that Mr Donne had been offered a 'post' at his old University—

252

chaplain in the college or something like that.

'How suitable,' said Belinda, 'but of course it will mean him leaving here, won't it?'

'Oh, yes, of course,' said Harriet casually. 'But don't you see, we shall get a new curate? The Archdeacon will never be able to manage by himself.'

'No, of course not,' agreed Belinda fervently, 'he couldn't possibly manage by himself. He will certainly have to get a new curate.'

'This is really a place for a young man,' said Harriet.

'Well, I don't know. A young man might want more scope, a more active parish with young people. Something in the East End of London, perhaps,' Belinda suggested. 'I should think this curacy might very well suit an older man.'

'Oh, I can't imagine that,' said Harriet in disgust. 'And anyway, curates are nearly always young.'

'Not necessarily,' said Belinda, feeling that she ought to help her sister to face up to the problem from every possible angle. 'Sometimes a man in middle life suddenly feels called upon to take Holy Orders. I always feel it must be so awkward and upsetting for his family.'

'Oh, dear,' Harriet's face clouded. 'I do hope it won't be anyone like that.'

'I'm not saying it will be, but it *could* be,' said Belinda. 'I think the Archdeacon would prefer a young man, though.'

'Yes, working with the Archdeacon must be a great experience,' said Harriet obscurely. 'A young man of good family, just ordained, that's what we really want. Do you suppose the Archdeacon will advertise in the *Church Times*?'

'He could hardly advertise for somebody of good family,' said Belinda smiling.

'They sometimes say "genuine Catholic" or "prayer-book Catholic",' mused Harriet, 'but of course we should hardly want that here.'

'Oh, Harriet, *look!*' Belinda held up the sheet of ravioli she had been rolling.

'But, Belinda, it's just like a piece of leather. I'm sure that can't be right,' protested Harriet.

'It is,' said Belinda joyfully, 'it's even finer than the finest chamois leather.'

CHAPTER TWENTY-ONE

The next few weeks were entirely taken up with preparations for the curate's wedding. It may be said without exaggeration that it was the only topic of conversation in the village at this time, and many a church worker's dingy life had been brightened by the silver and white invitation card, which was prominently displayed on many mantelpieces. The marriage of their dear Mr Donne was something in which all could share, for had he not at some time or another been to meals at all their houses? Many were the chickens which had been stuffed and roasted or boiled and smothered in white sauce in his honour.

One afternoon, a few days before the wedding, there was a gathering at the parish hall, the object of which was to make a presentation to Mr Donne and his fiancée. Miss Berridge was to stay at the vicarage and be married from there, as her parents were dead and Mrs Hoccleve, perhaps because of her niece's substantial contribution to Middle English studies, had always been particularly fond of her.

There was great excitement in the hall for nobody had yet seen Miss Berridge, though Edith Liversidge had caught a glimpse of her coming from the station the previous evening. As it had been a very dark night she had not been able to give a satisfactory description, except to say that she had been wearing a fur coat, a dark, rather bushy fur, musquash, she thought, and that she was very tall, perhaps taller than Mr Donne, who was only of middle height for a man.

'Taller than he is,' said Harriet in a disgusted tone, as they sat waiting for the proceedings to begin. 'What a pity! I always think it looks so bad.'

'Yes,' agreed Belinda, 'but of course it can't be helped. I mean, there are other things more important.'

'Tall women always droop,' said Edith sharply. 'I'm always telling Connie to hold herself up. It never had any effect until Bishop Grote said something about liking tall women—she's been better since then.'

'Did he say that?' asked Belinda, interested. 'I didn't think he really minded what people looked like—or expected much from people of our age, anyway.'

'Bishops ought not to mind or expect,' said Edith, 'but I suppose they're human. Besides, don't forget all those native women . . .' she paused darkly. 'He was describing their costume or lack of it when he came to tea with us the other day. Poor Connie was quite embarrassed.'

'Well, he's gone now,' said Belinda comfortably,

'and he'll probably be quite glad to be back among those dear, good fellows.'

'Agatha was sorry to see him go,' said Harriet. 'That was obvious. *Ah, quotiens illum doluit properare Calypso*—Ah, how many times did Calypso grieve at his hastening.'

'Connie was sorry too,' said Edith. 'If it hadn't been that she was due for her annual visit to Belgrave Square she would have been very low.'

'I do hope she will be back in time for Mr Donne's presentation,' said Harriet, 'she wouldn't want to miss his speech, I'm sure.'

'Her train is due in at a quarter to three, so I suppose she should be here for most of it—in at the death, you know.'

'Poor Mr Donne,' sighed Harriet, 'one almost feels that it *is* a death.'

At this moment there was a stir among the rows of waiting women, and the door on to the platform opened. Agatha Hoccleve, in a black tailored costume of good cut, came in, followed by a tall, pleasant-looking woman in the early or middle thirties, in a blue tweed costume of rather less good cut. She had a pale, rather long face and wore spectacles. Her hair was neatly arranged at the back of her head, though this was rather difficult to see as her navy felt hat was pulled down at a sensible angle.

Long, English gentlewoman's feet, thought Belinda noticing her shoes and good, heavy silk stockings.

Miss Berridge was followed by Mr Donne, looking rather sheepish, Father Plowman, whose parish had wished to join in the presentation, and, finally, the Archdeacon, smiling sardonically and

256

bearing in his arms a large square object shrouded in a cloth which he placed on a small table at one side of the platform.

'She *is* taller than he is,' whispered Harriet, 'and she looks much older. What a pity! She's rather plain, too, isn't she? Why doesn't she use lipstick?'

'Ladies and Gentlemen . . .' Agatha Hoccleve's clear voice rang out. She was a confident public speaker and this afternoon's audience of parish women with a few churchwardens and choirmen held no terrors for her. 'It gives me great pleasure to introduce my niece, Miss Berridge, soon to be Mrs Donne, to you all. I only wish she were going to stay longer with us, but we must not—I am sure we do not—grudge her to Mr Donne and I am equally sure that he'—she gave a sideways glance to where the curate was sitting looking down at his shoes—'will not grudge *us* the opportunity of getting to know her while she is here. Of course *I* know her already,' she added with a little laugh, and sat down amid the mild clapping which followed.

By this time the Archdeacon had got up and moved over to the side of the platform where the shrouded object stood and seemed about to uncover it, but he was prevented by an agitated gesture from Father Plowman. The situation was saved by Agatha stepping forward and saying in a loud voice, 'Before the Archdeacon makes the presentation, I think Mr Plowman has something to say.

'*Father* Plowman,' giggled Harriet.

'Yes, indeed I have,' said that clergyman with a grateful glance at Agatha and a rather baleful one at the Archdeacon. 'My parishioners and I felt that

257

we could not let this opportunity pass without adding our good wishes and our widow's mite, as it were, towards this gift. I think we shall not soon forget Father Donne's gifts to *us*. I mean,' he added, sensing a faint bewilderment among his hearers, 'his Sunday evening sermons. I can see him now, walking across the fields in the evening sunshine, his cassock and surplice over his arm . . .' Mr Donne himself now looked a little startled as Father Plowman's church was some seven or eight miles away and he had always gone over on his bicycle . . . 'pausing perhaps to drink in the beauty of our old church seen in that gracious evening light, pondering his message to us that evening, the *gift* he was bringing us.' Father Plowman paused, a little overcome by his eloquence. 'May he, with the help of Miss Berridge, go on from strength to strength, as I am sure he will. *From glory to glory advancing, we praise Thee, O Lord.*' He bowed his head. 'And now a prayer, *Prevent us O Lord in all our doings . . .*'

The obvious prayer, of course, thought Belinda, who had noted with anxiety the expression of irritation on the Archdeacon's face. Perhaps Father Plowman ought not to have said a prayer at all—it should have been left to the last speaker— the Archdeacon—who was now advancing once more towards the shrouded object.

As if in deliberate contrast, he adopted a more ominous tone, and dwelt, not so much on the parish's loss, though he did mention that Mr Donne's going would mean a great deal of extra work for *him*, as on the difficulties that Mr Donne might be expected to encounter in his new life. 'The University is a stony and barren soil,' he declared in a warning tone, 'one might almost say that the labourers are too many for the scanty harvest that is to be reaped there. The undergraduates are as in Anthony à Wood's day, much given over to drinking and gaming and vain brutish pleasures.' He looked as if he were warming to his subject, and Belinda began to fear that he might quote other and more unsuitable passages from that crabbed antiquary, but after a short pause he left the subject and went on. 'It is to be hoped that Mr Donne may succeed where others have failed. Indeed, with the help of Miss Berridge'—he gave her a most charming smile—'one feels that he may. I am certain too that with her considerable linguistic gift, she will be a great help to him if ever he feels called upon to labour in the Mission Field.'

There was a visible stir in the audience at these words and some indignant whispering.

From Greenland's icy mountains
From India's coral strand . . .

'It is not so very long since we were singing Bishop Heber's fine hymn in *our* fine old church.' The Archdeacon paused as if to let the significance of his words sink in and then began to fumble with the cloth which shrouded the square object.

'Isn't it the table cloth out of the morning-room at the vicarage?' whispered Harriet. 'How unsuitable!'

We take no note of time but from its loss.
To give it then a tongue is wise in man . . .

259

The Archdeacon paused—'Edward Young, the eighteenth-century poet and divine wrote those words nearly two hundred years ago. Not a *great* poet, you may say, no, one would hardly call him that, but I think his words are still true today. That is why we are giving this chiming clock to Mr Donne and Miss Berridge as a wedding present.' He flung aside the cloth with a dramatic gesture that Belinda thought very fine, if a little too theatrical for the occasion. 'May it do something to ease the burdens they will be called upon to bear in their new life.'

'I should think Mr Donne's burdens will be infinitely lighter in his new life than they have been here,' murmured Edith, 'but I suppose the Archdeacon cannot bear to think of anybody without some kind of burden.'

'Well, we know that life is never without them,' said Belinda loyally. 'It is perhaps just as well to remember that. And even if we appear to have none we really *ought* to have . . .' her voice trailed off obscurely, for Miss Berridge had come forward and was making a speech of thanks. Her voice was clear and ringing, as if she were used to giving lectures or addressing meetings. What an excellent clergyman's wife she would make with this splendid gift!

'Edgar and I are simply delighted . . .' there was comfort in the words, as if she were protecting Mr Donne in a sensible tweed coat or even woollen underwear. It was obvious that she would take care of him, not letting him cast a clout too soon. She would probably help with his sermons too, and embellish them with quotations rarer than her husband, with his Third Class in Theology, could be expected to know. A helpmeet indeed.

'Rather *toothy* when she smiles, isn't she,' whispered Harriet. 'I wonder what *he* will say.'

Mr Donne's speech was very short. 'Olivia has said exactly what I would have said,' he began. Here again the use of Christian names gave a cosy, intimate feeling. Agatha and Father Plowman were smiling and even the Archdeacon was looking benevolent.

Mr Donne concluded on a serious note. 'I think we shall both remember what the Archdeacon has said about the burdens we may have to bear in our new life. I hope we may not be found wanting at the testing time. And now, let us pray . . .'

Belinda wondered whether he would be able to think of another suitable prayer when Father Plowman had rather unfairly used the obvious one already. But she had to admit that his choice was an admirable one. *Lord, we pray Thee that Thy grace may always prevent and follow us, and make us continually to be given to all good works* . . . She bowed her head and could see out of the corner of her eye Miss Prior and Miss Jenner, creeping in through a side door carrying a tea-urn. When they realized that a prayer was being said, they stood stiffly with the urn, like children playing a game of 'statues'.

The prayer ended, and after a decent pause Miss Berridge and Mr Donne—or Olivia and Edgar as they had now become in the minds of their hearers—came down from the platform and moved among the audience, shaking hands and chatting.

Belinda found herself talking to Miss Berridge and offering her a cake from a plate which seemed to have got into her hand. She felt a glow of warm friendliness towards her, perhaps because of her rather plain, good-humoured face, her sensible felt hat, her not particularly well-cut tweed suit and her low-heeled shoes. Nothing from the 'best houses' here—all was as it should be in a clergyman's wife.

'Where will you live?' Belinda asked. 'I suppose suitable accommodation is provided for married chaplains even in a place that is in other ways as old-fashioned as our University.'

'Oh, we've already taken a very nice house, rather Gothic in style, but I think it will be comfortable and it has a large garden,' said Olivia. 'And Edgar will have rooms in college as well, of course. I hope you and your sister will come and see us when we are settled in. Edgar tells me you have been so good to him.'

Belinda managed to stop herself saying, 'Oh, it was really Harriet, my sister, she dotes on curates,' and asked instead whether it was decided who should come in place of Mr Donne. 'Will he be a young man or an older one who needs the quiet and country air of a little place like this?' she asked.

'Both, in a way,' said Olivia. 'He *is* young, but he has recently been ill—I think you'll like him very much. I believe he's a Balliol man and he's certainly very handsome, dark and rather Italian-looking, really. Edgar looks quite plain beside him.' She laughed affectionately. 'Anyway, you'll see him at our wedding.'

'How splendid! My sister will be delighted,' said Belinda with unguarded enthusiasm. 'She has such a respect for Balliol men,' she added hastily.

'Yes, it still maintains its great tradition of scholarship,' agreed Olivia. 'I had an idea that Archdeacon Hoccleve was a Balliol man.'

'No, he isn't, as a matter of fact,' said Belinda, 'but he is a very fine preacher. His knowledge of English literature is quite remarkable for a clergyman.'

'His sermons are full of quotations,' said Harriet bluntly. 'I consider Mr Donne a *much* better preacher.'

'I think that English Literature and Theology can be very happily combined,' said Olivia gracefully. 'I daresay I shall find myself encouraging Edgar to write more literary sermons.'

'Ah, yes,' said her fiancé, 'I expect Olivia will help me to outdo even the Archdeacon with obscure quotations from the *Ormulum*.'

'Whatever is that?' asked Harriet. 'It sounds very learned.'

'A kind of moral treatise, I believe.'

'Oh, well, I hope you won't listen to her,' said Harriet. 'I suppose people liked things like that in the old days.'

'And I hope that we in these days may still be said to like "things like that",' said Father Plowman, smiling indulgently at Harriet, as if she were a naughty child.

'Perhaps we would like them better if we could understand them,' said Belinda. 'I mean the language, of course.' She spoke rather hastily as she could see the Archdeacon approaching and thought it might be as well to change the subject before he came. 'I wish somebody would have another cake,' she said, offering the plate which

263

she was still holding. Harriet took it from her and began to encourage Mr Donne to eat a cake with pink icing, much to the amusement of Olivia, who did not appear to mind Harriet's proprietary attitude in the very least.

Belinda, feeling that she had monopolized the young couple for quite long enough, withdrew quietly and found herself near the tea-urn over which Miss Prior and Miss Jenner were presiding.

'Would you like another cup, Miss Bede?' asked Miss Prior. 'I know you're one for tea, like I am.'

'Yes, please, I would,' said Belinda, feeling this to be a comfortable classification. 'I'm sure we need plenty of tea after all this excitement.'

'We certainly do,' agreed Miss Prior. 'Miss Aspinall, too! *That* news was a surprise, I can tell you. A shock, you might almost say.'

'Oh, I always thought he had his eye on her,' said Miss Jenner in her shrill, arch voice. 'I said to mother only the other day that something would come of it.'

'Come of it?' asked Belinda, looking over to where, as she now realized, Connie Aspinall, fresh from Belgravia, was standing in the centre of a little crowd. She looked almost happy and was talking with unusual animation. Even Belgrave Square could hardly have made such a change in her. 'I don't quite understand,' Belinda went on, 'has something happened to Miss Aspinall? Is *she* getting married as well?'

'Didn't you know?' Miss Jenner almost shrieked. 'Miss Aspinall's got engaged to Bishop Grote. You remember, Miss Bede, he was staying at the vicarage not so long ago.'

Belinda had taken a large gulp of tea and

narrowly escaped choking, but she was able to indicate that she did remember Bishop Grote. 'But this is amazing, wonderful,' she emended, 'news. I must go and congratulate her immediately.' She put down her cup and made her way over to Miss Aspinall's corner.

'My *dear* Connie,' she said, 'I've just heard your wonderful news. I *am* glad.'

'Yes, I'm so happy,' said Connie. 'Theodore told me that as soon as he came here he felt that he was destined to find happiness, and that when he saw me he knew it was to *be*.' She gave a mysterious emphasis to these last words.

Belinda was silent for a moment in thankfulness and wonder. She did not now resent the Bishop's quoting of her favourite hymn *God moves in a mysterious way*. It was manifest that He did.

'But how did you come to meet again?' she asked, curiosity taking the place of wonder. 'Did he visit you in Belgrave Square?'

'No, we met one afternoon in the Army and Navy Stores,' said Connie. 'That was the wonderful part of it. I had gone into the garden-furniture department to buy a trowel and I was standing looking at a sweet little bird bath—you know they have such pretty carved stone ones—when I heard footsteps behind me—the place was *quite* deserted—I happened to look round and there was Theodore.'

'How extraordinary!' said Belinda, imagining the shock she herself would have felt.

'Yes, it seemed he had lost his way. He wanted to buy a new tin trunk to take back to Africa and found himself in the garden-furniture department by mistake. The man he asked had misdirected

265

him or the department had been moved, I believe.'

'How extraordinary life is,' Belinda interposed. 'To think that the moving of a department, if it *had* been moved . . .'

'And so then he asked me to go and have tea with him and luckily there was a Fuller's teashop quite near and he proposed to me over tea.'

'Did you have that lovely walnut cake?' asked Harriet, who had now joined them.

'I don't suppose Connie noticed what she was eating,' said Belinda. 'My dear, I'm so glad for you. I hope you will be very happy. I'm *sure* you will,' she added, feeling that she may have sounded doubtful.

'Well, I think we shall be,' said Connie. 'At first I naturally felt rather nervous—the importance of the position, you see—but Theodore assured me that I was quite equal to being a bishop's wife.'

'Yes, I am *sure* he did,' said Belinda, remembering. 'Are you to be married here or in London?'

'Oh, from Belgrave Square. Lady Grudge insisted on it. She's been so *very* kind and is most interested in the splendid work Theodore's been doing.'

'I feel that Connie's cup is almost too full,' said Belinda, as she and Harriet walked home together, 'but I'm very glad she's so happy. Perhaps they really do love each other, though he may have told her not to expect that. But perhaps it was only *I* who was not to expect love,' she added rather sadly.

'And being married from Belgrave Square!' said Harriet, who was in high spirits. 'One feels that is almost the best thing about it. *Hymen Io!*' she

266

chanted, producing a most appropriate left-over fragment of her classical education. 'That is suitable for weddings isn't it?'

'I suppose so,' said Belinda, who had not had the same advantages. 'Of course there are many beautiful Epithalamia in the English language, but one reels somehow that they are more for young people.'

But Harriet had lost interest in Connie and the Bishop. She was remembering Olivia Berridge's description of the new curate. 'Balliol and rather Italian-looking,' she breathed, 'and just recovered from an illness. Oh, Belinda, he will need such special care!' Later that evening she could be seen studying a book of Invalid Cookery, and was quite annoyed when Belinda pointed out that he would probably be eating with a normal appetite by the time he came to them.

CHAPTER TWENTY-TWO

Fortunately the wedding day was fine, one of those unexpected spring days that come too soon and deceive one into thinking that the winter is over. Belinda had great difficulty in restraining Harriet from casting off her woollen vest, and was only successful after she had pointed out, with great seriousness, that the curate would surely not be so foolish as to leave off his winter combinations in February.

'Oh, I suppose Miss Berridge would see to that,' said Harriet sulkily. 'It's quite obvious that she's going to fuss over him and turn him into a mollycoddle.'

Belinda could think of no answer to make to this, but could only wonder at the shortness of Harriet's memory. It seemed such a little time since she had thought of nothing but knitting and cooking special dishes for Mr Donne.

> *By many deeds of shame*
> *We learn that love grows cold,*

thought Belinda. Did the author of that fine hymn realize how often his lines had been frivolously applied? She turned to her prayer-book and saw that he had died in 1905: so he was beyond the realization. No doubt we are more frivolous now than we were then, she thought, feeling in her jewel-box for her little seed-pearl brooch. The neck of her new dress—a soft shade of blue that could not possibly make her look yellow—needed something to relieve its severity. Miss Prior had really made it very well; it even fitted quite closely as a result of Belinda's timid and carefully phrased request for something a little less shapeless than usual. Harriet had ordered a creation from Gorringe's which Belinda considered an unnecessary expense. She had not, however, mentioned this to her sister as she realized that the loss of a dear curate was something of an occasion and this was, as far as she could remember, the first time one had been lost by marriage. Usually it was the Mission Field or the East End of London that claimed them, or, more rarely, a comfortable living in the gift of a distant relative . . .

'Belinda! Are you ready?' Harriet stood in the room, magnificent in furs and veiled hat.

'Oh, yes, I just have to put on my hat and coat. There! You *do* look nice, Harriet. I wonder if a veil would suit me? One feels that it's *kinder* somehow—not that your complexion needs to be hidden, of course, but I sometimes think that for me . . . and yet, I don't know . . .' she broke off, wondering whether it would really make any difference now if she were to appear with her face softened by clouds of veiling. Henry knew the face underneath and would not be deceived and that was all that really mattered.

'Yes, I think it's one of my most successful hats,' said Harriet. 'Yours is nice too,' she added kindly. 'I think I should wear it just a *little* further back, though.'

Belinda adjusted it without looking in the mirror and they went downstairs.

'It's really a perfect day,' said Harriet, 'amazingly mild.'

'But I'm glad you kept on your vest,' said Belinda, 'it would have been most unwise to leave it off. It's certainly mild compared with what it has been, but it may be colder tonight.'

As they passed the vicarage she drew Harriet's attention to an almond tree in full blossom.

'Look, the almond tree's out,' she said. 'I always feel it looks lovelier every year, so beautiful that one can hardly bear it.'

Harriet looked at her sister apprehensively. She hoped Belinda wasn't going to cry too much at the wedding. They did not have many weddings in the village and it would hardly be surprising if Belinda began to distress herself by remembering that if Fate had willed otherwise she herself might have married the Archdeacon thirty years ago. She was relieved when Belinda went on to talk about ordinary things, whether it would be wise to take more than one glass of champagne at the reception, always assuming it were offered, what Agatha would be wearing and whether the new curate would be at the church.

The sisters arrived in good time so that they could choose their place carefully. Harriet looked round quite unashamedly to watch people coming into the church. Belinda occasionally turned her head, but most of the time she sat quietly with her hands folded in her lap, though she could not help showing her interest and even whispering to Harriet when Agatha came in, very elegant in dark red, with a fur coat and wide-brimmed hat. A group of nondescript-looking women—possibly relatives or friends of the bride, fellow workers in the field of Middle English studies—came behind Agatha and they sat together in one of the front pews.

Dr Nicholas Parnell had unfortunately not been able to come down for the wedding as he had to welcome to the Library some distinguished Russian visitors who were bringing with them a number of interesting relics. Mr Mold had recently left for China, where he was to make a tour of libraries and a special study of the heating systems employed in them. There was, however, to be one distinguished visitor, the University Professor of Middle English, who was to give the bride away.

'Perhaps he wanted Miss Berridge too,' Harriet had suggested, 'but hadn't the courage to speak.'

'Oh surely not,' said Belinda, 'or how could he bear to come to the wedding?' She could certainly not have attended Agatha and Henry's.

In the meantime the church was filling up. Count Bianco, whose gout was well enough now to allow him to go out, had chosen his seat carefully so that he could have a good view of Harriet. Edith Liversidge came in alone, for Connie Aspinall was in Belgravia, preparing for her own wedding in a few weeks time. Edith had honoured the occasion by wearing her best purple dress, and a kind of toque on her head, a little like a tea-cosy but dignified for all that. How dear John would have loved to see her, thought Belinda sadly. Being in church often made her think of John and his tragic death in Prague. They said it was a golden city, but how much more golden must it be from its associations with him.

She began to study the white and silver leaflet, announcing the marriage of Olivia Mary Berridge with Edgar Bernard Amberley Donne. The young couple had not chosen *God moves in a mysterious way* among the hymns, indeed, Belinda had hardly hoped for that. Their selection, except for a Middle English lyric to a setting by a relative of the bride's, was conventional. *Gracious Spirit, Holy Ghost* and *The voice that breathed o'er Eden* were very suitable. It was true that the latter was often sung to the tune of *Brief life is here our portion*, but it did no harm to be reminded of that. Brief life *was* here our portion . . . Belinda's eyes strayed to the rows of memorial tablets to past vicars. She could hardly bear to think that one day Henry's would be among them and that she might be there to see it.

At this moment there was a stir of excitement as the curate appeared with his best man, a stocky, red-haired young clergyman, a typical rowing man,

271

as Harriet whispered to Belinda.

Shortly afterwards the bride entered on the arm of the Professor of Middle English, a tall, thin man, ill at ease in his formal clothes. Belinda wondered whether Henry and Agatha were remembering their own wedding day. She had heard that people did on these occasions unless they were in a position to look forward rather than back. Count Bianco might be looking forward, but more quietly and with less rapture than a younger man. Was there anybody in the church without some romantic thought? Possibly Miss Prior, sitting with her old mother, was more interested in the bride's dress which, Belinda noticed with approval, was not white but sapphire-blue velvet, the kind of thing that would 'come in' afterwards and could if necessary be dyed and worn for years. She really looked very nice, almost pretty and not as tall as she had seemed to be at the presentation.

'If I'm ever married I shall certainly have *a fully* choral ceremony,' said Harriet enthusiastically as they filed out of the church. 'Or is there a special one for those of riper years?'

Belinda said nothing because she had been crying a little and could not trust herself to speak yet.

'No, that's only baptism,' said Edith cheerfully. 'I believe Connie and the Bishop are having quite an elaborate affair. You will be getting your invitations soon. She's having a dress made at Marshall's—embossed chenille velvet—though goodness knows what use that will be in the tropics,' she snorted.

'No, it doesn't seem as if it would be much use,' Belinda agreed. 'But of course he won't be Bishop

272

of Mbawawa all his life. I suppose he may retire and write a book about his experiences. They often do, don't they?'

'With cassock and surplice in Mbawawa-land,' retorted Edith. 'Yes, one knows the kind of thing only too well.'

'What a beautiful day,' said a gentle voice behind them. 'It is quite like Naples.'

'My dear Ricardo,' said Edith, looking round, 'where in Naples would you see such a very odd-looking crowd of people as are now coming out of this church?'

'I don't see the new curate among them,' said Harriet, looking worried. 'It can't be the best man, can it? Nobody would call him Italian-looking. Ricardo, Italians don't ever have red hair, do they?'

The Count considered the question seriously. 'Red hair is certainly not unknown in Italy,' he pronounced at length, 'but I do not think you would say that it is characteristic of the Italians. In the north of course it is sometimes found, but,' he paused impressively, 'I do not remember that I ever saw a red-haired man in Naples.'

'Oh, that's good,' said Harriet perfunctorily, 'it can't be him then. But I did hope he was going to be at the wedding.'

'I daresay there was some difficulty about the trains,' suggested Belinda. 'We shall probably find that he is at the reception.'

This was to be held at the parish hall. The curate had invited all the village, so that the vicarage drawing-room would hardly have contained them. The bride and bridegroom were in the doorway to shake hands with the guests as they filed in.

273

Belinda murmured what she hoped was a suitable greeting and passed on but she heard Harriet laughing loudly with Mr Donne, so that she wondered rather fearfully what her sister could have said. She found herself standing by Agatha and confronted by a tray of glasses of champagne which one of the hired waiters was holding in front of her.

'I must just have a sip, to drink their health, you know,' she said apologetically, feeling Agatha's eyes on her.

'Oh, certainly,' said Agatha. 'It is quite the thing.'

'I'm not really very used to drinking champagne,' Belinda admitted.

'Aren't you?' Agatha gave a little social laugh, which would normally have crushed Belinda and made her feel very gauche and inferior. But today she did not mind. She was almost glad to be able to see Agatha as her old self again. The socks not quite long enough in the foot, which the Bishop had so unkindly mentioned, had been worrying Belinda. She had suddenly seen Agatha as pathetic and the picture was disturbing. Now she knew that there could never be anything pathetic about Agatha. Poised and well-dressed, used to drinking champagne, the daughter of a bishop and the wife of an archdeacon—that was Agatha Hoccleve. It was Belinda Bede who was the pathetic one and it was so much easier to bear the burden of one's own pathos than that of somebody else. Indeed, perhaps the very recognition of it in oneself meant that it didn't really exist. Belinda took a rather large sip of champagne and looked round the hall with renewed courage.

Most of the guests were known to her, although some people from neighbouring villages had been invited. She noticed Father Plowman, near the food and with a well-filled glass, Lady Clara Boulding, putting a small *vol-au-vent* whole into her mouth, and a group of Sunday School teachers, Miss Beard, Miss Smiley and Miss Jenner, standing in a corner by themselves and looking suspiciously into their glasses. Agatha had left her now and was greeting some of the guests, so Belinda moved over to where Miss Prior and her mother were standing.

'Very nice, isn't it?' she said inadequately, nodding and smiling in their direction.

'Oh, yes, it's quite nice,' said Mrs Prior. 'It's nice to see everyone enjoying themselves. I like to see that.'

'Mother was saying she wished there was a cup of tea,' said Miss Prior in a low voice, 'but we'll have one when we get home. You see, Miss Bede, we're not really used to drinking champagne. It's different for you of course.'

'Well, I don't often have it,' Belinda admitted, feeling that she must stand midway between Agatha and the Priors in this matter, 'but of course we all want to drink the health of the bride and bridegroom in it.'

'Yes, of course,' Miss Prior agreed. 'She looks very sweet, doesn't she? That *Vogue* pattern makes up well in velvet, it was in the December book. Your dress has turned out quite nicely, too, Miss Bede. I had such trouble with the sleeves, you wouldn't believe it. I found I'd put them in the wrong way round!' Miss Prior laughed rather shrilly and took a gulp of champagne.

'Are they the right way round now?' asked Belinda.

'Oh, of course, Miss Bede. I took them out again. I couldn't let you wear a dress with the sleeves in the wrong way round.'

'No,' said Belinda, feeling all the same that this kind of thing might very well happen to her. 'Mrs Hoccleve's dress is very smart, isn't it?' she ventured, feeling that it was not at all the thing to discuss the guests' clothes with Miss Prior but being unable to resist the temptation. Perhaps, she thought, Miss Prior's profession will excuse me.

'Smart, yes, that's what I would call it too,' said Miss Prior. 'But red's not her colour. The material's good, I can see that, but you take a look at the seams inside—you won't find them finished off like mine are.'

'No, I dare say not,' said Belinda, realizing that she would certainly never have the opportunity of examining the dress so minutely, but feeling, none the less, that Agatha's splendour was considerably diminished.

'Oh, look, the Archdeacon's going to make a speech,' said Miss Prior. 'Pray silence for the Venerable Hoccleve,' she giggled.

The champagne was having a different effect on Belinda, who was now gazing very sentimentally at the Archdeacon, thinking how nice he looked and what a clever speech he was making, not at all obvious or vulgar as wedding speeches so often were. She had really no idea what he was talking about, but there were a great many quotations in it, including one from Spenser which really seemed to be quite appropriate, something about love being a celestial harmony of likely hearts

276

Which join together in sweet sympathy,
To work each others' joy and true content . . .

He was not saying anything about Burdens or sudden calls to the Mission Field.

The curate replied very nicely after the health had been drunk and was followed by the Professor of Middle English, who made an unintelligible but obviously clever little speech about *The Owl and the Nightingale*, embellished with quotations from that poem. Agatha and Olivia were smiling knowledgeably at each other, and Belinda turned away to meet Harriet, who was moving towards her through the crowd. Her face radiated joy and happiness. How nice it is that Harriet is entering so whole-heartedly into their feelings, thought Belinda, for she had been so afraid that her sister might be made unhappy by the curate's marriage and departure.

'The third from the left,' whispered Harriet eagerly.

Belinda looked about her, rather puzzled. Then she saw what her sister meant, for in a corner she saw five curates, all young and all pale and thin, with the exception of one, who was tall and muscular and a former Rugby Blue, as she afterwards learned.

The third from the left. How convenient of the curates to arrange themselves so that Belinda could so easily pick out Harriet's choice. He was dark and rather Italian-looking, paler and more hollow-cheeked than the others. Now Belinda understood her sister's joy and suddenly she realized that she too was happier than she had been for a long time.

For now everything would be as it had been before those two disturbing characters Mr Mold and Bishop Grote appeared in the village. In the future Belinda would continue to find such consolation as she needed in our greater English poets, when she was not gardening or making vests for the poor in Pimlico.

Harriet would accept the attentions of Count Bianco and listen patiently and kindly to his regular proposals of marriage. Belinda did not go any further than this in her plans for the future: she could only be grateful that their lives were to be so little changed. It was true that the curate on whom Harriet had lavished so much care and affection was now a married man and lost to them, but another had come in his place, so like, that they would hardly realize the difference, except that he was rather Italian-looking and had had a nervous breakdown.

> *Then she fretted, ah, she fretted,*
> *But 'ere six months had gone past,*
> *She had got another poodle dog*
> *Exactly like the last . . .*

thought Belinda frivolously, but the old song had come into her head and seemed appropriate. Some tame gazelle or some gentle dove or even a poodle dog—something to *love*, that was the point.

'I think I'll ask him after the reception, although it's rather soon. But we do want to make him welcome *at once*, don't we?' Harriet was speaking eagerly to her sister.

Belinda smiled. 'Of course, dear.' Asking the

278

new curate to supper seemed a particularly happy thought.

'I knew you would agree,' said Harriet, making boldly for the curates' corner.

Belinda was looking round the room to see if she could find some sympathetic person to whom she could say that Dr Johnson had been so right when he had said that all change is of itself an evil, when she saw Harriet approaching with the new curate.

She smiled and shook hands with him, but before either of them could utter a suitable platitude, Harriet had burst in with the news that the young man was coming to supper with them on his first Sunday evening in the village, which would be in about a fortnight's time.

'He says he is fond of boiled chicken,' she added.

Belinda laughed awkwardly and hoped that the new curate would not be embarrassed by Harriet's behaviour.

But he seemed completely at ease as Harriet confided to him that she always liked to eat chicken bones in her fingers.

'Like dear Queen Victoria used to,' she sighed.

'Now, I'm sure *you* don't remember Queen Victoria,' he said gallantly.

'We older people remember a great deal more than you think,' said Harriet coyly.

'Oh, *come*, now,' laughed the curate, and although his voice was rather weak as a result of his long illness, Belinda was overjoyed to hear that it had the authentic ring.